William Henry Venable

Let Him First be a Man

and other essays chiefly relating to education and culture

William Henry Venable

Let Him First be a Man
and other essays chiefly relating to education and culture

ISBN/EAN: 9783337423773

Printed in Europe, USA, Canada, Australia, Japan

Cover: Foto ©Andreas Hilbeck / pixelio.de

More available books at **www.hansebooks.com**

LET HIM FIRST BE A MAN

AND

OTHER ESSAYS

CHIEFLY RELATING TO

EDUCATION AND CULTURE

BY

W: H: VENABLE LL.D.

AUTHOR OF "THE TEACHER'S DREAM" "BEGINNINGS OF LITERARY CULTURE
IN THE OHIO VALLEY" "HISTORY OF THE UNITED STATES" ETC.

BOSTON

LEE AND SHEPARD PUBLISHERS

10 MILK STREET

1893

LET HIM FIRST BE A MAN

PREFACE

It is hoped that this book will encourage teachers, especially *young* teachers, and help that large class of self-helpful students who are seeking guidance in the broad field of general culture. The author has not attempted a formal statement of the science or philosophy of education; many excellent treatises on Pedagogy are already at the teacher's hand. But there is always room for one more volume of educational essays dealing with the common problems of teaching and learning, and derived from actual experience in school and out of school. One may obtain benefit from a new statement of old truth, or by comparing his thoughts with those of another who has striven, like himself, to answer the questions, "What is education? and Why do we educate?"

A glance at the contents of the following pages shows a considerable variety of topics, but the miscellany is not without plan. The opening chapters are intended to depict the potential man, the ideal being which it is the highest purpose of education to per fect. On the teacher's conception of the worth and dignity of human nature, and equally on the learner's self-respect, and reverence for the divine workmanship which makes his body the "quintessence of dust," and his soul "the infinite in faculties," — on these depend the processes of that nurture and training which fit men to live the best and most useful life.

After discussing, in brief, the nature and educability of man, and the motive of all education, the writer ventures to make a few suggestions concerning the special function of schools in the vast work of general education, and touches slightly upon methods of government and instruction, under the inclusive heading "Schoolmastery." Then follow brief essays on the essential elements of mental and moral development, and on the importance of reading as a means to superior culture. About a third part of the volume is taken up with studies in the history of education.

Many of the articles here printed were addressed originally to popular audiences or Teachers' Institutes, and might with propriety be called familiar

"Talks," rather than essays. Some of the pieces have appeared in "Education," the "Ohio Educational Monthly," "Intelligence," and other journals. The dominant purpose of the several essays and of the collection is to oppose the deadening influence of mere mechanical routine in the training of children, whether in school or at home. The "Procrustean bedstead," the "cramming-machine," the "conservative groove," still find a place in the generality of schoolhouses, and there is still need of abolitionists to urge their removal.

The incentive that led to the making of this book is the same that induced the author to compose the several sections originally, — the wish to be of some service, even the slightest, to the vital cause of popular education. The melioration of the children of the people is the reform that underlies all other reforms.

CONTENTS

―――――

"The discipline of Slavery is unknown
   Amongst us, — hence the more do we require
   The discipline of virtue; order else
   Cannot subsist, nor confidence, nor peace.
   Thus, duties rising out of good possessed,
   And prudent caution needful to avert
   Impending evil, do alike require
   That permanent provision should be made
   For the whole people to be taught and trained.
   So shall licentiousness and black resolve
   Be rooted out, and virtuous habits take
   Their place; and genuine piety descend,
   Like an inheritance, from age to age.

   .   .   .   .

   Change wide and deep, and silently performed,
   This land shall witness; and, as days roll on,
   Earth's universal frame shall feel th' effect,
   Even till the smallest habitable rock,
   Beaten by lonely billows, hears the songs
   Of humanized society; and bloom
   With civil arts, and send their fragrance forth,
   A grateful tribute to all-ruling Heaven.
   From culture, universally bestowed,
   Expect these mighty issues; from the pains
   And quiet care of unambitious schools
   Instructing simple childhood's ready ear,
   Thence look for these magnificent results!"
                WORDSWORTH. *The Excursion, Book IX.*

ix

ESSAYS

I

LET HIM FIRST BE A MAN

I. THE END AND THE MEANS

OF many passages that shine like gold in a cabinet of less precious ores in Rousseau's celebrated Essay on Education, the following is one : " According to the order of nature, men being equal, their common vocation is the profession of humanity ; and whoever is well educated to discharge the duty of a man cannot be badly prepared to fill up any of those offices that have a relation to him. It matters little to me whether my pupil be designed for the army, the pulpit, or the bar. Nature has destined us to the offices of human life antecedent to our destination concerning society. *To live* is the profession I would teach him. When I have done with him, it is true he will be neither a soldier, a lawyer, nor a divine. LET HIM FIRST BE A MAN ; he will, on occasion, as soon become anything else that a man ought to be as any person whatever. Fortune may remove him

I

from one rank to another as she pleases, he will be always found in his place."

The doctrine thus proclaimed by Rousseau had been announced centuries before by Plato, who says in the sixth book of the Laws that "a nurture perfectly correct ought to show itself able to render both bodies and souls the most beautiful and best." What is such a nurture but adequate preparation for the "profession of humanity"? This comprehensive view of the purpose of education is always held by those who march in the van of civilization. It is a general truth to inscribe on the ever-advancing banner of educational progress. Like the gospel of religion, it must be preached anew in every age.

The child is born into the world ignorant, feeble, plastic, — a mere lump of organized protoplasm, — yet living and endowed with germs of all human powers, — a potential man. His education begins with his first breath. His parents are his primary educators; they must nurture his body and nourish his mind. The cradle is the first room in the school of life. The Kindergarten of home is the real preparatory department. Unless the child's early training, and the parents' ideas of the purpose of education, be correct, later teachers must work at great disadvantage. The father and mother give their child his constitution, his health, his habits. They call forth and direct the first motions of his mind, foster his tastes, set up standards for him, furnish his surroundings, determine his associations, advise him, control him. How important, then, that parents adhere to the best-known principles of education in dealing with their children, and in relations with those to whom their children are intrusted after they leave the nursery for the schoolroom. Right systems of education will be adopted by teachers if right demands are made by parents. Popular opinion determines the character of the schools. The best and wisest teacher in the world cannot bring his goodness and wisdom to the proof when the prevailing sentiment is against him, or not with him. Superior teachers need sympathy in their purposes and aspirations more than they need co-operation in the actual discharge of their duties.

The vital question is not what books to use, or what subjects to teach, or what classes to form, but what is the ultimate object of teaching? What do we want to do with or for boys and girls? What *is* education?

"Give our children a practical education" is the exhortation of many parents; and little miss and master in the infant grade "tackle" the schoolma'am with, "What good 'll it do us?" The schoolma'am does not easily give little miss and master a satisfactory answer to their question. Nor does the superintendent find it possible to explain the utility of the course of study to the anxious, inquiring father, especially if the father be pertinaciously practical.

What good ? What use ? *Cui bono ?* The old stumbling-block.

Suppose we permit the school-boy to erase from his schedule of studies all subjects that appear to him useless, how much is left ? The boy cannot know what he needs. The chances are he is prejudiced against all studies that tax his pleasure and freedom. He obeys the call of his blood, not the sedate voices of forethought and wisdom. If our extremely practical philosopher advises the lad, the advice and argument may be something like this : " Of what advantage is it to study geography? The ignorant emigrant is carried over the sea as safely and swiftly as are Ritter and Guyot with all their grand conceptions of continents and seas. Tea comes to us from China whether we know where China is or not. And what real benefit can you get from grammar ? So long as you make your meaning understood, who cares whether verbs agree with their subjects or not, or that there are such things as verbs and subjects ? Again, why waste time in learning the $x + y$ of algebra ? Who keeps accounts in algebra ? Will reading history provide you food, or pay debts, or cure cholera ? Why, even reading, writing, and arithmetic are of very little practical use. You will generally hear the news told, and may avoid the trouble and expense of a daily paper. Your ' mark ' will secure legal rights. You may calculate interest and add up sums in your head. Common sense is all the education you need.

My father never went to school a day, and yet he became a rich man. Learning spoils a man for business."

Such is the absurd logic, pushed to the extreme, of a certain class of self-styled practical men, when they talk about education. Nor is our imaginary case much overdrawn. There are hundreds of well-to-do men and women, of average intelligence, who act as if they really esteem education in the abstract as a sort of evil, or, at best, an unnecessary good. They seek schooling for their children, not from a conscious belief that schooling is in itself valuable, like money, and land, and office, and respectable family connection, but because custom compels them to send their boys and girls to school. They seem to begrudge the time and money spent in education. And, therefore, cheap and rapid transit through schools is much in demand. If thorough education takes time and labor, let us have a superficial education that looks like the genuine article. Walnut and mahogany are expensive, — will not veneer answer every practical purpose? veneer, or even paint, in imitation of the true grain?

The end of education is, indeed, practical, but the means to that end are not simple and easy. The making of a child into a complete MAN is a process requiring time, skill, science, and wisdom. The most *useful* knowledge, and the most valuable process of education, furnish facilities to ward the boy in his progress toward ideal manhood.

2. THE FOUNDATION AND THE SUPERSTRUCTURE.

The ardor of professional teachers is perpetually checked by the popular clamor for easy education, simplified education — education that anybody may obtain without study and use without skill. The call is for a commodity that no man can supply — a commodity that does not exist. Education is not an article that one may buy at a shop and carry away in a basket. The training and storing of the mind require a long process. It is a vital, cumulative, continuous effort. The results of education — the fruits — cannot precede the conditions that produce them. First the bud, then the blade, then the ear. The applications of power imply — power. Let the boy become a man, mentally, before expecting him to do a man's mental work. The whole object of the teacher should be to train the *man ;* not the artisan, the merchant, the professor. To train the whole man — not the hand alone, the head alone, the heart alone.

Nature demands of the faculties disinterested activity. She is exacting, and will not pay until the work is done. The student shall not know the joy of victory until he conquers. He shall not overcome the hard problem until he has wrestled and strained with it. He shall not express a thought clearly before he has conceived it clearly. He shall not become a scholar without the probation of the student. He shall not be master except through the tasks of apprenticeship. He shall not be competent to do independent and special duties until he has enfranchised his faculties by discipline, and learned to distinguish the particular from the general. The school catalogues propose to fit boys for the duties of life. This is the legitimate work of preparatory schools, academies, and colleges. They are introductory to life itself, not to stations in life — not to vocations. There is necessity of commercial schools for mercantile training, law schools for lawyers, medical schools for physicians, normal schools for teachers, theological schools for divines ; but before all there is need of educational schools for men and women. The special school is supplementary or complementary to the general school. Neither is a full substitute for the other, though the training for life is the foundation of any training for a living. The person who is without the developed power that the fundamental training of his faculties gives, cannot make good use of the opportunities afforded by schools devoted to special objects. Every building, be it designed for residence or factory, castle or cathedral, requires a firm foundation. Solid stone walls first, deep laid and level. This lower work is much the same for all houses.

Well-grown wood makes reliable timber, and a stick of timber may be turned to various uses ; it may be fashioned into a mast, a beam, a piano, a pulpit, an exquisite carving. But it must become

timber first.   Sap-wood cannot be wrought into durable forms.   Time must elaborate the tissues of the
tree.

Education in school is the building of basement
walls — it is the growing of sound timber — it is the
confirming of tissue, physical, mental, moral.   The
child must be educated because he is a man — to-
morrow.   He must be educated simply because he
can be educated ; because it is the nature of man to
improve by culture.   As Ruskin epigrammatically
says, "There is an education which in itself *is*
advancement in life."

This education, though it does not aim to fit men
for any station, goes far to fit them for all stations.
But not by special training for particular vocations.
As John Stuart Mill puts it, "Education makes a
man a better shoemaker, but not by teaching him to
make shoes."   Is this a hard saying ?   Cannot our
practical philosophers see that education must educate before it can claim to have benefited its subjects ?
What is it that teachers, books, schools, studies,
recitations, examinations, gymnasia, should be expected to do for youth ?   What does education bestow ?

We answer, education gives general increase of
power — discrimination, versatility, command.   It
gives each faculty habitual exercise of its function.   No
one knows his destiny, — what he may be required to
become, do, or endure, — and if he neglects any power
of body or mind it may be the very power he will
have greatest need to employ at some important

crisis. Predominant talents become more effective by general training. Though Pascal learns geometry by intuition, and Burns sings spontaneously as a bird, and Mozart's baby fingers know, untaught, every secret of the clavier, it does not follow that education is wasted on Pascal, Burns, and Mozart. The fine nature is the one most hurt by wrong, and most benefited by right culture. The highest achievements of genius depend somewhat upon the general strength and health of the faculties, as the perfection of a flower depends upon the condition of roots, branches, leaves, and all the other organs of the flowering plant. Wrong culture is ruinous, but right culture invariably adds to the gifts of nature. Educated genius is indomitable.

3. CUI BONO ?

The more complete and extensive a man's education, the more able is he to accomplish whatever he undertakes. If he be naturally well endowed, and then thoroughly educated, failure can scarcely surprise him. Each part and power of man is educable. The educated hand is strong, steady, active, graceful, and sensitive. The educated eye is alert, telescopic, microscopic, discriminating, capable of many tasks, accomplished in many arts. The educated memory is comprehensive, unconfused, accurate, retentive, quick. The educated reason is ready, logical, tranquil, profound, masterly. The educated affections are tender, constant, vigilant to seek and do their office, beautiful, robust. The educated will is decisive, prompt, unwavering — immovable in its rest, irresistible in its god-like motion. An educated man is a grand congeries of organs and forces, material and spiritual, working together in health and harmony, mutually dependent, mutually helpful, — many in one, — subordinate only to Him who is Supreme. To educate a man is to give his hand, brain, and heart their maximum life, power, and facility. "Know thyself" is the theoretical end of education ; — use thyself is the practical end. The Orient said *know and be :* the Occident says know, be, and do.

Practical education! it is not the knowledge of crafts, trades, and professions. It is not that which confers skill in the use of this or that instrument ; it confers upon man the right understanding and ready use of himself. That is a practical education, worthy of the name, which enables a person to maintain bodily health, strength, and comeliness ; to command his own muscles and nerves ; to employ his organs of sense with accuracy and effect ; to adapt himself to outward physical conditions ; to subdue unruly appetites ; to compel the material world to yield most benefit at least expense. That is practical education which enables a man to transact miscellaneous business with ease and despatch ; to preside with dignity at the called meeting ; to perform the duty of trustee or guardian ; to meet the requirements of family relations ; to plan a house ; to choose a book ; to select a picture ; to derive profit or pleasure from

travel. Practical education introduces a man to
mankind, and acquaints him intimately with himself.
That is practical education which assists one to rise
above prejudice, bigotry, partisanship, superstition,
and conventional folly ; to estimate himself and others
with candor and correctness ; to discern the signifi-
cancy of actions and the tendency of opinions and
events ; to sift the speech of the demagogue ; to vote
for the right man ; to advocate the best measure.
That is practical education which educates a human
being to think his own way to conclusions, and to
express conclusions with forcible accuracy ; to ask
and answer questions pertinently ; to generalize without vagueness, and to specialize without triviality ;
to marshal his mental forces for attack or defence in
a sudden emergency as an able commander marshals
his regiments.

Yes, practical education should make of each man
the most that the limits of his constitution will admit. Education, like religion, offers a second birth
to the soul. A good schooling regenerates the intellect, adding to the natural man an inestimable growth.
The school is truly a second mother to nourish youth
to manhood. Let the boy become a man. Then
will he remain a man, not dwindle to a manikin nor
lapse into a brute. Then may he trust himself and
be trusted by his fellows. Then may he master the
art of living, having served his rigorous apprenticeship. Then may he confidently meet the years,
clasping their friendly hands as, one by one, they

welcome him onward to success. For education helps to preserve body and soul from functional feebleness and decay. One of the sages of the Talmud declares that " As the wise grow old their minds become more substantiated." When boys and girls grow restive in school, and over-anxious to escape the discipline of study, they should be reminded that the acquisitions of eighteen may prove the most precious resource of eighty.

4. YOUNG AMERICA AT SCHOOL.

The American boy considers himself a man at about the age of sixteen. To him the idea of remaining in school after his voice begins to change is preposterous. He will never consent to squander the prime of life in humdrum exercises with slate and lexicon. That sort of thing is for children, but men of sixteen must be doing for themselves in the arena of actual life. There is something pathetically ludicrous in this young American scheme of doing for self. How many, alas! have *done for themselves* by engaging prematurely in the tasks that should have followed practical education! 'Tis a delusive precept that urges youth to grasp frantically at the forelock of Time, — a capillary remnant much abused. *Time flies*, says the impatient father and more impatient mother, therefore our son must fly.

Let us have a school on wings to bear him through an aërial course of study. The brief flight ended, the boy begins life. He esteems himself not only a

gentleman and a scholar, but a man of business, a
lion in society, a politician, a critic, a philosopher.
He has graduated into the self-importance of inex-
perienced ignorance. He sits cross-legged before
the Sunday newspaper, sucking cigarettes ; he has a
theory of "finance," and talks ironically on the
" woman question ;" he bluffs his seniors in conversation, and indulges in a thousand other manly
performances.

Young America feminine is the counterpart of her
precocious brother. She, too, is impatient, — even
more impatient of the school restraints, and longs
to cast them off. She gets through the seminary
before you supposed her through the Third Reader.
Her mental acquisitions culminate in the graduating
essay, — thrilling production ! — elegant flower of
originality that blossoms, alas ! only to exhaust the
parent stock which flowers so no more forever.
After Commencement all study ceases, all reading
drops excepting the lighter novels ; even the piano
lessons intermit, like the chills of a half-defeated ague.
For is not Esmeralda's education finished ? She
finished that at school. And now Esmeralda is
doing for herself. She is practically educated. She
is accomplished. *She is done for.* She is ready to
marry.

The eagerness of parents for immediate results in
education defeats its purpose by communicating a
feverish restlessness to the youth, who, instead of
regarding their school duties as regular business to

be discharged with fidelity, are constantly looking
beyond their books to an imaginary "actual life" of
business or pleasure. This illustrates exactly the
national fault which Herbert Spencer criticised when
he visited the United States. He observed as a
general fact, "the American, eagerly pursuing a
future good, almost ignores what good the passing
day offers him; and, when the future good is gained,
he neglects that while striving for some still remoter
good." The dreadful delirium for early participation
in what are called the actual affairs of life prevents
all moderate living.

Actual affairs! What affair can be more actual
than that of bringing youth to the state of manhood
and womanhood? What business can be so important as the acquisition of power to do business? It
is not education to send children through school, or
to send school through them. The pupil must
absorb the school; must digest and assimilate the
elements of knowledge and virtue. This takes time.
The boys and girls who "go through" are sometimes
diseducated: they lose their natural aptitude for
the very pursuits which schools profess to fit them
for. They go through and come out half-developed
physically, not half-developed mentally, without established moral principles or power of self-government;
without the strong armor of experience, or the sharp
weapons of discipline, and, rushing into the conflict
for subsistence, for pre-eminence, for riches, for
happiness, they miserably fail.

5. WHAT IS A MAN?

"Let him first be a man." But what is a man? There are so many ideas and so few ideals. Some one relates that an English school-girl answered the question "What is the difference between man and brute?" by saying, "The brute is an imperfect beast; man is a perfect beast." Shall our education develop such an animal? What kind of man shall our American boy become before he begins the special duties of life? What shall be his preconceived notion of success? To judge by the Plutonic standards which many follow, success consists mainly in acquiring riches. "How much is he worth?" means not at all what is his intrinsic value, but how much money has he? If the power to pile up wealth is the chief end of school-training, being the chief end of man, then should the conscientious schoolmaster train his pupil to be sharp and shrewd and self-seeking. The boys should be taught to spell the word educate e-d-g-e-u-c-a-t-e, to give *edge* to the mind. He who would cut his way to the many-mansioned place of the millionnaire must be a keen blade. But how if the young man don't want to be a money-maker? Perhaps, like Matthew Arnold, he would prefer the heaven of "sweetness and light" to the Eden of riches. When Arnold died his estate was valued at only a few thousand dollars, yet who will say this great lifter-up of civilization was an unsuccessful man or that he left the world no rich bequest?

Who will say that Agassiz, who whimsically said he
had no time to waste in making money, was not
a winner in life's battle? How beautifully other men
drew golden swords for him that he might pursue
the paths of science and so aid mankind! He
needs must be about his Father's business. Or, take
the case of Emerson, who, though he gained material
fortune, did not seek it, but devoted himself to amass-
ing a capital of thoughts and dreams, — a millionnaire
of ideas.

"Planter of celestial plants,
What he has nobody wants."

Is it the object of our schools, or should it be, to
make Vanderbilts, or Arnolds, or Emersons? or to
make Grants, or Gladstones, or Beechers? When we
say, "let him first be a man," do we have any particular man or class in view? Not at all. The shining
lights of the world may serve to guide and illuminate all men; but each man must work out his own
destiny self-impelled and directed by the inner lamp
of individuality, or he can never become a "success"
in any sense. It is wrong to deceive children or
college students with the belief that the general
training they receive from books and teachers will
make them poets, or presidents, or railroad kings, or
this or that. The knowledge, the study, the physical exercise, the discipline of body and soul, which
the school should afford, are to preserve an ideal type,
not to differentiate a unit. First, the typical man,
sound in body, sound in mind, endowed with the

possessions which the wisdom of ancient authority and the prescience of modern reason have agreed to consider the BEST CULTURE, and then the practical man, exercising his special talent according to the bent of his will.

II

THE PARAGON OF ANIMALS

In the Book of Genesis we read that "The Lord God formed man of the dust of the ground."

Josephus says more particularly, that Adam was made of red clay. According to Grecian mythology, Prometheus compounded the first man of clay and particles taken from various animals. The Mohammedans say that God made Adam of seven handfuls of earth from different depths and of different colors, collected by the angel Azrael. The alchemists and astrologers, in their vague but bold speculations, wrote much of the human body, the Microcosm, or little world, supposed to be made up of every element to be found in the three kingdoms of nature, — in the Macrocosm, or great world. The modern, ingenious, and beautiful theory of evolution — recognizing the kinship of man to all that lies below him — was it not symbolized and foreshadowed by the old philosophies ?

Francis Bacon, commenting curiously on the belief of the alchemists, remarks that "the body of man is of all existing things the most mixed and the most organic," and that "this, indeed, is the reason it is capable of such wonderful powers and faculties; . . . abundance and excellence of powers reside in mixture and composition."

Science determines with accuracy the kind of material of which the body is made. About twenty simple substances have been detected by the chemical analysis of the human organism ; these combine to form between eighty and ninety physically different components, technically called "immediate principles." The immediate principles make "structural elements," such as cells and fibres, and from "structural elements" are developed all the tissues, such as fat, muscle, nerve, and bone. Of tissues are fashioned the organs of motion, digestion, circulation, respiration, sensation, generation, that are severally called systems, and that collectively make a complex mechanism named *the system.*

The human body comprises about two hundred bones, — rods, plates, levers, shields, — deftly articulated, bound together by silvery ligaments ; four hundred red elastic muscles — lithe, half-reasoning laborers that serve King Brain ; veins pulsing purple currents, and arteries conducting crimson streams — the bright brooks that water the Little World and purify themselves in their own swift-running ; innumerable pearly nerves — the telegraphic wires of the Microcosm. Hundreds of millions of these wires run from the brain ; by their means any part of the "skin of the hand is brought into connection with, perhaps, two hundred muscles."

Within the body, by mysterious processes, bread is

transformed into blood, and blood into flesh and bone and brain. Fluids of subtile quality thread their intricate way through a thousand "natural gates and alleys," building and destroying ; vital air permeates minutest vessels, diffusing heat and energy to every fibre. A man requires three thousand pounds, or a ton and a half, of food a year to keep his body in repair and to keep it alive and warm. Twenty millions of blood cells are born, and as many die, at each beat of pulse. In the lungs are six hundred million air cells, presenting an aggregate surface of seventy-four hundred square feet with which oxygen comes in contact. We use in a lifetime about one million cubic feet of air — enough to form a solid air-castle a hundred feet square and a hundred feet high.

The surface drain-pipes of the body, the sweat-tubes of the skin, taken together, Carpenter computes, are twenty-eight miles in length! What extents! What forces! What effects! Is the delicate body of yonder slight school-girl the storehouse of so much material? Is it the theatre of such enormous activity? Is it such a power-hall? Yes ; the physical forces which we unconsciously employ are vastly greater than those controlled by the will.

The stark, cold corpse of man, the cadaver, awakens in the reflective mind admiration and reverence. The surgeon dissects it with ever-increasing interest. He is never done inspecting its parts, contemplating its structure.

The prying microscope, the delicate knife and

probe, the searching chemical test — all the fine appliances of science, are employed in the study of anatomy and physiology. But how much is imperfectly known, how much undiscovered in the mysterious "little world," even after the incessant explorations of thousands of years !

Regard the body as divided into extremities, trunk and head ; or into locomotive, vital and thinking organs. It will aid us to form a conception of the perfect and admirable structure of man, if we make a brief examination of a single representative in each of the divisions named. No more interesting member of the locomotive or mechanical group of organs can be named than the hand. So suggestive a topic is the hand, and so prolific in "proofs of design," that Sir Charles Bell made it the subject of one of the Bridgewater Treatises, devoting two hundred pages to an account of its mechanism and vital endowment. Bell and many other writers define the hand as belonging exclusively to man, and from comparing it with the paw, or other prehensile instrument of the brute creation, they deduce some of the most convincing proofs of the essential superiority of man. The number, form, and adjustment of its parts ; the freedom, variety, and celerity of its movements ; the firmness of its texture ; the peculiar power it possesses of resisting the injurious action of poisonous or corrosive substances; its exquisite sensibility, — all tend to make the hand the most perfect instrument conceivable for the purposes to which it is applied.

Should we survey the group of organs termed vital, we would at once single out the heart — that "metropolitan city of the blood," as it has been poetically called. The heart is strong and tough, yet smooth, soft, and elastic. Its muscular coats consist of several layers, each made up of an incredible number of fibres twisted, inwound, and woven together in the most compact and intricate way; its partitioned cavities, each of peculiar form, communicate by various openings with one another, and with the great veins and arteries; its variform valves open and close with rhythmic precision that the skill of mechanic art cannot imitate. Even after the brain and spinal cord have ceased to act — when life is extinct — the heart will sometimes throb. (Faithful servant, beating the march of life to the end — yea, and even the funeral march of dead life!)

We are, when in good health, unconscious of the action or presence of the heart in our breast, so gently and noiselessly it performs its unceasing labor. And what a mighty labor it performs! Small as it is and light, only about five inches in length, and not more than ten or eleven ounces in weight, it yet pumps eighteen pounds of blood from itself to itself in less than two minutes.

Calculations made by Professor Houghton demonstrate that "the daily work of the human heart is one hundred and twenty-four tons lifted through one foot." In other words, the heart exerts one-third as much muscle power in one day as does a stout man engaged in hard labor. Or, to employ another of Professor Houghton's illustrations, "If we suppose the heart expends its entire force in lifting its own weight vertically, then the total height to which it could lift itself in one hour is 19,754 feet," and that is twenty times as high as an active pedestrian can lift himself in ascending a mountain.

Sovereign in the highest group of bodily organs is the brain. No brief description can convey an idea of this. Occupying the highest place in the structure, the dome of the temple, it is the medium through which the soul acts and enjoys. To reason and to will are its supreme functions. Chemistry and microscopy have labored diligently to dissect, magnify, and analyze the fine forms, textures, and substances of this extremely interesting organ. It remains in many respects a puzzle to the scientific investigator. To those unacquainted with anatomy, a mere enumeration of the terms used in a description of the brain is bewildering. A thorough and exact knowledge of the complicated organ itself is only to be acquired by years of industrious and scrutinizing application. Its several parts, the medulla oblongata, the pons, the cerebellum, the cerebrum, are each great chapters of a greater volume.

The brain is composed of several peculiar substances, differing in consistency, color, and texture. It is massed in hemispheres, lobes, and convolutions; and cut up by ventricles, fissues, and sinuses. The average weight of the human brain is three pounds. The exterior surface, owing to numerous convolutions, presents an area of about five square feet to the action of the blood. Some physiologists believe that intellectual forces are generated upon this brain surface in a manner similar to that in which electric currents are developed upon metallic plates. The brain is hence regarded as a great galvanic battery of thought. Wilkinson, in his book, " The Human Body and its Connection with Man," says the brain " is the heart of hearts, for it receives from the body and the universe spiritual blood, which its cortices pulse out in infinite streams ; " that " it is the lung of lungs, for its animation is the breathing of the soul in the all-communicable ether ; " that " it is the stomach of stomachs, because of its bold chemistry in the preparation of the food of food, which is the nerve, spirit ; ay, and it is the primal womb of life and thought."

Consider the organs of sense, the instruments by which the mind receives the world.

The acuteness of sight and hearing is often spoken of and needs no illustration. The lower senses — feeling, taste, and smell — are not so much studied or so well appreciated as their nobler sisters. By the touch, the blind not only read, they have been known to model portrait busts, to distinguish genuine coins and medals from spurious ones, to recognize the different specimens in a large conchological cabinet, and even to distinguish the colors of woven fabrics.

A blind man at Indianapolis turned aside to avoid
a wood-pile, which, unknown to him, had been placed
in the line of his usual walk.   When asked how he
knew there was an obstruction before him, he replied,
"I felt it."   Perhaps he should have said he heard it.

The sense of pressure enables a man to use his
hand as an accurate balance.   Experiment proves
that we are able to distinguish nineteen and one-
half from twenty ounces by muscular sensibility.

Exact calculations also show that the finger can
perceive a difference of temperature of about one-
fourth degree C. ; a sensibility, says Bernstein,
"greater than we should have expected, since it is
greater than that of an ordinary thermometer."

By the sense of taste we can detect "one part
of sulphuric acid in one thousand parts of water."
Carpenter   states   that   "the   experienced   wine-
taster can distinguish differences in age, purity,
place of growth, etc., between liquors that to ordinary judgments are alike ; and the epicure gives an
exact determination of the spices that are combined
in a particular sauce, or the manner in which the
animal on which he is feeding was killed "

Bernstein asserts that the sense of smell has a
delicacy surpassing that of any of the other senses.
He says, "No chemical reaction can detect such
minute particles as those which we perceive in the
sense of smell, and even spectrum analysis, which
can recognize fifteen-millionths of a grain, is far
surpassed in delicacy by our organ of smell."

Bacon says, in the "Advancement of Learning," that he thinks "it would contribute much to magnanimity and the honor of humanity if a collection were made of what the schoolmen call *ultimities*, and Pindar, the tops or summits of human nature, especially from true history, showing what is the ultimate and highest point which human nature has of itself attained in the several gifts of body and mind." Bacon further states that such a collection had been designed in ancient times by Valerius Maximus and Caius Pliny.

Influenced by Bacon's suggestions, one Thomas Wanley, an Englishman, about a century ago compiled a work which he called "The Wonders of the Little World; or, A General History of Man." In the introduction to this work we are told that its author ransacked the history of all times and nations and at a great expense of labor and learning, which renders him as great an instance of human industry as is to be found in his own book; he gleaned several thousand facts which he had disposed in such order as to form a complete system of the mental and corporal powers and defects of man.

Upon examination, I find Wanley's book, though quaint and entertaining, by no means authentic, nor is it made up of matter sufficiently important. It deals largely in the traditional, the marvellous, and the monstrous, and entirely fails of furnishing "that volume of human triumphs" which the great author of "The Advancement of Learning" says is wanting to finish what Valerius Maximus and Pliny the Elder had begun.

The first and most general reason why we admire man is that he presents himself to our view as the paragon of animals. Whatever may be the origin of the human species, that species is now, by many degrees, superior to the brute. However perfect the missing link may be, we know how much the average man of this period surpasses the average ape. Man "is the only living creature that can walk or stand erect. His face and eyes look straight to the front." His anatomical structure is in many ways different from that of the ape. The facts are all old but strong.

The great distinction of man, however, is that the range and quality of his reason and his power of language lift him immeasurably above the brute creation. His glorious body, quintessence of dust, is worthy of the faculties which manifest themselves through it — reason, imagination, love, will power, speech. Man is majestic. His power over *things* is absolute.

The grandest statue, the most impressive portrait, cannot compare with the reality which it strives to imitate.

Praxiteles carves well; Raphael paints skilfully; but what artist can compare with the Divine Master? No colored outline or chiselled form can express power, stateliness, symmetry, as does the person of a Coriolanus, an Alexander, a Napoleon, a Webster. Long before Goethe was celebrated as a writer, he was admired as an Apollo. We read that when he entered a restaurant people laid down their knives and forks to look at him. Plutarch relates that "Caius Marcius, being in the depth of winter, and in great hazard of his life, was saved by the majesty of his person; for while he lived in a private house at Minturn, there was a public officer, a Cambrian by nation, that was sent to be his executioner; he came to this unarmed old man, with his sword drawn, but, astonished by his noble presence, he cast away his sword, and ran trembling and amazed."

What glowing canvas or shapen marble reveals queenliness and grace as do the form, attitude, and movement of a splendid woman! Marlowe, the painter, writing of Mrs. Siddons, said that when, in the character of Queen Katherine, she addressed Wolsey in the words, "Lord Cardinal, to you I speak," her statuesque attitude was the sublimest thing in ancient or modern sculpture.

What in nature or art so satisfying to the æsthetic sense as a perfect human form or face! Tradition says that Apelles, ambitious to paint a picture that should worthily represent the Goddess of Beauty, travelled for many years, and, having beheld innumerable fair women, he mingled the charming features of all in a composition of surpassing loveliness, and produced an ideal Venus to which all Greece yielded adoration. There is another account of the origin

of both this work, the Venus of Cos, and the equally
celebrated Venus of Cnidos, executed in marble by
Praxiteles. Alexander Walker informs us in his
"Analysis of Female Beauty," that "both these
productions are said to have represented Phryne
coming out of the sea on the beach of Sciron,
in the Saronic Gulf, where she was wont to
bathe."

Madame Récamier was so beautiful that the French
people all but worshipped her. Once she consented
to carry around the purse at St. Roche for a charit-
able object. The church was crowded, the people
standing upon chairs and pillars to get sight of her
as she moved down the aisles. Twenty thousand
francs were dropped into her box. At the reception
of Bonaparte, on his return from Italy, she rose from
her seat to get a good view of him, the crowd caught
sight of her, and, turning from the conquering general, gave a long murmur of admiration.

We pass from the contemplation of beauty to the
study of strength and endurance. What can the
" Paragon of Animals " do and bear ? What can he
not ? Though man in infancy is helpless, he becomes at maturity very powerful for a creature of
his size. A man's power is estimated to be one-fifth
of a horse-power ; that is, the daily labor of a
workingman is performed at the expense of force
sufficient to lift three hundred and fifty-four tons
through one foot. A man of ordinary strength may,
by the advantageous application of his muscular

energy, lift two thousand pounds at a single effort.
Dr. Winship of Boston was enabled, by patient practice, to raise the enormous weight of twenty-seven
hundred pounds.

Dr. Bellows says, in his letters from Europe, that
the Alpine climbers of the Rifel make their twenty
miles' tramp over glaciers and cols eleven or twelve
thousand feet high without serious fatigue and with
great enjoyment. Frederick Hassaurek reports similarly of the Equadorean arrieros, "who trot fourteen
or fifteen leagues a day over rugged mountain roads,
now ascending steep acclivities, now hurrying down
steep and muddy ravines." Byron and his friend
swam the Hellespont in emulation of Leander; Ida
Pfaff crossed the Andes on foot; Marie Mathsdotter
made a journey of six hundred miles alone on skates;
a diver won a wager by walking several miles at the
bottom of the Hudson.

There is something more than amusement in the
equestrian performances of the circus, the perilous
leaps of the Hanlons, the difficult evolutions of the
ballet-dancers, the skill of accomplished swordsmen.
Yet not in miraculous feats of trained gymnasts
and athletes does human strength show at its best.
The application of man-power and endurance to
useful purposes gives dignity to muscle. Bodily
strength and fortitude make it possible for man
to obtain and hold dominion over the lower animals
and over the substances and forces of nature. Read
Victor Hugo's iron description of the man and the

canon, *Vis et Vir.* Not alone to brain and heart belongs the credit of the conqueror ; the God who makes soul makes sinew too. Samson has a mission to perform as well as Solomon or Isaiah. There is fitness in the just worship of Hercules and Thor.

Whoso honors labor must honor muscle and nerve. Thanks for the working hand. It is this that piles the wharf with box and bale, builds up the mason's solid stony wall, controls the locomotive's course, flings from his rocking boat the whaler's spear, overcomes the frenzy of the rearing horse, hauls the deep anchor from the ocean bed, holds fast the ship's helm in the roaring storm, directs the musket's flying shot, and wields the flashing sabre in defence of liberty and truth. The body is as remarkable for fortitude as for active power. It has the endurance of St. Simeon Stylites :

> "Patient on this tall pillar,
> I have borne rain, wind, frost, heat, hail, damp and snow."

The only cosmopolitan, man is at home on the scorching sands of Sahara, and among the wind-beaten crags of Labrador. He explores the marshy tundras of Siberia, and the pestilential jungles of the Dark Continent. He plies his task in the deep, dread mine, and scales the snowy height of Chimbo-razo. He dives to the pearl-strewn bottom of the sea, and rises with Mongolfier's silken ball, above the storm cloud, into the dizzy, empty spaces of eternal silence and cold.

Men have been known to survive for days, weeks, and even months without sleep; and numerous examples are on record of persons whose daily slumbers did not exceed four or five hours. Fred- erick the Great was one of these. Soldiers sleep on the frozen ground and rise instantly to arms at the bugle-call. The tough Britons slept on beds of sticks, scorning a softer couch. Canadian lumbermen sleep soundly with their bodies half submerged in the water of a raft, their head pillowed on a log of wood.

Life may be prolonged from twenty to forty days without food, and from eight to twelve days without either food or drink. Fairly authentic reports assure us that certain Indian fakirs retain vitality for six weeks buried in underground cells of stone.

The fortitude with which the body suffers pain is amply exemplified in the history of martyrdom. Even more to be admired than physical strength and fortitude, even more than beauty, is manual dexterity. What cannot the hand make and manip- ulate? Observe the skill of the base-ball player, the oarsman, the archer, the rifleman, the composi- tor, the engraver, the phonographer, the micro- scopist. Not to weary you with illustration, let only the art of the musician engage your mind for a moment. Can we conceive a finer and more com- plex mechanical accomplishment than is exhibited by the violin-playing of a master like Wilhelmj? Think of what his fingers can do!

The human hand becomes a thing divine. Even more wonderful are the vocal organs. A trained singer can determine the contraction of the vocal organs to the seventeen-thousandth part of an inch, so nicely is the instrument tuned. Then hear it play! Listen to Cary or Kellogg or Patti : —

> " The melting voice thro' mazes running,
> Untwisting all the chains that tie
> The hidden soul of harmony."

Do we ask more proof that the human body, with all its infinite capabilities, is the master-work of the Creator?

Shakespeare portrays man in a few sublime sentences : —

"What a piece of work is man! How noble in reason! How infinite in faculties! In form, and moving, how express and admirable! In action how like an angel! In apprehension how like a God! The beauty of the world! The paragon of animals!"

If the temple wherein the soul dwells for a time is so perfect, if it is so deserving of honor and admiration and care, how much more perfect and wonderful and worthy of care is the soul itself, and what inexpressible perfection and wealth are comprised in body and soul together, — in man, — in the august creature who was made only a little lower than the angels.

What a theme is this to invite research, to excite imagination, to inspire reverence for the master-work of the Master-worker! Mind of Man! Who can estimate its forces or enumerate its modes of action? In what language can we portray the intelligence which informs the body, making dust divine?

Is the body beautiful — how can we paint the ineffable loveliness of the spirit? Is muscle swift and strong? Thought flashes in an instant to the verge of space. Thought is stronger than Titan, heaving the earth when he breathes. Does the body endure a hundred years? The mind endures forever. Is nerve sensitive? Can the ear discern whispers, and the eye catch the gleam of distant stars? The mind receives the music of the spheres and sees the procession of ages filing along the shore of time.

If from the pages of history we should select examples showing the vast intellectual and moral achievements that individuals have actually made, as we have attempted to show by authentic facts what physical accomplishments men really possess, what an overwhelming array of evidence would we have of the possibilities of human nature. Whatever faculties or powers have been manifested in any human being exist in embryo, or in a more or less developed state, in every complete individual.

The thorough development of all the faculties, bodily and mental, of a complete man, would furnish the world with a perfect man. Human culture embraces all the processes by which we approximate to such development.   These processes are the means of culture.   The ends are as numerous and diverse.

Culture aims to secure every true, good, and beautiful thing, mortal and immortal, to which man can aspire.

III

FUNCTIONS OF THE PREPARATORY SCHOOL

. THE preparatory school, because it *is* preparatory, holds a position of peculiar trust among educational institutions. No one loses the impress made upon him, the impulse given him, by the first schooling he receives.

What is the main purpose of education ? What the essential duty of the teacher ? —To develop mind, brain power, mental and moral force. This development is effected not merely by accumulating knowledge, as one puts gold in bank, but also by training the powers of thought and feeling, by arousing the faculties to original action and conscious achievement. The subjects taught are of a value proportioned to their good effect on the mind. Lessons, like food, are taken for their nourishing quality. They must enter into the intellectual circulation. Not the studies, but the study educates. 'Tis labor lost to store facts in the brain if they serve no other use than when in books.

Your pupil is fitted for college when he knows how to answer the entrance examination questions, and, besides this, knows how to think, how to listen, how to learn, how to co-operate with books and teachers, and how, in some degree, to direct his own course.

For, as Quintilian says, " Why do we teach pupils but that they may not always require to be taught ? "

Much is it desired that some plan be devised by which competitive examinations shall test the powers as well as the possessions of the mind.

None know better than college professors how important it is that the freshmen start with right habits, motives, and aspirations. Some educators make a strange distinction between fitting for college and fitting for life, as if one fitting were incompatible with the other. Better not fit for college at all if that fitting unfits for life, present or prospective.

Do the most for your pupil to-day, and he will have the best possible preparation for to-morrow. Each day's mental growth should be a beautiful conclusion to all preceding growths and a hopeful beginning to all following.

The object of all schooling is to strengthen and enrich the human faculties. The best education gives to man's natural powers the right direction and greatest efficiency. The superior teacher endeavors to impart to his pupils both knowledge and the art of getting knowledge. He conveys by his teaching, not only the contents of books, but also correct habits of study, thought, and speech. He seeks to expand the intellect, regulate the affections, and impel the will of his pupils, so that they may be trusted to use their minds and acquisitions rightly, at all times and places, without supervision.

The cramming system, fostered, I fear, as much by the colleges as by the lower schools, is opposed to every axiom of pedagogics, and earnest teachers everywhere protest against it.

In Strasburg a method prevails of compelling geese to eat in order to increase enormously the size of the liver, for *pâtés de foies gras — fat liver pies.* The unhappy goose is shut up in a box barely large enough to hold him, and is crammed with food several times a day. His bill is forced open, and the pabulum is poked down his throat with the finger. Alas for the poor goose or gosling who is crammed with indigestible knowledge, be it science, mathematics or classics ; whose memory grows prodigious at the expense of health, reason, wit, fancy, feeling, taste, manner, and conscience.

This process of cramming is part of the compli-. cated operation known as machine education, so much, but not enough, criticised and condemned. The terrible " machine," though found in the most mischievous perfection in large public schools, in cities whence it is difficult to remove it, is set up also in many schools, where there is no excuse for tolerating it. Teachers are not so much to blame for the existence of the "machine" as are the people, too many of whom, though theoretically opposed to it, practically regard it as a useful and necessary part of school apparatus, and, unless they see the usual forms, papers, reports, per cents, text-books, and external routine in general, are apt to take alarm and suspect something visionary. Too often the friends of better education are like the temperance man in Maine, who was in favor of the prohibition law, but opposed to its enforcement.

Reforms go forward but slowly when not encouraged by public sentiment. Nevertheless, as a German philosopher says, " To elevate above the spirit of the age must be regarded as the end of education." We must pursue in patience the path of our feet.

Education should proceed with free steps along a broad way. Learners, properly instructed, take an active, happy interest in their work. Teachers often quench desire by pouring in knowledge. They should create thirst for knowledge, and the pupil's eagerness will lead him to the fountains. The only thoroughness possible proceeds from willing effort. The boy who does not care for his own progress does not advance. You *cannot* teach a pupil what he *will not* learn. A humble mood is the first requisite of the student. Only the docile have discovered the secret of power. Obedience is victory. The demands of a good school are rigorous and exacting. True are the words of Joubert : " Education should be tender and severe, and not cold and soft."

Youth needs guidance ; no greater evil can befall a boy than to be left to do as he pleases. The duties that a preparatory school prescribes are imperative, and should be done with scrupulous integrity. Let no one hope to reap the sheaf of scholarship except with the sickle of toil.

One of the functions of a preparatory school is to discover and respect the individuality of pupils. We cannot fashion all characters in the same way, and if we could, we should not. We defy nature when we force John to be James, or either of them to imitate ourself. You must be you ; he, he ; and I, I. Nature fixes that ; education must accept nature's condition. Yet children cannot know themselves or their own bent ; teachers must discover the natural tendency, and act from a knowledge of it. Diversity in disposition does not necessarily call for great difference in treatment. A beginner in learning cannot be a correct judge of what he ought to study or not to study. The young are almost certain to mistake their wishes for capacities.

The competent educator recognizes diversity of ability in young people, as in older ones, whether owing to hereditary influence, state of health, or other cause. It is not to be expected that pupils develop with equal rapidity or in the same degree under similar schooling. Enough if each works up to the limits of his power. 'Tis a misfortune, not a vice, to be, like Snug the joiner, "slow of study."

The merit of a teacher is tested by what he does for the tortoise, not by the fact that he causes the hare to run swiftly. Take care of the blockheads and the heads will take care of themselves.

Yet the blockheads and the incorrigibles may, in the long run, win the goal of scholarship and virtue. Stupidity, stolidity, inaptitude for special studies, vicious tendencies, are to be regarded as chronic diseases; the wise physician of mind may cure them by patient treatment.

The perfect work of education cannot be accomplished except in the individual who comes from a stock prudently cultivated for generations. Training your pupil you are continuing the work of his ancestors' teachers, and you are possibly educating his posterity. Seed brain, like seed corn, propagates its kind, improved or deteriorated by culture. When we grade our pupils, is it not just to bear in mind what share of their success or failure depends upon birth and family influence, and what upon their own independent effort?

Finally, the preparatory school must take time and pains to cultivate goodness, courtesy, and delicacy in pupils. Every class should be a class in conduct, though no precepts need be announced. Every relation of teacher and learner should induce in both gentle and gracious behavior, self-respect, dignity, and sense of honor. The greatest value of any education is its moral value. The schools are the foremost promoters of civilization. They should illustrate the best habits of the best society.

In a word, the ideal duty of the educator is to make the best of his pupils by preventing all perversions and assisting all normal faculties to attain their true functions. Beautiful and inspiring is that sentence of a wise French thinker : —

" Man might be so educated that all his prepossessions would be truths, and all his feelings virtues."

Sacred is the task of the teacher ; let us approach it with reverence, and discharge it with religious fidelity, for education is the science of life, and conduct is its cognate art.

IV

SCHOOLMASTERY

I. GUIDE, SHEPHERD, AND PILOT

THE word *paidagogos*, from which we derive pedagogue, a teacher, and pedagogics, the science of education, means primarily, " child-leader." The Greek pedagogue, as is well known, walked with the children to and from school, took care of them, helped carry their books and harps, taught and protected them.

The Anglo-Saxon term for pedagogue is *child-herd*, shepherd of human lambs.

The word schoolmaster is a strong, serviceable compound containing both Roman and English blood. *Master* is derived from *magis*, greater, and *stoer*, to steer, and hence means chief steerer, principal pilot, or ruling director ; in other words, one who is able to control his affairs so as to obtain successful results, to helm his ship to the desired port. There is a suggestive antithesis between the words *magister* and *minister*, the greater and the lesser pilot. The fact that we say schoolmaster and church minister suggests that the teacher has more absolute power than the preacher. The former commands and controls the young and plastic ; the latter persuades the mature and fixed.

The function of the teacher has widened, and the dignity of his office has been magnified in modern times. We call the teacher not only pedagogue, child-herd, schoolmaster, but also instructor, preceptor, disciplinarian, educator. The efficacy of his work has doubled because it has come to include *her* work ; for girls now go to school with the boys, and women teach with men. What an accession to the civilizing forces of the world! There once was a time when literature was addressed to men only, and when women who wrote or read were considered out of their proper sphere. Now men and women write alike for women and men, and both sexes participate in teaching and learning.

2. WHAT THE SCHOOLMASTER MASTERS.

Schoolmastery is a double mastery. It puts and keeps the school, as a whole, and every pupil, in the best condition to learn, and also causes all to learn what is best to know. Further than this and more important, it compels the school and every pupil to do the things they know, thus making bodily, intellectual, and emotional acquirements, practical forces in bettering society and self.

The dual purposes of his office will be present constantly to the mind of the master. His duties are both impersonal and personal, — the class he teaches is a *thing;* the members of it are persons, boys and girls. The school must be regarded as a community working out a problem of social and political duty, and as a number of individuals each destined to a personal existence and bound to pursue a special ideal. The master fashions the opinion and colors the conduct of his small republic. He masters both brain and heart. The schoolmaster masters the school's will.

All this he does, not despotically, not to oppress or to suppress, but to strengthen and expand the powers of his subjects. He bears them up on eagle's wings, for the sake of teaching them to fly.

3. TEACHING AND GOVERNING.

Usually the excellent instructor is the successful ruler. The teaching faculty seems to carry with it authority. The disciplined mind makes itself felt as a disciplining mind. Whatever regulates the thoughts of a pupil also regulates his outer conduct. When a boy is thinking, he " comes to order." Skill in imparting knowledge commands respect and elicits attention. The teacher whose stock of knowledge is large and varied, and whose method of communicating ideas is clear, captures his school by charming their intellect, and thus he escapes conflict with their passions.

Yet it must be conceded that skill in teaching is not always associated with ability to govern. The pulses of the blood cannot be reached by appeals

to reason. Man is an animal, especially when he
is a boy. The schoolmaster must learn the "art
Napoleon," which, though difficult to acquire, is
learnable. Some are born to rule. Equally true
is it that some are born with tact for teaching.
Now and then one appears in the flesh, endowed
with special gifts of rulership and teachership. But
if the schools wait for Providence to send them
miraculous masters, they must wait too long.

The professor of pedagogy should give his scheme
scope enough to include the art of governing youth
as a necessary part of the teacher's preparation.
The normal-school graduate, when he goes forth to
seek a position, ought to bear with him as distinct
understanding of how to govern as of how to teach.
He must widen his conception of the training that
fits him to educate boys and girls. How can he
educate them in the elements of learning, unless he
knows how to hold them in a receptive attitude?
He must *get at them* in order to instruct them. *Perhaps more than half the teaching we do is wasted
because we do not, by controlling their wills, prepare
pupils to receive knowledge.*

4. PERSUASION AND FORCE.

Themistocles, the Athenian general, demanding
tribute of the revolted cities, gave it out that "he
had on board his ships two powerful divinities — Persuasion and Force ; and whoever would not follow
the former must submit to the latter." The school-

master relies on the same "two powerful divinities," to secure obedience to the necessary laws by which the intellect, the affections, and the will of youth are rightly educated.

Obedience to proper authority for just and desirable objects is necessary from every one. The teacher should assume that every salutary school law is sacred, and must be observed, not because he commands so, but because it *is* salutary. The teacher is as imperatively bound to execute good laws as his pupils are to comply with them. No personal issue need be made. The law is impersonal; the teacher reveres the law because it is the means of doing good to his pupil; he says, like Paul, "The law is *our* schoolmaster," — yours and mine; he rejoices when the pupil conforms to the rule of right; he is sorry when the pupil falls below the required standard and compels the lawgiver to become judge and executive.

The teacher, like the parent, unites in his office the three governmental functions. He must define what is to be done; he must decide the manner of doing it; he must enforce the duties demanded. There is constant danger that he will abuse his unlimited power, through ignorance or want of self-control. Therefore he should be forever on his guard. The history of education shows too many examples of the mistakes of the pedagogue in the art of rulership. The records unhappily prove that Force has often been appealed to when Persuasion should have been sought. If this were not so, the literature of the world would not present so frightful a gallery of the pictures of ill-tempered and despotic schoolmasters.

Books on school government repeat the maxim that force should be resorted to only after other means are exhausted. This is often, but not always, true. Force should occasionally be the first resort, especially with very young pupils and with older ones in whom, as Plato says, "The fountain of reason is not opened." It is impossible to persuade a mind incapable of reasoning, or to move feelings incapable of activity. The object of both persuasion and force is to set the wrong right. When the wrong is set right, both persuasion and force become useless.

The purpose of government, and therefore of its agencies, persuasion and force, is twofold, having reference to scholarship and to conduct. The student must study — must obey the laws that regulate the development of memory, reason, judgment, language. But since conduct is more than learning, he must also behave properly — must obey the laws of his moral nature. The kind of persuasion and the kind of force that induce him to master his lessons and to control his general conduct, visible and invisible, is what the schoolmaster must go in quest of, and seek till he finds. That secret is his holy grail.

5. DR. ARNOLD'S WAY.

Mr. Stanley, in his biography of Thomas Arnold, says of that celebrated teacher : —

" He recognized in the peculiar vices of boys the same evils which, when grown, become the source of so much social mischief. He governed his school on precisely the same principles he would have governed a great empire ; and constantly exemplified to his own mind, or the minds of his scholars, the highest truths in the simplest relations of boys towards each other and towards him. The boys were treated as school-boys, but as school-boys who must grow up to be Christian men; whose age did not prevent their faults from being sins, or their excellences from being noble and Christian virtues, whose situation did not make the application of principles to their daily life an impractical vision. . . . In proportion as he disliked an assumption of false manliness in boys was his desire to cultivate in them true manliness, as the only step to something higher, and to dwell upon earnest principles and moral thoughtfulness as the great and distinguishing mark between good and evil. Hence his wish that as much as possible should be done *by* the boys, and nothing *for* them; hence arose his practice of treating the boys as gentlemen and reasonable beings, of making them respect themselves by the mere respect he showed them, of showing that he appealed to their own common sense and conscience."

Dr. Arnold's method of dealing with the boys of Rugby has been applied in more than one American school with the most beneficial results. Indeed, the plan seems more American than English, being founded on a democratic idea. Mr. Hughes tells us that the Rugby boys told Dr. Arnold no lies because *they knew he would believe them.* Confidence begets confidence, suspicion excites suspicion. The conflict, open or secret, that goes on between teacher and pupils in many, if not in most schools, is unnatural and unnecessary. The majority of boys and girls will co-operate fully and sincerely with a competent teacher who, without reserve, takes them at their word, in full faith, and acts upon the theory of mutual trust. The minority he can master completely with the aid and sympathy of the majority.

The emphasis that Arnold placed upon inculcating "earnest principles and moral thoughtfulness" in his pupils points to the central fact in the science and art of school government. Boys and girls can never be trusted by parent or teacher who does not rely on their own moral sense, and learn to exercise their minds in the direction of conscious, thoughtful self-government. In other words, individual charac-ter must be educated and developed in boys and girls.

6. HOW NOT TO GOVERN A SCHOOL.

A gentleman owning suburban grounds, with fruit orchard and flower garden, put up at conspicuous points on the border of his premises, the warning inscription, "No Trespass," painted in threatening capitals of black on a white board. The purpose of these imperative notices was to prevent depredation; the effect was to provoke the wanton spirit of all the boys of the neighborhood. The curt notice was con-strued into a challenge; the boards were battered to pieces with stones; raids were organized to spoliate the unwise gentleman's vineyard and water-melon patch. His vigilance to anticipate trouble antagonized Tom, Dick, and Harry, and precipitated the evil it was eager to avert.

The gentleman's wife employed a different and more successful method of protecting the place. She caused a hedge of rose-bushes to be planted around the premises, and the obnoxious warnings were removed. When the next June came, "the boys" came also; but instead of marauding, they paused to admire the beautiful and friendly barrier of blossoms, and, after consultation, concluded that it would be a shame to destroy what Mrs. Thompson had provided for the pleasure of the wayfarer. The prudence of Mrs. Thompson had quite changed the disposition of Thomas, Richard, and Henry.

Prohibitory orders, when uncalled for, are sure to bring out antagonism. Forbidden fruit is ever sought, whether it be good or evil. Blue Beard's wife looks into the closet. Tell a boy that a few drops of nitro-glycerine will blow his head off — he straightway studies chemistry to find out how to make nitro-glycerine. Tell him you will skin him alive if he don't behave himself, and he will set all his wits to invent ways and means of misdemeanor.

Therefore think twice before you threaten to punish for prospective violations of the law. Expect your pupils to do right, yet be prepared for them to do wrong. Neither require nor prohibit acts that you are unable to control.

7. THE TRUE STORY OF "RUSTY NAILS."

A very unpromising lad, reputed incorrigible,
applied for admission to a certain city school. He
sullenly admitted that he had been expelled. The
urchin rejoiced in the peculiar nickname "Rusty
Nails." Rusty Nails had been rattaned until his
body was all callous. He had won some reputation
as a teacher-fighter. The proprietor of the new
school decided to take him on probation, at the
beseeching solicitation of his father, an eccentric
gentleman of frail will but stalwart affections. So
on Monday morning Rusty Nails entered the new
school, filled from crown to toe top full of direst
insubordination. Now, it happened that the first day
glided by under influences strangely pleasant, and
no occasion arose for any sort of conflict. The
teachers and schoolmates of the notorious bad
boy acted towards him just as if he were one of
the family, showing him perhaps a little special
courtesy because he was a stranger. The second
day shed its civilizing light and warmth on him, and
a curious change began to take place in Rusty
Nails. A month elapsed, and the boy carried home
a "Report," giving his father the astonishing
intelligence that his son's "deportment" was "excellent," and that he had ninety-four per cent in
"problems."

"What is the meaning of this?" asked the in-
credulous parent. "There must be some mistake ;

your 'Reports' before this always gave your conduct
as very bad. Were they true, or is this?"

"Well, pa," said Rusty Nails with a broad grin,
"I'll tell you how it is. Them 'Reports' was true,
and this here one is true. The fact is, nobody in
the new school seemed to want to lick me, and there
was no use in being bad."

8. THE IDEAL TEACHER.

The model teacher should be — should he not be a
perfect man? Surely should the teacher whose mission it is to point the way to perfection, whose special
work in life is so grand in its scope and objects,
surely should he be a developer of men. Yes, "let
him first be a man" in the full and vigorous exercise
of all those qualities that go to make up human
nature. Let him be a man armed at all points for
the varying fortunes of the battle of life. Let him,
so far as in him lies, be such a man as in his own conception excellent education may produce, so that he
may stand both as guide and example. Let him be
a man each day rising towards his ever-receding
ideal, each day realizing his highest possible destiny
in the constant endeavor to attain unto the unattain-
able, each day approximating unto perfection.

Within the circumference of his activity as a
human being and professor of humanity is included
the smaller circle of his particular vocation as an
educator of the young. But each special calling demands some peculiar qualities in its votary, and some

distinctive adaptations. While practising his chosen profession, art, or trade, every man should be appropriately costumed and equipped, and should give himself up with all his mind and with all his might to the duties of the day. The soldier, armed and uniformed for war, is familiar with the manual of tactics, and is prepared to march and to fight. The surgeon, differently trained, attired, and provided, has mastered anatomy and knows how to use his case of instruments. The priest has a preparation, apparel, and manner suited to the pulpit. The teacher, likewise, requires a professional outfit adapted to his field of operations. This field is the school and its environments. The obligation of the schoolmaster is to educate to the best of his ability an assemblage of children, over whom he exercises an almost unlimited authority. This authority is not natural, but delegated, and, acting in the place of many parents, the teacher occupies a very delicate position, beset with difficulties. He holds responsible relations to private confidences and to public trusts; he links families to the State. At once he is nominally parent and magistrate, yet suffers the disadvantage of being neither of these in reality. He has no blood claim to the obedience and affection of his pupils, and seldom thinks of appealing to police force or judicial intervention in the management of his small community. In fact, the family and the State both stand aloof and trust him, or, rather, require him to sustain his position, and establish his reputation by virtue of independent judgment, skill, and sagacity. The tenure of his office depends upon the results he achieves. In many schools, especially country and village schools, everything is trusted to the teacher. ·He can do as he pleases, provided only that he gives satisfaction. He is expected to understand what he is about. "Nothing succeeds like success;" but how achieve success? How acquire the mastery of the situation and the confidence of pupil, parent, trustee, and people?

Circumstances may do much to aid the teacher: an intelligent and liberal community, a good school-house eligibly located, convenient furniture and apparatus, attractive books to study and read, pictures on the wall, a piano, flowers. But all these are non-essential: the teacher is more than circumstances — he is centre. Circumstances are things which stand around; the master creates circumstances for his necessity. Garfield's noted and notable saying cannot be quoted too often — "A bench with Mark Hopkins seated on it becomes a university." The teacher who ascribes his failure to the schoolhouse, or the text-book, or the incorrigible boy, resembles the farmer who condemned the prairie because it was destitute of trees, and the forest because it was covered with woods. We must take things as they are.

Leaving out of consideration the teacher's dealings with his employers, patrons, and the neighborhood in general, let us inquire what qualifications and deportment will best promote his success in the specific work of his six or eight hours' daily educating within the schoolroom. Happy for him if nature has cut him out for the business he has chosen. Unhappy for him and his charge if he is unfit in body or mind for that business. To win and sway his school, to secure respect and love, he should possess an attractive exterior, a dignified bearing, a pleasant face, an agreeable voice, a charming manner : to command obedience and inspire awe, he should also have the look and manner pertaining to authority, —must be every inch a king, and ready to sacrifice inclination and sentimental softness to order and law. The sternest are sometimes the gentlest. He must be a benignant angel to loyal and trusty pupils, but a terror to the shirk, the sneak, the liar. Yet there need be no putting-on of threatening airs, or clothing the offended powers with thunder. Napoleon did not " swell round."

Too much emphasis cannot be placed upon the necessity to the teacher of bodily vigor, activity, and vigilance. The master, or mistress, must have good eyes and ears — keen senses generally, and know how to employ them. Ever on the alert, and yet never perturbed, he must know what is going on and what is *coming* on. His will, like a reserved military force, must rise at call, if need be, to meet and overthrow the combined rebellious will of his school ; for, be he never so just, there will tumults arise on occasion, and the very best pupils will sometimes conspire to resist their own good. Veterans in teaching will tell you that when everything seems perfectly serene in school, and all goes, as it were, without effort or friction, then look out for trouble!

It is bad policy for the teacher to appeal to the school for personal sympathy by alluding to tasks, sacrifices, headaches, or the like. But if it should hap to become known to the pupils that the teacher suffered and made no complaint, the moral effect is powerful. Boys especially admire one who takes hurts without "squealing."

Due attention to external appearance and what may be called physical accomplishments, no less than to social arts, is quite as necessary as the regular mental and moral preparation for which the teacher's license vouches. The certificate may testify that its bearer's character is irreproachable and his scholarship superior, but in spite of all that, boorish behavior, slovenly habits, vulgar associations, will counteract every paper recommendation, and defeat every ambition of the candidate for high position in the teacher's profession. In saying this I do not underrate the supreme importance of complete intellectual equipment.

The usual preparation of teachers for the practice of their profession is desultory and confused. It should be definite and methodical.

The special training, the professional fitting or finishing, should be preceded by a sound education. The young man or woman who contemplates becoming a teacher should first obtain a clear and full knowledge of the leading facts and principles of science, language, and literature ; should get a good academic education, a large fund of information, a ready facility in mental operations. Such fundamental schooling is what every cultivated man and woman nowadays is assumed to possess. This is the usual American stepping-stone to the professions.

But the person of sound general education is not a teacher any more than he is a lawyer, a doctor, a theologian, an artist, an actor. There may be " born teachers," as there are born musicians and orators ; but I am now writing of the rule, not the exception, of *made* teachers, not the miraculous few who came into the world labelled *First Class Educator.* Was there, in fact, ever such prodigy, or is the "born teacher " a myth ? The "born teacher," if there be such, will not bring a knowledge of algebra and parsing into the world with him, and therefore he, too, must go to school awhile. The basilar education furnishes whomsoever has it a pedestal on which to erect any tower of particular knowledge, but is not itself a professional fitting. It it true, however, that as teachers deal with the elements of learning, the experience of every student is, in some sense, a preparation to teach, wherefore all good schools partake of the nature of normal schools, and especially so when they exemplify the best methods of instruction. The scholar who has been taught and trained by an expert will not fail, if he becomes a teacher, to imitate the example of his own preceptor.

Nevertheless, no matter how fortunate may have been the general education of a student, he needs his special course before entering a special profession. It should be the function of the Normal School, or the pedagogical Chair of the University, to conduct him along this special course, just as special institutions and professors guide students to the degree of Medical Doctor, Civil Engineer, or Bachelor of Laws. The student who, on account of poverty, or any other cause, cannot go to normal school or university, may study at home. He will miss the advantage of lectures, quiz, and examination, and the benefit which comes from attrition with other minds, but there are some compensations for his loss. Books know everything that is known. Books are not expensive. Books rival the professors and compete with the university. What must the student read in order to learn the business of teaching?

Of course he must master, in detail, the branches he is expecting to teach. These he has studied already, in the childish way, at the common school. They must be restudied in the manly way. The maturer mind will discover in the elementary text-books much that escaped the beginner. The one or two manuals to which the school-boy's lessons were confined will be supplemented and corrected by many others which the grown-up investigator will peruse.

But it is not enough to know accurately the contents of the text-books. The pupil reads to acquire and memorize; the teacher reads to impart. His vocation requires him to know how to teach in general, and how to teach every particular branch with the best economy of his own and the pupil's time and strength. This requisition calls for a close, clear, and complete study of methods of teaching.

Furthermore, since the great object of education is to develop the human mind, the teacher must know the structure and nature of the mind, — must know psychology, the science of mind.

And as the mind is manifested through the bodily organism, and is dependent on the brain, the teacher should know, thoroughly as possible, the science of physiology and collateral branches. An understanding of psychology and physiology — mind and body — must underlie any scheme of education that can justly be called scientific.

Educational practice, as now conducted, is largely empirical. Yet much of it rests upon sound maxims derived from successful experiment. Perhaps it can be said with truth that modern education is an experimental science, and that our progress depends not alone upon the direct study of the faculties of mind, but also upon what has been demonstrated in the past by actual trial. The History of Education therefore contains the philosophy of education, and the teacher must give hundreds of hours to the study of that history.

V

NATURE THE SOVEREIGN SCHOOL-
MISTRESS

I.

MOTHER NATURE is the sovereign schoolmistress. The teacher who does not co-operate with her fails; who does co-operate with her, succeeds, for she is the authorized principal of all the schools. Her credentials come from on high. Her certificates are signed by the Great Examiner.

Man has his part in training his fellow-man; he is his brother's keeper; but his duty is limited by his ignorance. Human responsibility extends to the verge of human wisdom and virtue, which is soon reached, and beyond that verge Divine hands relieve us of our tasks and cares. Children come out of the mystery of Heaven, and are consigned to our trust to be nurtured, taught, made ready for the career called living, and the destiny called dying. From God we come into the world; out of the world we go to God. From the infinite unknown to the infinite unknown is the brief flight called mortal existence.

Nature, the daughter of God, sits in the earth to interpret her Father's will. Her lap is filled with

the records of centuries, and she opens to man sibyl-
line chapters foretelling what humanity shall become.
She is the Sovereign Schoolmistress. Hear ye her
voice.

Man's first duty is to educate his kind; and to
educate is to assist nature, not to supplant her, not
to oppose her. Could we only know how to adjust
ourselves to the laws of God (which are nature's
laws), we might hope to educate with a potency
hitherto not dreamed of.

We must educate children — must instruct, control, inspire, direct them, by the wisest means we
know; but we must not forget that they also educate
themselves, or are educated by inworking forces;
that the very structure of their being determines
their culture; that nature gives impulse to every
faculty, and defines every function of body and mind.

Teachers cannot create mental and moral elements
in pupils; as well may they try to create physical
organs by gymnastic training. We may retard, develop, regulate, harmonize existing organs and forces,
but that is all we can do. The educator's utmost
science is to know nature's laws; his supreme art is
to co-operate with them. This is the economy of
economies.

Boys and girls should not be left to run wild;
nevertheless, the same instinct and energy which
runs them wild is the power on which to rely in pro-
pelling them up the hill of civilization. The misap-
plication of power is evil, but power itself is good.

As where there is life there is hope, so where there is mental force there is promise.   It is a radical mistake to regard the faculties of the soul as essentially bad or wrong.   There are no evil passions or base propensities.   The complete man possesses all the faculties named or not named in mental and moral philosophy.   The perfect man uses all, misuses none, of these faculties.   Evil springs from misuse, and misuse is the result of ignorance more than of conscious law-breaking.   The teacher has cause for discouragement and grieving when he discovers a strong faculty perverted; yet he should take heart from the reflection that *conversion* is always possible ; that, in fact, the best skill of his days must be employed in converting.   One may deal confidently with a developed faculty, — with an active, positive, vigorous force ; but how much more difficult and perplexing it is to germinate an embryo, to hatch an egg of the mind, and feed the chick through the gaps of infantile feebleness !

There must be some natural order of development in man.   Each individual grows, feels, wills, acts, according to the tendency and possibility of his nature.   As observations in meteorology bring us nearer and nearer to the realization that every change in the weather depends on fixed laws, and that even the variable winds and electric storms obey an invariable force, so the study of man's nature tends to prove that what seems accidental and irregular in character and conduct may be in accordance with persistent forces understood and applied by superior wisdom. Men are alike in elementary constitution, but diverse in development. From unity education produces infinite variety. Nature seems to abhor sameness. She differentiates, and we err when we oppose her method.

The organization of the human being is so intricate, so complicated, so multitudinous, that science is foiled in her attempts to discover the law of its operation. Here is a clock-work which no one but the maker understands. It has been running for thousands of years, — some say for millions, — and yet it has not revealed the mystery of its structure. We can see the index moving, but we cannot see the wheels and springs, the weights and pulleys, within. We observe eccentric attachments, but know not how they are organically connected with the machine. We may break open the case, and curiously pry within, and learnedly name the parts, — *protoplasm*, and *gray matter*, and *nerve-force ;* but, alas! when the clock is broken, it is not a clock.

The most pedagogical pedagogue must frankly own that man is a mystery. But this mystery is not all mysterious. Some things we know, and much we may learn, and all is known to the Creator. Using what we know, learning what we can, and trusting Him for the rest, let us enter our schoolrooms and do our work

II.

Much time is wasted at school in attempting to teach children what they are not old enough to learn. The farmer is not so unwise as to plant corn in January. And how foolish the parent or teacher who thinks to grow, in the child's brain, the reasoning powers, the conscience, the moral sense, before the season! When my pupil was six years old he could not comprehend the simple elements of arithmetic and grammar, though he studied by the hour, and stained his slate with tears. When he was twelve he found no difficulty in elementary arithmetic and grammar ; and he wondered that he had ever regarded these studies with disgust. Nature, thou patient schoolmistress, why didst thou not teach me not to teach ?

We do not look for ripe fruit on succulent sprouts. Why expect the elaborate essence of morality in early youth? Green apples are bitter and sour. The fond mother weeps at what she deems the depravity of her young son. Remember the boy is a boy, not a man. He is yet in the savage state of his individual life. The marvellous insight of Plato long ago discovered the real state of the case. "The boy is the most unmanageable of all animals. He is the most insidious, sharp-witted, and insubordinate of animals." But hear how the wise Greek explained the fact. The boy is thus, because "he has the fountain of reason in him not yet regulated."

Yes, boyhood is the primitive period of human life. It is a heroic age, a dramatic era, a time of war and love, but not civilized, much less enlightened. Shall we call it the Thor period, of which the leading idea is *hammer?* Boy as boy is interesting to contemplate, but who could bear to exist with a perpetual boy? He is a never-ending noise, and a ceaseless explosion of dynamical violence. Our mental ejaculation to the average boy is that of Dickens's benevolent Cheeryble to his brother: "Devil take you, Ned, God bless you!"

Have patience with these obdurate young brethren. Their ugly transitional traits will not last. Let the surgent blood leap while it will, and let the animal grow. Bear and forbear. Yes, be thankful that Sam is Thor, hammering thunder out of the sky; not pale Narcissus, drooping by the brook of death. The finer principles of benevolence, pity, piety, gentleness, self-sacrifice, are of slow culture. You, there, who sit at the teacher's desk, have *you* quite tamed the savage in you?

Trust Mother Nature to punish the boys. Gracious Matron! she forever whispers deep lessons to their hearts. Sam weeps on her consolatory bosom, after disdaining his mother's plea, his father's condemnation, and his master's rod. Yes, rigorous yet gentle nature knows the boys will not forever stone the pigs, slay the cats, and pull off the birds' heads; they will not always monopolize the nicest of the apples, and beat their sisters for reporting the facts.

Experience discovers limitations to their tyranny, and teaches even their selfishness to seek gratification in less objectionable ways. They throw away the Thor hammer of their own accord, seeing it is not the best instrument with which to win happiness.

The farmer finds it almost impossible to crush, with roller, harrow, and hoe, the stubborn clods of his field; but under the action of rain, frost, sunshine, and gravity, how often those same stubborn clods fall to pieces of themselves, and crumble down about the roots of the wheat and the barley! So the teacher finds it difficult to subdue and reform incorrigible propensities that, if left alone, will soften, yield, and disappear, under the beneficent influences which commonly bear upon youth. How many efficient assistants every teacher might have if he· were wise enough to recognize them! The first assistant ought always to be the teacher's own pupil. Ah! I spoke without reflection, and should have said the teacher is only first assistant to the learner; for real education must always be, in the main, self-help.

III.

He who co-operates with nature in the work of educating the young will discover that nature's text-book is illuminated on every page with the inspiring word, Freedom. Freedom is the best good. Freedom is good for the body, good for the soul, good for

man — for each organ and part of him, even to the
minutest atom that enters into his composition, and
for every motion of life or spirit that stirs his being.
Freedom is strength, activity, life, — loss of freedom
is feebleness, paralysis, death. Freedom is neither
license nor constraint ; neither stimulation nor stu-
pefaction ; nor the condition of the over-nourished,
hot-house plant, nor of the neglected weed by the
barren wayside ; nor of the rank, untended wild vine
of the forest ; but it is the state of the cultivated
vegetation of the fertile, sunny garden bed. Freedom is the condition which allows man to become
his perfect self in the happiest way. It is favorable
opportunity to conform to the law of individuality,
to adjust man's faculties to their natural and proper
use; to seek and find one's own physical and spiritual
heritage, and to reach the full stature of independent
manhood. Freedom is not the right to do as you
please ; it is the liberty to do and become what you
are capable of in the legitimate exercise of your own
powers — the privilege of obeying the eternal com-
mandments inscribed by the Creator upon your
members and your mind. Freedom, ideal and absolute, is the glorious liberty of the sons of God.

There can be no true obedience without freedom.
To obey the laws of health I must be permitted to
obtain proper food, practise suitable exercise, breathe
pure air, and sleep in peace. The mind's health,
also, requires wholesome surroundings and opportunity to enjoy them. Elegantly has Holmes elabo-

rated an old, familiar figure illustrating my subject:
"Look at the flower of a morning glory the evening
before the dawn which is to see it unfold. The delicate petals are twisted into a spiral which, at the
appointed hour, when the sunlight touches the hid-
den springs of its life, will uncoil itself, and let the
daylight into the chambers of its virgin heart. But
the spiral must unwind by its own law, and the hand
that shall try to hasten the process will only spoil
the blossom that would have expanded in symmetrical beauty under the rosy fingers of the morning."

Not only must the plant blossom in its own way,
it must remain of its own species. Shall one say in
obstinate pride or blind conceit, " I will make of this
plant what I please. I will conform it to my ideal, —
it shall bear peaches, — it shall bloom roses, — it
shall ripen corn, — it shall grow, like Jack's bean, a
hundred miles high, — it shall be a creeping moss " ?
Or shall we reflect, with humility, as co-workers with
God, "What will come of this marvellous perennial
that I am permitted to train ? What lovely and here-
tofore unheard-of blossom may it unfold ? How can
I best nurture and protect its tender leaves ? How
can I discover what soil, situation, and culture are
best adapted to it ? "

Let us emancipate ourselves from the slavery of a
mechanical system which ignores nature, forgets
God, and reduces us to tasked operatives, supervis-
ing a spinning-jenny. Emancipate the children from
the tread-mill task of grinding out lessons for the

sake of recording the grists. Lead them back to the freedom of nature; make them conscious of mind, thought, affection, duty, and joy. Feed them not on husks, but call them to the fruity orchard of vital knowledge, and to the flowing waters of living virtue. Measure success, not by the number of sub-jects taught, but by the number of minds roused to action. Count it no merit to have "passed" a class with an average per cent of 99, unless you can claim also that the class has learned to love learning. Show one boy or one girl whom you have induced to study as a pleasure rather than a tax, and you de-serve the crown of praise. Make of this boy an original man; make of this girl a woman whose mind to her shall Kingdom be, and no crown of praise can add glory to your brow.

Oh, that some blessed revival could come upon the brain and heart of our profession; could fall like sunlight from heaven and illuminate and warm us for our duty! For we forget the principal things we should remember. We lapse into unconsciousness of our greatest privileges. The teacher should more than teach, more than govern, more than love; he should *inspire* his school. Inspire, breathe into the pupil the animative principle, the soul-breath, the awakening spirit that gives consciousness of the need of activity, power, culture, education.

VI

TOPICS OF THE TIME

I. "EXPERIMENTS OF LIGHT"

"God, on the first day of creation, created light only, giving to that work an entire day, in which no material substance was created. So must we likewise, from experience of every kind, first endeavor to discover true causes and axioms, and seek for experiments of light, not for experiments of fruit. For axioms rightly discovered and established supply practice with its instruments, not one by one, but in clusters, and draw after them trains and troops of works."

This text, from that inspired, philosophic bible, Bacon's "Novum Organum," suggests a sermon, not more important to the scientific explorer than to the practical educator. That ignorant men should fail to see the worth of "Experiments of Light" is to be expected, for they do not reason far enough to comprehend general principles. But that educated men — men educated to educate others — should hold a prejudice against such "experiments" is almost incredible. Yet we know that many teachers *do* mistrust and disparage speculative discussions on pedagogics, and emphatically call for "experiments of fruit" *before* "experiments of light."

It is noticeable that the majority of those who attend teachers' institutes and normal schools seek methods rather than systems, and are impatient with even the most fruitful axioms, though grateful for even the barrenest rule or regulation to imitate. Young teachers are apt to regard the very terms Theory and Practice as antithetic. What is theoretical they assume is impractical. To such an opinion a wise rebuke is to be found in a very ancient Hindoo poem, in which the deity himself is made to say, "Children only, and not the learned, speak of the speculative and the practical doctrines as two."

All intelligent practice must grow out of theory; that is to say, thought must precede correct action. That workman bungles who does what he is told without knowing why he does it. The teacher who follows his master's advice, not comprehending the motive, aim, and end of that advice, can never succeed. Such a teacher is an automaton — a mechanism of springs and wheels that must soon run down and cannot wind itself up again.

Imitating what another does is not *doing*, but only pretending to do. The teacher's art, like all arts, depends on its science. How profoundly true and how encouraging is Bacon's assertion that "theories supply practice with its instruments, *not one by one, but in clusters, and draw after them trains and troops of works.*"

No sadder delusion can becloud the brain than that broad, philosophical thinking unfits the thinker for practical details of work. Experience proves that the men who comprehend subjects in their general relations are the men who set a true value on particulars.

How may a teacher train a mind if he doesn't know what mind is? How can he educate without conceiving an idea of education in the abstract? In a word, what is it to acquire the teacher's profession if it be not to master a comprehensive science; namely, the science of teaching?'

To possess a good education is not to be a good educator. The teacher should possess knowledge — the more the better — for, as Goethe says, "There is nothing more frightful than a teacher who knows only what his scholars are intended to know." But no amount of learning minus the science of education can make a person master of the teacher's *profession*. The knowledge that distinguishes the educator from other educated men is the knowledge of the principles of pedagogics, theoretic and applied.

The physician who thoroughly understands anatomy, physiology, chemistry, medicine, surgery, who has studied the body in health and disease, is prepared to practise his art.

The lawyer who comprehends the fundamental principles of law and justice, who realizes the full meaning of his text-books, is ready to undertake a suit in court.

The teacher who has patiently examined the history, philosophy, and literature of education, who has formed a definite conception of the human faculties, and of why and how they may be developed best, may begin to teach school.

The objection that the region of speculative pedagogics is a land of fogs, should incite explorers to clearer discoveries. If we must walk in the fog, it is better to light a lantern. Better, it would seem, to pursue the divine method recommended by Bacon, and illuminate our way. And if the teacher must choose between the visionary and the empirical, is it not barely possible that the visionary may prove the more hopeful of the two? Happier he who sees visions and dreams dreams of professional progress than he who is content to plod on, not knowing or caring whither his steps tend, not sure that they tend any whither except around a tread-mill.

2. BOTH SIDES ARE RIGHT.

There is much wisdom in taking both sides of a disputed question, not in a partisan, but in a philosophic spirit, and by taking both sides, learning the truth and the error each contains. Every debatable question is debatable because its affirmative and its negative statement both appear right to some and wrong to others, and may, in fact, both be true and both false in some part or degree.

Dogmas in political economy, sociology, ethics, religion, education, are seldom absolutely demonstrable, by logical process, like a mathematical proposition. The science of pedagogics is not yet an exact science. The scope of it is infinite; the themes it discusses are too numerous and complicated and too subtle to be caught in the net of definition.

How admirable is that magnanimity which, while sincerely holding its own view, and even ready to die for its convictions, can yet candidly say, " The other view may be right, and, if I saw so, I would change."

The conflict of theories, in the pedagogical arena, is productive of practical good; and every attempt to deduce first principles in education is a step in the direction of reform. Yet it is never to be forgotten that theory is theory, and is true only so far as it can be verified by fact. We must have theories in education, as in physics or chemistry, and for the same reason; namely, to give unity and direction to our work.

A favorite dogma in the modern science of education appears to be that the purpose of schooling is not *learning* but *development.* Pupils used to go to school to store their minds with knowledge; now they go, as we say, to strengthen their faculties, to cultivate the power of thought and the habit of duty.

Are not both ideas correct, and is there not danger that, in putting so much emphasis on the new statement, we may underrate the value of the old? The end of education is the same now as it used to be; that is, to benefit the educated individual by imparting to him knowledge, in which process power must necessarily be imparted. There is no such thing conceivable as mind-development unaccompanied by the acquisition of ideas. Learning is the food of the brain by which all thought and feeling are nourished. The measure of a mind's actual knowledge will be also the measure of its acquired ability. A confusion arises, in our reasoning, from misunderstanding what is meant by knowledge. Knowledge means more than the memorized facts. The scholar comprehends principles, causes, effects, differences, similarities, and all the relations and combinations of facts.

The protest against mechanical education, against cramming and working for per cents, is timely, and cannot be too strongly put. This protest, however, is hurled, properly, not against knowledge, but against a false method of. imparting knowledge. If the mechanical methods were successful in conveying knowledge, the fact that they are mechanical would not stand against them. If you *can* cram knowledge into the children, in God's name do it; but you cannot. The student who is crammed is not intelligent; he does not know facts; he gains neither information nor discipline. There is no mechanical way of producing intellectual results. Dean Swift's Academy of Laputa is not what is, but only what Gulliver saw. Why should we try the experiment of writing a geometrical problem on a wafer and compelling our pupil to swallow it, in order to impress the demonstration on his brain?

Fire hot volleys all along the line of discussion,

against the stupid, old or new methods of teaching; but have a care that you do not hit what you do not aim at, and wound the dignity of solid learning. Both sides are right. The object of education *is* to store the mind with knowledge, and it is also to develop mental power and moral character. The acquisition and retention of exact, systematic, true, good and beautiful knowledge create a clear mind and a pure heart. Knowledge and power are one; they coalesce and become wisdom, the prize that is precious above rubies.

3. DISCO.

Disco means to know, to learn, in the widest sense. From the word are derived *disciple*, a learner, and *discipline*, learning, or the result of learning. Discipline and knowledge are one.

When, therefore, we speak of subjects as having special value in disciplining the mind, we do not mean that such subjects are of a different nature from other kinds of knowledge, or that they can be learned or used in a peculiar way. That scholar is disciplined, in a degree, who knows how to calculate the interest on a note, or how to roast a turkey. Discipline is required in order to write one's own name, or to tell the difference between a ball and a cube. Greater discipline is called for in doing more difficult things, or thinking more difficult thoughts.

One must learn before he can do. The more one

learns the more can he do.   All knowledge is discipline; there is no discipline outside of knowledge.

It is a delusion to suppose that mental power can be acquired by any exercise of the faculties that does not imply the possession of ideas.   How can we conceive of a mathematical ability severed from a comprehension of mathematics? or of logical skill without logic? or of linguistic power apart from knowledge of language?   To assume that the results of knowledge can be obtained without knowledge is to assume that the whole is less than the sum of its parts.

All knowledge is not of equal value, but power comes only in proportion to acquisition.   The question is not, Can knowledge and discipline be separated? but, What knowledge, i.e., discipline, is most valuable?

The original forms in which a certain kind of knowledge may have entered the mind may be obliterated or forgotten, while the essential knowledge may be retained, as an algebraic formula contains, in permanent, usable result, many particular examples once solved but afterwards not thought of.   The mastery of the formula was the binding of many straws into one sheaf — was gathering knowledge in principle.

This grasping of principles or general truths is what scholars understand by mental discipline.   There is no royal road to it.   There is no short road to it. There is no smooth road to it.   The superficial and inaccurate student can never attain it.

Teachers and learners should divest themselves of the notion that education is only a key to unlock the treasury of knowledge, or that discipline consists in the mere effort of unlocking a treasury. Education is not the key or the treasury — it is key, treasury, and treasure.

4. NATURAL ABILITY PLUS EDUCATION.

Going to school or college may indeed spoil the boy, but good education spoils him not. The fortune left to young Princely was his ruin, yet how good a thing is money!

Education may subtract some efficient qualities from natural ability, but adds ten where it takes away one. The wild peach has lovelier blossoms and fruit of more piquant flavor than the cultivated tree, yet the latter is most valued. An edge-tool, as Quintilian says, loses something in the process of sharpening, but who therefore thinks a dull tool is best? The marble loses substance and strength when hewn into a statue. Rough stone is better adapted to some purposes than polished blocks, nevertheless the polished block is alone fit for finest uses.

What can a keen blade do that a dull one cannot? What can a microscope do that the naked eye cannot? The dull knife may be fine steel; it must be sharpened, tempered, ground, whetted for the engraver's hand or the surgeon's. The shaping, tempering, grinding, whetting educate the good steel for its exquisite functions. Something is lost, much is gained. The eye must be a good eye before it can be helped by the microscope or the telescope; but never can the naked eye, however good, see a blood corpuscle or the rings of Saturn. Optical instruments magnify and multiply vision.

Uncultured natural talent or genius is the naked eye, the native iron. Education cannot create original force. Falstaff longed to know where a "commodity of good names could be bought." 'Tis easier to buy a good name than a good capacity. Schools cannot furnish the stuff; they only manufacture it. Out of pot-metal pots can be made — most excellent pots. Damascus steel will make Damascus blades.

Every mind is bettered by correct education; the greater the natural ability the more right culture will add.

5. THE QUICK COAL.

> " Man is no starre, but a quick coal
> Of mortal fire :
> Who blows it not, nor doth controll
> A faint desire,
> Lets his own ashes choke his soul."

These quaint but piercing lines from rare George Herbert's poem "Employment" afford the student a warning, the scholar an incentive. Activity is the price of culture; the intellect must be kept alive by the breath of the will ; the faculties disused fall to decay. It is a common observation that mechanical

skill is acquired and retained only by habitual practice. Wilhelmj, the celebrated violinist, said : " If I
remit rehearsal for one day, I am conscious of dete-
rioration ; if I neglect practice for two days, the
critics observe it ; if I neglect for three days, my
audience notice it." The right hand loses its cun-
ning, so also do the memory, the inventive faculty,
the reasoning power. I used to know how, but I
forget — I have lost facility. Facts and processes
acquired at school seem to vanish from the mind.
One man discovers with dismay that his Greek and
Latin have flitted from him ; another cannot recall
the once familiar method of solving a quadratic
equation. One says, "I am rusty ;" another says,
" The cares of this world choke out the seeds of
culture." And so they do. Culture is a jealous
god, and demands earnest and constant worship.
To him that hath shall be given, and from him that
hath not shall be taken away. Old Confucius said,
" Learn as if you could not reach your object, and
were always fearing, also, lest you should lose it."
And again, " If a man keeps cherishing his old
knowledge, so as to be constantly acquiring new, he
may be a teacher of others."

The student's soul may be all aglow at the end
of his school days. The day after commencement
brings a crisis. Will the " honor man " then blow
the quick coal without his teachers' prompting ?
without the enthusiasm of class influences ? without
the motives which emulation and ambition create ?

Will he control a *faint* desire for self-improvement, or will he let his own ashes choke his soul?—his own ashes : sordid pursuits, sensual pleasures, dull indolence.

6. DOES IT EDUCATE?

The core of one of Matthew Arnold's best books is that "The object of religion is conduct," conduct being at least three-fourths of life. The object of education—the main object—is conduct. The men and women that the teachers make of boys and girls at school should be men and women who can do the things of common life well, whether these things be of the hand, the head, or the heart. Conduct is the art of living. What is it that we value most in our fellow-beings? Is it not their facility in doing daily and hourly duties in a happy and generous way? We like the person who is able and agreeable ; who applies his nature and his acquired powers to doing right things pleasantly.

The child should learn to speak because speech is conduct, is the means of humanization, concord, love, and social service. He should learn to read for the good that reading may do to himself and to others ; for the meliorating, civilizing, sweetening use of books. He should write in order to write legibly, easily, for the convenience of life. To think clearly, to desire purely, to perform beautifully,—these are the purposes of training.

All that is attempted or done in giving tasks,

hearing recitations, advising or restraining pupils, should aim at the golden centre of the target — conduct. That is the best subject to teach which imparts the most usable knowledge of the most durable kind for common practice in affairs. That text-book is best which wastes the least time on non-essentials. Give something to each pupil at every lesson-time, — something worth giving, — and that will fashion his life in some degree for the better. Clinch the nail instruction. Illuminate the boy's mind. Quicken his moral perception. Sweeten his disposition. Modulate and beautify his manner. Do anything and everything that will tend to make him a lucid-minded, clean-hearted, versatile, thoroughly useful and happy citizen of the earth, heaven-bound.

The branches of learning, as we call them, are all one in their grand purpose. They may all be committed to memory and do no good. To learn is to learn. The book must be poured into the very veins of the pupil and circulated through him from brain to finger-nail. What is needed is the juice of the book, not the husk. He who teaches arithmetic well has taught all mathematics by anticipation. Who teaches the First Reader rightly has given his pupil a clew to Shakespeare, to Herodotus, to Confucius. Education is all one — it is feeding a soul, it is bestowing upon faculties the readiest and noblest use of their functions.

The school should put its pupils at once into the conscious exercise of their educable organs, habits, ideals. To-day this girl ought to walk, talk, look, think, feel, wish, hope, better than she did yesterday. These children, when they quit school, must move in the world — work, play, earn, spend, sustain a thousand relations to others. They must do their tasks, they must bear their burdens, they must live the life, die the death, and leave the record of a mortal.

Education should fit them for all this. Does it ?

7. THE BEGINNINGS OF EDUCATION.

It is curious to observe the first efforts of the child to exercise his powers and enlarge his range of experience. He begins to manifest his innate tendency to *do* something, and to connect his little intelligence with things around him, by vague, unsteady motions of limbs and body, and by inarticulate crying or crowing. The tiny fingers presently become busy. The baby picks and pries into everything, makes his mouth a universal test-tube, tears paper, throws his spoon, likes to make something tumble. His activity is incessant, like his quick heart-beats. He rolls and sprawls, he babbles and blinks. The first attempts to walk are most feeble and ludicrous. After hundreds of trials he learns to creep. After thousands of falls he is able to stand. How little control he has over his motions ! Starting to go forward, he staggers backwards — tipsy fellow !

The child's endeavor to utter words is as wide of

its aim as the primary efforts to handle or to walk. The organs of speech are unformed, — still less formed the mind-power which sets the machine in motion. Nature prompts the infant to imitate, and he makes the oddest approximations to correct speech. The tongue and lips must clamber and stumble, as do the puny hands and feet.

The later attempts and struggles of the boy to acquire a surer and stronger control over his muscles, nerves, and mental faculties, are very similar to the earlier trials of the infant. The boy of ten is a baby when he grapples with hard studies or difficult arts. The mind is trained to severer thinking by repetition and practice only. And what are the highest mental exertions of the logician or philosopher? They are baby endeavors to stand on insecure ground, with unsteady feet — baby efforts to articulate unfamiliar language. The whole course of education, from first to last, seems to be a series of endeavors and approximations — a training of the faculties to higher and higher uses. The baby begins, but he has eternity to progress in.

8. EDUCATION AND TEMPERANCE.

The most profoundly efficacious "temperance man" is the temperate man. Not by wind-power, nor by water-power, but by power of example he reforms others. His practice preaches. His conduct is a moral prohibitory act. His influence enforces constitutional amendments to the habits of his associates and observers.

Self-control is temperance. The mind should be the body's king. The temperate man is temperate at the top. He reasons, decides, and then acts. He administers the laws' of moderation to his subjects, the desires. Two giants, Will and Won't, guard his appetites and propensities as the lion-tamer rules caged beasts ; they drive or stop his passions, those flying fire-steeds of the brain. These desires, these appetites, these propensities, these passions are the driving-wheels of character. They are the heat, light, electricity of the human engine, all convertible into beneficent working force, yet ever liable to produce conflagration, explosion, and death.

Man should be educated to run his own machine, namely, his body, according to the laws of its structure. The greatest man, when he loses self-control, makes the greatest wreck and ruin. 'Tis the consummation of wisdom to conserve human power.

Few take the trouble to be moderate. Eternal vigilance is the price of liberty in the world of individual existence. The moment a man ceases to set sentries at the gates of his palace, the enemy will steal in. The temperance pledge must be taken anew every hour and kept every minute. License, excess, dissipation are every man's enemy always. Whosoever is out of temptation is out of this world. Temperance is as difficult as climbing a mountain, or rowing against the stream. We float or fall to the devil, but we toil and sweat on the road to redemption. The oarsman is a fool who complains because the stream flows downward ; it is right that the stream flow downward and necessary that the oarsman pull hard against the rapid.

A temperate life is the consequence of a good education. A good education gives men self-control. A good education means correct habits early begun and firmly established. Sensuality, drunkenness, lust are dreadful diseases, hardly curable ; but they are preventable. Physicians use what they call "prophylactics" to lessen the probability of disease. The prophylactic for intemperance is education, — moral education. Begin with the children.

9. UNIVERSAL EDUCATION.

Education cannot confer every benefit upon a nation, but it can confer incalculable good. / Neither population nor products, money nor machinery, bullets nor ballots, will secure lasting prosperity to any people. Nor will all these together secure it, unless they become the agents of general intelligence and sound morality.// True education has never disappointed the expectations of individual, / community, or State. It has always helped man in proportion to his faithfulness in seeking its good offices. The more general the diffusion of knowledge among the multitude, and the higher the popular standard of education, the better in every way will be the condition of man, whether in private or public life. Vast material resources, / unless controlled by intellectual and moral influences, are as systems of worlds destitute of the attraction of gravitation. Education is not everything ; yet without it a nation is nothing.

They who put their trust in legislation as a sure means of maintaining good and preventing evil, are no wiser than they who have implicit faith in the saving power of wealth and enterprise. Solon, when asked if he had given the Athenians the *best* laws, replied : " Yes ; the best the Athenians are capable of receiving." In a republic the citizens fashion the government more than the government fashions the citizens. They are their own Solons, and dictate laws for themselves. But they cannot devise laws above their own capacity, nor will they obey such laws. Constitutions and statutes, banks and rail-roads, farms and warehouses, reflect the spirit and character of the men who make and manage them. Acts of Congress and decisions of courts are only marks upon the barometer scale of Popular Opinion, and serve to indicate the state of the intellectual and moral atmosphere. It is vain to expect wisdom and purity to rule at the Capitol unless wisdom and purity dwell at our firesides. Party corruption rages among the ignorant and vicious, as cholera infects the weak and debauched. Only education can depose spurious office-holders and amend evil measures. Intelligence desires excellent rule — petitions for reform of abuses — is a good law unto itself when thrown upon its own option. Ignorance hates all rule — demands license — demands anarchy — gravi-

tates to barbarism. No statesmanship can save an
ignorant people from ruin. Exclaims the historian,
Michelet, "What is the first part of politics? Education. And the second? Education. And the
third? Education."

There are multitudes of uneducated men and
women in the United States. They weaken society,
as rotten threads impair the fabric in which they are
woven. And there are other multitudes so poorly
and superficially educated that they are not capable of
intelligent self-government. This nation, notwith-
standing its boasted educational facilities, permits
the existence of an immense class of foreigners,
native whites, and negroes, who can neither read nor
write, not to speak of that yet larger class of persons
who, though they read and write, are far from being
able to think rationally or act virtuously. These
classes are hostile to good institutions, whether they
know it or not, whether they wish to be so or not.
The State must lift them up or they will drag it
down. Universal suffrage is a doubtful good, unless
accompanied by universal education. To extend the
right of voting to the ignorant is to open new fields
to the spoliating hands of the demagogue. Would
we have the freedman appreciate his privilege? Educate him. Would we better the condition of woman?
Educate her, and she will better her condition for
herself. Would we save the expense of poorhouse
and prison? We must incur the expense of schoolhouses and library. Would we avoid civil war, estab-

lish business upon a sure basis, abolish the evils of
caste, repress sensuality, and induce men and women
to live rational, beneficial, and happy lives? We
must let education do its perfect work for high and
low, rich and poor, male and female, black and white.

General education is general uplifting. The more
complete the culture, the higher the elevation. Universal and complete education is universal and complete elevation — is human perfection on earth — is
the millennium of enthusiasts realized.

Material resources may fail, banks break, and cor-
porations go down ; trade may languish, and mechanic
invention slumber ; blight may fasten upon the grain-
fields, and drought dwindle the running streams ; the
army may disband, and the navy lie idle upon the
barren sea ; courts and congress may dissolve, and
the sacred ballot-box moulder from disuse — but yon
humble schoolhouse must not be abandoned nor neglected. To sacrifice that were fatal indeed. To stab
the people's Free School is to pierce our country in
the heart — is matricide.

VII

BOOKS AND READING`

Books, the main instruments with which teachers work, are themselves substitutes for teachers. "The true University of these days is a Collection of Books," said Carlyle; and Emerson repeated the same idea in other language.

"Strong book-mindedness," as Wordsworth forcibly calls it, is a great, if not the greatest, element of scholarship and means of education. The student graduates from the seminary, but from the library never. Original men begin self-education where school education ends. Books are their post-collegiate professors.

The ignorant disparage book-knowledge; but, in fact, books teach everything except, as Bacon says, "their own use." He who knows how to use books efficaciously has acquired a fruitful art. Books are repositories of universal experience. They record the wisdom and the folly of mankind. They perpetuate generations. In them the past lives and the present moves. Whatever men know or do, books tell. A book is an image of the mind that conceived it. Authors reproduce themselves in their writings. Books are phonographs that repeat the message origi-

nally received by them. Do not printed pages communicate to us the diverse brain product of the race?
They instruct, argue, exhort, and amuse. They phi-
losophize — they prattle; they soothe — they inflame;
they laugh — they lament.

Plato objects to written discourses; that they, like
pictures, though seeming to possess life, are silent, and
answer no questions. They do not continue the discussions in which they have awakened our interest;
cannot explain or defend themselves when challenged.
This disadvantage of books is counterbalanced by
the negative merit that they do not take offence
when shut up, and have not the tenacious persistence
of a living bore. A man cannot always choose his
flesh-and-blood companions; but his associates in
printer's ink he may command absolutely. The
humblest reader may own the highest book.

Though books are silent, their voices are audible
to imagination. The charm of Plato illustrates this.
The art of his Dialogue is such that it illudes the
senses. The reader is absorbed, rapt; he walks with
Socrates and Phædrus by the Ilissus and worships
Pan. He reclines at the Symposium in the house
of Agathon, hearing eloquent discourse of love, and
is disturbed and amused by the troop of revellers
led by tipsy Alcibiades. He stands in the court
listening with breathless attention to the unavailing
Apology; he beholds Socrates drain the cup of hem-
lock, and hears the last dying syllables of the tranquil
martyr.

My bookcase is like the enchanted table in Faust, from which, at pleasure, were drawn Rhenish wine, champagne, Tokay.

"The choice is free: make up your minds."

Would I taste the vintage of science or history or philosophy? Here are the works of the masters. Here, in little space, is the labor of a life. Spencer's forty years of toil and thought are in those few volumes. There is Bacon. There is Gibbon. What did Milton say? "Books are not absolutely dead things, but doe contain a potencie of life in them to be as active as that soul whose progeny they are; nay, they doe preserve as in a vial the purest efficasie and extraction of that living intellect. that bred them."

Here are the essayists, the novelists, the poets, the dramatists. They proffer the honey and wine of their genius. I have only to wish. I have only to take my books from the shelves, and sit down, and read.

Do I desire to hear eloquent speeches? These volumes pass me to the floors of senate, parliament, court. I may call for whatever eloquent orator I prefer, living or dead, and he will make for me his greatest effort. Stand up, Demosthenes, and while away my time.

Where shall we go to church to-day? Already have Spurgeon and Beecher been to my house this morning, flying on the wings of the press, and they have prayed and preached the prayer and the sermon of the living present. This afternoon I shall hear Jeremy Taylor.

Milton uses the word "unbookishness" to denote a certain rudeness of mind. In these days it is a disgrace not to be able to read. A taste for reading is regarded as a mark of refinement. The mere "dipper into books" takes higher rank than his wholly illiterate neighbor. Victor Hugo gives a *quasi* dignity to an unlettered oddity, by making him delight in knowing simply the names of philosophers and poets. The smatterer is a plane above the ignoramus. A little knowledge is not dangerous, though danger is incurred by mistaking a taste of the Pierian Spring for a deep draught. Even the wish to learn is commendable.

To possess books is not to possess their contents. An author's writings are properly called his works. It takes work to compose a substantial book, and proportional work to read it. How presumptuous that I should expect to understand in a day the volume I could not have produced in a lifetime!

Sir Walter Scott says in "Waverley," "I believe one reason why such numerous instances of erudition occur among the lower ranks is, that with the same powers of mind the poor student is limited to a narrow circle for indulging his passion for books and must necessarily make himself master of the few he possesses ere he can acquire more." Michelet says, "The workman loves his books, because he has few

of them. Maybe he has but one; and if it be a
sound work, he gets on all the better for having but
one. One book read and read over again, which you
ruminate upon and digest, often develops the intellect
more than a vast, indigested mass of reading. I
lived for years with a Virgil, and found my account
in it."

The "Autobiography" of Stuart Mill, in its "record of an education that was unusual and remarkable," shows what an enormous amount of difficult
reading one man may do thoroughly. The complete
and exact reading of one solid book makes the reading of a second easier. An experienced student,
whose mind is disciplined by systematic application,
acquires a grasp and facility of thought that bears
him on rapidly through labored discussions and intricate mazes of knowledge. The scholar, like the
artisan, must take time and pains to learn the use of
his implements.

With what varying results do different readers
peruse the same book! One man brings riches from
a barren page; another comes away poor from the
very treasure-troves of literature. There are few
mental phenomena more puzzling than that of a sane
man or woman reading by rote from a sense of duty.
Is it not extremely curious that any one should conceive it to be a virtue merely to read perfunctorily,
automatically, without comprehending the words
seen or uttered? Yet this is done, not only by
school-children, in their parrot-like lessons, but also

out of school, by grown people who seem to have good sense on other matters. Persons impose upon themselves the weary task of poring over number- less, bulky volumes of history or science, under the delusion that they are improving their minds, when, in fact, they are only wasting precious time, and inflaming their eyes. I once knew a young school- master who had got it into his conscientious pate that reading was the proper thing to do, and that the more pages he pronounced, the more nearly he discharged his duty to himself, his profession, his country, and mankind. He plodded through Josephus, Rollin, and Dick's works with incredible patience, and with a scrupulous attention to notes and references that was morally sublime. No tome was too massy for him ; no subject was out of his range. He would not have hesitated, I am sure, to undertake the national poem of the Kalmucks, which De Quincey says measures seventeen English miles in length. I can hear the sigh of tired triumph with which Josiah (for that was his name) closed a finished volume of Patent Office Reports. "There !" he exclaimed, "I am through that !" On a well-remem- bered·occasion a roguish girl put Josiah's bookmark from volume ii. of Kane's "Arctic Explorations" to the corresponding page in volume i. The patient plodder, when he came home from school on the day of this trick, turned to the bookmark and continued reading the whole evening, unconscious that he was reviewing what he had gone over a week or so before.

When, however, the sly maid by whose stratagem he lost so much time, demurely asked in her Quaker fashion, "How does thee like Dr. Kane?" Josiah answered that it seemed to him there was a good deal of sameness in the book.

The young schoolmaster regarded himself as a remarkably well-read man. He plumed himself on his useful reading. He imagined that he derived from books as much benefit as any person whatever. Yet he no more assimilated his crude acquisitions than the mill-stone assimilates the corn it grinds. The corn wears out the mill-stone, giving it a mealy smell; the books wore out the young man, imparting to him only the faintest odor of literary culture.

Reading, if it answers its true end, nourishes and vitalizes the mind; it goes into the intellectual circulation, and is secreted in new forms of thought, imagination, and emotion. It quickens the perceptive powers and deepens the reflective. He who reads profitably absorbs from his book such ideas and such use of language as are adapted to his capacity and want. He reads actively, consciously: every increment of knowledge falls into its place and becomes usable. The more facts he accumulates, the better does he see the value and bearings of each.

The reader who speaks or writes may unknowingly appropriate the ideas and even the sentences of his favorite books. It sometimes happens that what one has read in his youth and forgotten comes back by some subtle association, rising in the mature mind as if formed there. No writer altogether avoids betraying the dominant influence of the books that educate him. The tendency to imitate that which we strongly admire is almost irresistible. Carlyle is original to a fault, — defiantly original, — and yet critics say Richter's style reappears in Herr Teufeldröckh. Originality of language does not consist in artful arrangement of words, much less in paraphrase. It depends upon the organic structure of the idea expressed, and upon the form in which that idea figures itself on the mirror of conception. The mode of expression is dictated at once by the commanding thought itself. Seneca says, "Great thought must have suitable expression ; and there ought to be a kind of transport in the one to answer to the other." Perhaps a man's most original thoughts are those he is least conscious of evolving. As dead, structureless chyle becomes living, cellular blood, through the operation of biological causes, so knowledge changes to thought — originality is the vitalization of the mind's food ; it is the last process of mental digestion.

Literary history does not show that invention flags as erudition advances. On the contrary, the great writers have been, generally, great readers. Rabelais, Cervantes, Montaigne, — men of their class — feed themselves on books.

To understand an author, we must understand more than his words. We must seize the spirit of his thought. His words are the best vehicles the writer could command to carry to us his meaning. But be sure, no thinker ever was satisfied with the words he uses. Days of thinking brought to the printed page one or two sentences. Reading those sentences, we may be provoked or allured to other days of thinking. The ability to think is the measure of our natural capacity with the effects of education superadded. To read much and think little may weaken the mind, not strengthen it. You cannot always have a book to read, or a companion to talk with ; but you can think without book or companion, by daylight or in darkness, with or without the aid of the senses. The mind takes up no room in a travelling-bag, and yet it holds the world and all. It holds the thinking apparatus.

The book that stimulates and enlightens Julius may prove intolerable to Felix. Lady Jane Grey likes Plato, Matthew Arnold likes Burke, Ruskin likes Coventry Patmore. Beecher declares that for twenty years Herbert Spencer's works had been " meat and bread " to him. Macaulay, a gormand of books, praises many, but places the seventh book of Thucydides above all others. He calls it " the *ne plus ultra* of human art." Carlyle names the Book of Job as the first of literary productions.

Ruskin says in one of the two charming lectures in " Sesame and Lilies " (a book of diamond lustre and value), "And if she can have access to a good library of old and classical books, there need be no choosing at all ; . . . turn your girl loose into the old library every wet day, and let her alone."

The formation of a library of standard books in every private house would work wonders in education and culture. The presence of books in a house is civilizing. The father who provides wholesome mental food for his family performs a duty at once political, social, and individual. He supports his children's souls. Fortunate the youth whose days and nights are, in part, given to the dignified influences of high literature.

IN THE LIBRARY.

. . . "Loved associates, chiefs of elder art,
Teachers of wisdom." — *Roscoe.*

I.

Once more the task-imposing sun
His proud imperious course has run.
I saw his blood-red royal crown
Beyond the dreary hills sink down ;
While from a chariot of cloud,
Her stormy trumpet sounding loud,
The Amazonian Night made war
Against the moon and every star.

My jealous curtains, drooping, hide
Repose within from storm outside.
Rave on, thou wintry tempest ! beat
The flying snow from street to street ;

Against the rattling shutter dash,
And madly buffet window sash;
Thy baffled pinions strive in vain
My still retreat serene to gain.
A safe redoubt this study chair,
From arrows of the icy air;
My tranquil Argand's yellow ray
Creates a supernatural day;
My Youghiogheny sunshine glows
Defiance to the boreal snows,
And, flushing, fills my tropic room
With rays that make the roses bloom.

Hence, haggard cares that vex the day,
Blind aches of head and heart, away!
Vague sorrows that the memory haunt,
Pale ghosts of early griefs, avaunt!
Forebodings of disastrous things,
Ye phantom brood, take wings, take wings!
All sordid thoughts of loss or gain,
Alluring hopes, ambitions vain,
Delusive dreams — whate'er ye be,
Depart and leave my spirit free,
For I would consecrate the hour
To books and their restoring power!

II.

Here, in my social solitude,
I make a new beatitude:
And Blessèd are the Books, I say;
The Muses' harvest sheaves are they;
They are the vials that contain
The attar of Time's heart and brain,
The fragrance of the blossomed hours,
One drop drained from a hundred flowers;
The sacred lanterns that emit
The light of science, wisdom, wit;
The caskets and the shrines that hold
Thought's diadems and learning's gold;

The full-brimmed beakers whence is quaffed
Imagination's sparkling draught;
The living-fountain-heads, where move
Deep waters of perennial love.

Enchanted heroes of the pen,
These books are living souls of men;
Awake! illustrious guests, spellbound,
Ye sons of genius, laurel crowned,
Your long, mysterious silence break;
I conjure you, arouse! awake!
Lo! from each scroll and massy tome
The spirits of the masters come!
They consecrate my humble home!
Immortal sages, seers, and bards;
They utter inspiration's words;
They whisper meanings manifold
That printed pages never told;
They break the esoteric seal,
And occult mysteries reveal;
My marred ideals they renew;
They speak, they sing the good and true;
As many stars give one pure light,
Their diverse messages unite;
Me to my fate they reconcile,
And prove life worth the living, while
Their lofty faith and converse high
Assure me soul can never die.

III.

My Youghiogheny coal aglow
Illumes my treasures row on row;
There Plato stands, half deified;
There Burke and Bacon, side by side;
Intense Carlyle by Goethe great;
There Shakespeare grand — for him no mate;
Montaigne and white-light Emerson;
Cervantes, Spain's immortal one;

Wit Fielding and French Hugo, too,
Elected with the Golden Few;
There genial Dickens, clad in green,
Beside romantic Scott is seen;
Satiric Thackeray is there,
And introspective Hawthorne rare;
The poets, too, a troop divine,
From honored shelves and alcoves shine;
And all these precious leaves are mine.

IV.

No bookworm blind and cold am I;
No friend to grim misanthropy.
That author best contents my mind
Who draws me nearest to mankind.
Not with a scientific greed,
For store of useful facts I read;
Not with a pedant's pride, to know
That I my ample lore may show;
Not with a worldling's lust of gain,
To gather gold by moil of brain;
Not with the critic's art, to scan,
And praise or blame because I can; —
Not do I pore for ends like these;
I read my books myself to please.
The wise King Solomon, I wis,
Said ne'er a sager thing than this:
" Eat honey, thou, for it is good."
Sweet reading is a dainty food;
Good honey is my book to me —
My author is good honey bee;
Good honey, and because 'tis sweet,
That is the reason why I eat.

V.

Reposing in my charmèd chair,
I exorcise the demon Care;
All yesterdays are past and gone,
And never did to-morrow dawn;

Is not this moment infinite?
Here, now, immortal do I sit.
Without is black December night;
Within is summer warmth and light;
I bend my fond, contented looks
On glimmering titles of my books,
As from the shelves they shine to me
In mute and dreamy sympathy.
"We are all here," they seem to say,
"Not comrades of a fleeting day,
But friends, unalienable, old,
Yet young forever, and warm-souled."
My soul, exalted, answers, " Yes,
Ye are the sons of blessedness."
I find upon the lettered page
More than the fabled Golden Age,
More than did Jove's symposia yield
To Lucian in the Elysian Field,
For all the best that men have thought
Or hoped or dreamed, have letters caught,
And God's own revelations shine
From holy books in words divine.

VIII

UNCLASSIFIED TRIFLES

I. STRAY THOUGHTS

MANY teachers of morality destroy the good effect of judicious counsel by too much talk, as a chemical precipitate is re-dissolved in an excess of the precipitating agent.

————

Repression is sometimes better than expansion. A rose is but a crowded cluster of repressed leaves.

————

Wild fruits lose an·exquisite flavor by the garden culture which causes them to become large and beautiful. So the mind may lose agreeable qualities by the process of education.

————

In burning delicate pottery the utmost care is taken to regulate the temperature of the oven, as excess or insufficiency of heat ruins the ware. Similarly, the nicest judgment is requisite in disciplining sensitive children, for one may injure their very nature by too much or too little severity. Virgil says the same fire that makes soft clay hard makes hard wax soft.

A successful fruit-grower was asked how it happened that he always obtained an abundant crop of peaches while his neighbors, with apparently better facilities, so often failed to raise even half a crop, and never got superior fruit. He replied: "I know my trees; they tell me what they want; I have a special interest in every twig of this orchard. A peach-tree won't produce unless it is loved."

If love brings forth the best that is in trees, will it not much more develop the best that is in men?

———

Some people practise their virtues so viciously that it is a pity they have virtues to abuse.

———

Books are called the tools of teachers. Teachers may become the tools of books.

———

Children are pleased with gay prints of high color and with the discordant, loud melody of the grind-organ. Gairish, gaudy hues and noisy sounds pain the cultivated senses. As the eye and ear learn to discriminate between harmony and inharmony, taste grows more exacting. In like manner mental training brings the mind to desire truth and enables it to detect and abhor error. The scholar demands coherence and logical connection of words. To the trained thinker a bad argument jars on the mind as an instrument out of tune distresses the ear. Education puts the mind in tune so that its strings answer to corresponding chords of truth.

———

It would seem reasonable that the teacher should be recognized everywhere as the highest authority on the subject of education, and that he should dictate how his pupils ought to be trained. In Germany that parent is considered impertinent who advises the professor in regard to pedagogical matters. In this country everybody considers it anybody's business to teach the teacher. Editors, clergymen, doctors, lawyers, merchants, mechanics, farmers, — all know how to teach school better than the schoolmaster does, and they all interfere, injudiciously, with his art. There should be co-operation between parent and teacher, but the school must proceed on general principles to which the individuality of families and single pupils must conform.

———

Wherefore fret if heedless Tom
Loses half the words I say?
What if sometimes dreamy Ben
Fails to learn his algebra?

Culture is not everything;
Farmers must not always hoe;
Undisturbed the roots of mind
Oftentimes the deepest grow.

Action is not always gain;
Crystals form when left at rest;
What the teacher leaves undone
May perchance be done the best.

> Haply inattentive Tom
>   Thinks a thought beyond my reach ;
> Peradventure Ben may dream
>   More than algebra can teach.

————

Purer than the mountain dew, whiter than sky-born flakes be the atmosphere of education. The sentiment and the language of instruction should be such that no blot or stain can touch the soul of the pupil. A holy light should pervade tuition. Might not boys and girls grow up with principles so sensitive to truth and purity that they would be forever self-shielded from the false and the foul?

They are benefactors of youth who use pure words. "Is not mine host a witty man?" asks the hunter of the fisherman in Walton's "Angler." The fisherman replies, "To speak truly, he is not to me a good companion. A companion that feasts his company with wit and mirth, and leaves out the sin which is usually mixed with them, *he is the man.* And let me tell you, *good company and good discourse are the very sinews of virtue.* But *for such discourse as we heard last night, it infects others.*"

Whatever is obscene, vulgar, degrading, or of questionable delicacy, infects the young. Blood poisoning is not so perilous as mind poisoning. What germicide can destroy the microbe vile imagination? We know temptation must be met, nevertheless, "lead us not into temptation." The school is the temple of safety. Within its sacred walls we are delivered from evil. There only good counsels and examples

and books and pictures and symbols should come.
There every low desire and every tainted fancy
should feel rebuked. There purity, like a guardian
angel, should abide.

———

We wish our sons and daughters to become superior men and women, and hope that school education
will contribute to that result. Therefore parents
confide in teachers with anxious trust. The teacher
stands in the parents' place, and has been called the
parent of his pupil's mind.

Yet the teacher's responsibility is much limited;
he is, at most, but minister plenipotentiary, not chief
ruler. Seven-eighths of the school-boy's hours are
disposed of by direct will of parents — only one-
eighth under the immediate control of the teacher.
No amount of vigilance can secure the true ends of
education without vigilant home rule at the hearth-
stone. It is hardly to be expected that any teacher
can maintain a stronger influence with his pupil than
an equally intelligent and conscientious parent can
exercise over his own child. Mother, father, schoolmaster — these are the educational trinity, — these,
in complete co-operation, are the agents of Providence to train the child.

The schooling which the young obtain out of
school is no less essential than that received on the
recitation benches. Bodily exercise and deportment;
skill in work and play; walking, riding, rowing,
swimming, dancing; public amusements, such as the

theatre, the concert, and the museum afford ; familiarity with social usages ; conversation ; general reading; travel, — these are branches of useful education, quite as important as the contents of text-books. Deprived of such schooling out of school, the mere student of books is not prepared to enjoy himself or to perform his duties. The teacher who disparages these extra accomplishments forgets the breadth of life. The parent mistakes the true relations of things when he undervalues the worth and dignity of school-training, and subordinates solid learning to superficial accomplishments. There should be harmony between what is done outside and what is done inside the seminary walls. Each set of tasks and recreations should have its bounds, so as not to trench on another set.   ____

Because its time is limited and its authority curtailed by many outside influences, a school, to be efficient, must be rigorous. The teacher needs economize his opportunity, and use his five or six hours a day with systematic efficiency. He knows that it is not possible for any one to acquire mental strength or accuracy, or to secure thorough knowledge of any sort, without concentration and continuity of effort. No matter how smart a boy may be, he acquires scholarship only by steadfast devotion to study, from day to day, week to week, year to year. No matter how able his parents, the heir does not inherit his A B C's. Stuart Mill says truly, that "the children of energetic parents frequently grow up unenergetic, because they lean on their parents and the parents are energetic for them." How gladly the father marks in his children every indication that they will some time be able to fight the battle of life unaided, if need be; and yet indulgence often robs the loved boy and the idolized girl of the weapon that alone makes success possible — self-reliance. Relaxation is necessary; but there should be no break in general purpose, no cooling of interest, no dissipation of force. To suppose that teachers or schools can impart a good education to a boy who scatters his energy by idleness or other vice is as absurd as to expect a plant to thrive that is pulled up by the roots every night, though carefully reset every morning. The wisest conservation of force is the conservation of brain force. If the boy squanders himself, becoming the slave of his own feebleness, no outside strength can save him. Why do we control our children at all if it is not to invest them with self-control? The restraints of school are like the stake that holds up a young tree that it may grow strong and straight.

I conceive of a school in which the motives, ambitions, and conduct are tuned to the same key and play together the melody of reciprocal service and good will. The teachers are exacting, but kind and just; the pupils docile, eager, persistent; the parents unremitting in their intellectual and moral support. Believing knowledge to be, as the Bible says, "more precious than rubies," the learners will toil and strive for knowledge ; will collect mental treasures and wish to become millionnaires of thought. Imbued with the sincerest sentiment of honor and purity, they will respond with quick enthusiasm to every generous and heroic idea.

——

2. WOMAN'S RIGHTS.

Rights spring from native powers, brute or human,
   And vary as the powers rise or fall;
   The flying angels and the worms that crawl
Have meted rights. The liberties of woman,
   Of man, of seraph, with their longings, grow.
   Our brain and heart are torches to illumine
   The path of duty ; by their inner glow
We ken the way we should have right to go.
He lives the best whose faculties are free
   To do, and think, and feel, as God designed,
   Who made the mortal members and the mind.
Each sex best knows its nature's mystery.
   Most feminine is she whose free-winged soul
   Feels no constraint except Divine control.

3. PAST, PRESENT, AND FUTURE.

One of the sublimest thoughts of Carlyle is that every day is the confluence of two eternities, the infinite past and the infinite future. That man narrows the scope of his existence who is concerned only with things local and temporary. The far distant and the long past may be more important to him than the present and what he is doing in it. How the wind is blowing a thousand miles away forewarns the sailor to cast anchor or to set sail. What is going on in Europe or Asia, in politics or in society, may affect my happiness to-morrow. What went on in Egypt, or India, or Palestine ages ago, transmitted through the lives of nations and of men, and through history, may control the thoughts and events of to-day. The stream of influences flowing from the past indicates what the tendency of the future may be. Realizing what has been accomplished towards civilization, and by what means, the individual man may order his life according to knowledge, and move forward with some assurance of making a real advance. He will know that the passing is the fruitage of the past, and will believe that he can plant the future now.   ·

4. PROGRESS OF CIVILIZATION.

Much has been accomplished within the past century for human amelioration. The average length of man's life has been increased by better sanitary conditions. The material comforts of living have multiplied beyond conception. What ancient king could command such powerful and willing slaves as every common citizen now calls to his service — steam and electricity. Steam carries me around the world ; lightning lights my candle. But what are the triumphs of material discovery and invention compared with the moral conquests and products of the century? Fetters have fallen from millions of slaves ; the wheels, keels, and wires of commerce mix up the interests of mankind and create a cosmopolitan sentiment of friendliness; the rights of suffrage have been greatly extended, and the sovereignty of the majority has been conceded without depriving minorities of just representation. Persecution in its grosser forms has ceased, and religious toleration, like sunshine, has melted the frosts of bigotry.

5. USE OF THE IDEAL.

When Thomas More wrote " Utopia " his contemporaries thought him a dreamer. He was not a dreamer, but a seer, and the vision he saw and pictured in words succeeding generations beheld materialized in beneficent institutions. Like an architect's drawing, the book furnished a working plan, by which political and social life in England built itself a new house. If More had not projected his speculative system on the imagination of readers, the reforms he desired might not so soon have been realized. Forever the conception of a better state leads men to practical endeavors to improve the existing condition of things. Said Fichte, " The actual must be judged by the ideal." Compelled to live among things as they are, man grows stronger and more helpful by drawing inspiration from things as they ought to be. The teacher who is content with things as they are, and does not see what might be and ought to be and labor for it always, is dead and ready for burial.

6. COMBINATIONS *vs.* INDIVIDUALS.

The present era of combinations does not indicate the final extinction of individual influence; it forecasts the approach of a day of universal concession to the natural rights of each and all.   Individuals combine and organize class interests for the remote object of liberating the individual from class oppression.   When the battles are won, the regiments will disband, and the privates will go each to his legitimate place.   How happy that condition of society in which every person will count for what he is worth, and will estimate his fellows at their full value! Honor will go to whom honor is due, and blame will fall upon the wrong-doer.   No man will be misplaced or without a place.   Special aptitudes will be stimulated by generous emulation, and the diverse energies of the race will be utilized for the common good.

7. A COLLECTION OF MEN.

Practical men are aware that success in life depends upon a knowledge of human nature.   The world is not unlike a menagerie, and the man of the world makes it a profit and a pleasure to see, not only the elephant, but all the living wonders on exhibition.   Let us pass into the big tent and hear the lion roar, the hyena howl, the eagle scream, the magpie chatter, the donkey bray, and the fox bark. Having seen the typical animals, it will not be amiss

to enter the side-shows and look upon the mon-
strosities.

We make but one voyage on the Ship of Time —
why not become acquainted with our fellow-passen-
gers ? The excursion is free — who has more right
on deck than yourself ? He lives most who has
most to do with mankind. The science of human
nature is best learned by the study of representative
men — good and bad. There are specialists who
delight in collecting birds' eggs, or postage stamps,
or buttons. Mark Twain made a collection of echoes,
and he is not the only author who has done that. A
collection of photographs is valuable, for it brings to
the eye the image of men's faces ; a library is better,
for it gives portraits of men's minds ; but, best of all,
is a collection of men and women — a choice assort-
ment of fine specimens gathered by observation, and
classified in the glass-case of memory, for reference
and instruction. Only in gathering such a noble
cabinet, the student of human nature must not fail
to carry with him what Goethe calls the Three Rev-
erences ; namely, reverence for that which is below
us, for that which is around us, for that which is
above.

8. EDUCATION OUT OF SCHOOL.

Teachers are the radical reformers of political and
social abuses. They are the builders of permanent
nations. But the education of schools is not the
only education that life in a democratic state affords.

The citizen of a republic feels himself really a part of a majestic system, and is conscious that his own life, liberty, and happiness are bound up in the bundle of the common destiny. Hence he learns to respect institutions more than rulers. He will criticise his senator, his judge, his priest; but he believes in law, justice, and religion, and will not permit these to be slighted. He fights for the Constitution. The Declaration of Independence is not a "glittering generality" to him. The school system, the press, the ballot-box — these he holds sacred. Nor does the existence of humbug, fraud, and corruption prove that sincerity, honesty, and purity are slumbering. The prevailing sentiment is right; the general conscience is true.

The free mingling of all elements, possible only in a democracy, tends not to level the mass down, but to level it up. Intelligence, morality — these are qualities that benefit all. It is good for the refined gentleman and for the rude laborer that they discuss together the questions of the day. When all classes become acquainted they agree better.

Just after the last presidential election, before the returns were in, and while the whole country was waiting with anxious excitement to learn who would be president, two little boys were observed on a by-street in Cincinnati, talking together earnestly. One was a colored lad, ragged and pathetically small; the other a sturdy white urchin, neatly dressed, and with the air of one born in a stone-front house. Said

the white boy to the dark, "What is the news?"
"We sha'n't know anything for certain," was the
reply, "until six o'clock." — "Sha'n't we? Then,
Charley, meet me here at just six, for I want to know
all about it!" The little "nigger" promised, and
the two young Americans separated.

Here was an instance, sublimely simple, of the
workings of democratic institutions ; of the reaction
of mind upon mind in the beginning place of vote-
making. So long as Charley meets his brother baby
at just six o'clock to inquire all about the state of
politics, the republic will be safe. This is popular
education.

9. THE OLD-FASHIONED ELOCUTIONIST.

The old-fashioned elocutionist culminated about
the time of the civil war, and since then he has
gradually lost public favor. The species has declined,
though individuals of it are still to be seen rocketing
in the oratorial sky.

In a stray volume of the Philadelphia *Port Folio*
for the year 1815, we read that Mr. Ogilvie of South
Carolina College had recently established "a new
branch of education," which was no other than a
course on oratory, and that he had "opened for himself a most splendid and useful career." The trus-
tees of the college testified over their official signatures
that there were none among Mr. Ogilvie's pupils
"who could not recite with justness and intelligence;

and some seemed to have made considerable advances in the higher walks of impassioned eloquence."

We will not venture to assume that Mr. Ogilvie was the founder of an actually "new branch of education," and the father of American elocutionists. But since he figured as long ago as 1815, we may safely conclude that the old-fashioned elocutionists have been illustrating the splendors of " impassioned eloquence" for nearly a hundred years in this New World.

"Impassioned eloquence," both in writing and speech, was the glory of the period beginning with the close of the Second War of Independence. The school of "our eloquent ancestors " was the political press, the stump, and the revival pulpit.

" Impassioned eloquence " by degrees passed from the domain of serious persuasion to the stage, the lyceum, and the academy. It became ornamental rather than useful. Fourth of July oratory retained a sort of *quasi* meaning for a long time, and even yet we occasionally see the spread eagle soar from a rustic platform and flap his broad wings in the high altitude of sublime noise.

Well do we remember the elocutionist of our school-days — his name was legion ; — we speak of the species, not of any particular specimens. He it was, wonderful-voiced, many-sounding man, who amazed our youthful ears by rending, not rendering, " Collins's Ode to the Passions," " Rienzi's Address to the Romans," and " Catiline's Defiance." Methinks I see him now in the act of clinching his fist at the imaginary Conscript Fathers and exclaiming,

> "He dares not touch a hair of Catiline."

"Parrhasius" was in his fierce repertory, and who that once saw and heard could ever forget the unqualified delight that the lively artist took in commanding his attendant to —

> "Press down the poisoned links into his flesh,
> And tear agape those healing wounds afresh!"

The impression upon small boys was ineradicable. Every urchin old enough to articulate was saying, in such sepulchral tones as he could simulate, —

> "Gods! if I could but paint a dying groan!"

The recollection of one other "piece" of declamatory "impassioned eloquence" comes back like Banquo's ghost. 'Twas called "The Seminole's Defiance," a great favorite with the old-fashioned elocutionist, and with nervous boys. By the way, how curious the fact that it is not the big, rough, savage boy who affects the terrific style, but rather the pale and slender fellow. The "Seminole's Defiance" is ferocious from beginning to end, but the closing verse was the climax and the crucial test of the orator's art. It runs thus : —

> "I ne'er will ask for quarter,
> I ne'er will be your slave,
> But I'll swim the sea of slaughter
> 'Till I sink beneath its wave!"

Language cannot convey an adequate conception of the gesticular strokes with which our old teacher plunged into the " sea of slaughter," as though that crimson flood actually rolled before us ; much less can words reproduce the exaggerated gurgle with which he sank beneath the wave.

The old-fashioned elocutionist rather disdained humor, regarding it as frivolous and undignified. Blood was his chosen element. Yet often he resorted to the other impassioned fluid — tears. A throng of recollections clamor to be told, but we forbear. Suffice it to say our old friend's pathos was more harrowing than his tragedy. There *was* a sort of grim pleasure in listening to his murders and defiances and death-rattles, but his tender speeches gave unmitigated misery to the audience. Yet, paradoxical as it seems, the popular taste was such that we enjoyed the pain.

Perhaps the most remarkable quality of old-fashioned " impassioned eloquence " was its parliamentary or senatorial element. The elocutionist considered it his bounden duty to instruct his audience in the principles and practice of parliamentary persuasion. As a rule, he preferred perorations rather than plain argument. Pitt, Burke, and Webster were the models he taught us to imitate, and the elocutionist gave brilliant examples of the style of those famous orators. Sometimes, also, he displayed samples of the art of Demosthenes or Cicero. Randolph, Calhoun, and Clay often appeared before us in the person of our lecturer. Demosthenes, Cicero, and Burke were represented as very solemn and even pompous. Webster and Pitt rolled their R's, and emphasized all the big words, and flourished their arms with great energy, and so far forgot their dignity in moments of excitement as to beat their bosoms and to storm. When it came the turn of Randolph, or Clay, or Patrick Henry, to take the floor, "impassioned eloquence" found full vent. These worthy statesmen were regarded as *naturally* eloquent; they were fiery and untamed; they tore every passion to tatters; they ranted like mad men, and when, exhausted with vociferation and frantic exercise, Randolph or Clay dropped into his chair, the audience thundered round after round of applause.

The recollection of these "elocutionary entertainments" brings with it a sense of their irresistible absurdity. What could be more ludicrous? Imagine Burke in the British parliament, or Webster in Congress, looking, acting, and speaking as the old-fashioned elocutionist represented him! Had Clay or Calhoun behaved on any public occasion as the professional declaimer used to personate him, his friends would have consigned him to the nearest sanitarium.

In these latter days elocution is more rational. Teachers of vocal culture are striving to base their art on a natural foundation. The old-fashioned elocutionist can no longer please an enlightened audience. Perhaps the new-fashioned professor of oratory runs to another extreme of refined artificiality, and has too much to say about the philosophy of expression and the subtilities of Delsarte. As the "blood-and-thunder" novel of yore has changed into the introspective tale of Howells and James, so the rant of the stage and the "spouting" of the "school exhibition" are supplanted by realistic acting and recitations in a quiet style.

10. "IT'S BOOKS."

"It's books." Such was the idiom of our district. The phrase was familiar to my ears in boyhood. Perhaps the expression has become obsolete; maybe it was narrowly provincial and "countryfied." I do not know. But I distinctly recollect that, in the quiet precincts of old Ridgeville (an Ohio village fondly remembered as the scene of my first schoolgoing), we used to say "It's books." We meant by the words that the hours of study and recitation had begun; that playtime was over; that, to use another peculiar form of "English as she is spoke," school had "took up."

I recollect pedagogues who used to call in their pupils by rapping sharply with a ferule on the window-sash, and others who sent messengers to the playgrounds to tell us that *it was books*. The schoolmaster who first used a hand-bell to ring the children in from Riley's Woods was regarded as quite a magician; and we fancied that he must be very rich to possess a bell.

On the morning of the first opening of the city

schools in autumn, the streets present a lively and suggestive picture. The official announcement that it will be " books " on a stated Monday morning in September produces a flutter of preparation among the school-goers, and no little stir and anxiety among the school-senders. The various employments of vacation are cut short. The children's wardrobes are overhauled, repaired, and replenished. Tommy's out-grown suit is fitted, perhaps, to his younger brother. Lizzie is supplied with a new dress ; and her last fall's hat is done over in the style of the coming season. The family talk is of teachers, text-books, and grades. The tents of rest are folded, and the educational camp buzzes with the sound of preparation for another year's active campaign. The antici- pated opening day arrives. Then, betimes, the boys and girls issue from their places of abode and flock together, laden with baskets, satchels, slates, and books. The sidewalks are musical with the patter of elastic feet. In the bustle and excitement of the occasion, most are filled with hope and vivacity. Here and there a reluctant urchin, opposed to the school system in general, and perhaps personally prejudiced against Miss Goad, the kind but firm young lady who rules his room, creeps unwillingly "and with heavy looks " toward the big brick edifice ·which he considers not the goal, but the gaol, of his wishes. An excess of forward-moving energy propels the majority, causing the observer to wonder at the force stored in young blood. Almost every lad or lass seems to belong to the fittest, having such manifest power to survive. Yet the discriminating eye may see in the crowd more than one timid, shrinking child, to whom the rush and flurry of the noisy procession is like the rude bluster of March winds to the tender and tremulous violet. At the home door stands the mother, her heart following with infinite solicitude the darling who this day for the first time ventures from the all-protecting enclosure of the household walls to enter upon untried scenes. Full of pathos to the parent's heart is this first day of school. The mother may cry a little in the lonely nursery when her baby is out of sight. Ah, innocent, ignorant child, rejoicing in her embroidered cloak, proud of her pictorial primer, how can she anticipate the realities of the long way that lies before her! Perhaps she may discover an appalling difference between home and school; between mother, whose love-kiss yet lingers on her lips, and Miss Goad, who sets her to learn the twos in the multiplication-table. Even father, undemonstrative as he is, betrays some interest in the children's movements on opening day; and he cannot help drawing a long breath over his high desk at the office, as he recalls to mind the air of his five-year-old namesake, who, after breakfast, set off so sturdily towards the hill of science, his pocket plethoric of tops and strings, his jacket and pants buttoned together around the waist.

It is not the infants only that interest and amuse

the observer on the morning when school begins.
Not only Minnie in her A B C's, but also

"Almira in the upper class,"

who studies chemistry, music, and French, and who
wears her hair in the most outlandish style of the
extreme mode ; not only little Fred, whose mind,
yet in the soft cartilage stage, is sorely confused by
the simplest object lesson, but also Charles Edwin,
with misty mustache on lip and Latin lexicon in
hand, with golden charms hanging to his watch-
chain, and, as he humbly conceives, manly dignity
stamped on his studious brow.   Now roll the private
seminary omnibuses along, bearing the lilies and
roses that toil not nor spin ; and the roses and lilies
bend and nod with peculiar sweetness as they pass
Charles Edwin by, and that linguistic beau moves
gracefully on, a taller and happier man.

Meanwhile the swarms gather and increase in the
vicinity of the schoolhouses.   There assemble the
children of the people — the rich, the poor — American, German, Irish ; the robust, the feeble, the beautiful, the deformed, the intelligent, the stupid, the
virtuous, the vicious, the children of the people.
They will be men and women — to-morrow.   They
have come from the privacy of the family to the
publicity of the school.   They have stepped into
the world.   They are weaving the individual threads
of life into the tissue of society and state.

The hour strikes, the bells ring out their summons, the multitudes separate into orderly ranks, and march to their appointed place. And "it's books."

II. THE CULTURED SNOB.

Young Mr. Acme Sweetlight, having completed his college course and perhaps European tour, has returned home to rest and recuperate. Sweetlight is an illustrious example of what education and culture may accomplish for a man. He manifests his superiority in every way. His dress and demeanor proclaim him finished. Acme has absorbed the learning of his times. Any one may see at a glance that he is saturated with information and intellectual power.

True, he does not say much, or read much, or do much in any sort, to demonstrate his ability; but he looks very much indeed, and what he does utter is oracular and final. Acme is a contemplator of other men's defects, not a producer. He sits in judgment on the words and works of lesser men. He sits apart in a region of inaccessible refinement, surveys, condemns, but never creates. Perpetual disapproval perches at the sensitive corners of Sweetlight's mouth. Censure and disparagement are written on his classic forehead. Infinite scorn of crudity and vulgarity lurks in the exquisite curl of his nose. He takes it for granted that anybody who tries to do anything is, according to the eternal fitness of things, a special target for his cynical arrows.

There is that in Acme Sweetlight which may be likened to what physicists call potential energy ; he seems charged with some mighty force, which, however, has not yet vented itself in positive work. The man is like a bent bow or a loaded gun, or ever so much superheated steam confined in a strong boiler. The piston of actual achievement moves not, though certain spirts of hissing criticism do escape now and then through the safety-valve of speech. He smiles disdainfully at false syntax or bad rhetoric, though he will not write himself. He goes to the lecture and pronounces it a failure ; and he attends church occasionally in a condescending mood, but is visibly bored by the sermon and excruciated by the singing. Doubtless this supreme being can do all things better than anything has ever been done. Conscious of latent ability, he cares not so far to identify himself with the " rascal multitude " as even to set an example.

12. NATURAL SCIENCE TEACHING IN THE COMMON SCHOOLS.

Children should become acquainted with natural objects, as parts of a complete whole, interesting and important not only in themselves, but also in their relation to other things. A stone-quarry teaches more than a cabinet of minerals ; a woodland walk more than a *hortus siccus ;* an ant-hill more than a card of beetles displaying their transfixed bodies through glass. Collections, classifications, specific and generic names are very useful in their way ; but nature and her works are best studied, loved, and appreciated in action, — in life, not in death. Even the inorganic world has its vital phenomena, — its force in action.

Much better it is for a child to learn crystalography by observing the manner in which solids are born of liquid solutions, than by looking at a few labelled specimens in a dusty box. Plants and animals should be seen, if possible, in their native haunts. What the beginner most needs is a taste for nature, habits of observation, and a method of investigation, — not laws, conclusions, scientific categories and results. The summing up of facts and final statement of principles is the work of trained thinkers, not of unpractised school-children.

The tyro needs knowledge — abundance of definite knowledge. The reason it is so hard to interest boys and girls in scientific text-books may be seen, when we recollect that these books are mainly summaries and general statements, dependent upon a vast accumulation of facts and experiments, that the boys and girls have not witnessed. On the very first page of the book the pupil is told that "science is knowledge reduced to system ;" it is the teacher's duty to draw the inference that, without some knowledge to begin with, it is absurd to suppose it possible to possess any science whatever. Science is not ignorance reduced to system. The pupils must be induced to take notice of what lies around them, or else all at-

tempt to teach principles and laws is hopeless. They
must study things and their properties, and learn to
distinguish what is significant in nature from what
is not.

Country teachers have peculiar facilities for ac-
quainting themselves and their pupils with the material of natural science, and they are scarcely
excusable if they neglect their opportunity. Soils,
stones, springs, trees, moss, birds, insects, snails, —
ten thousand objects of interest may be brought under
the observation of the farmer's children. Let the
scholars be induced to study the natural history of
their own homes. Put into their hands such books
as Wood's " Selbourne," and "The Fairy Land of
Science." Ask them to write compositions about
familiar natural objects. Take them on excursions.
Make them realize the significance and worth of the
familiar. Teach them the use of the eye, the microscope, — but, above all, the use of their mind. Bring
them close down to nature that they may feel her
mysterious life, and catch the spirit of her operations. There is a just complaint that scientific
teaching is apt to be sapless and soulless. It is a
pity if instruction tends to narrow the pupil's mind,
— to make him underrate other knowledge than
that of bare facts, — and to depreciate other than
scientific culture.

The practice of amusing children with the curiosities of natural history, chemistry, etc., without cre-
ating correct habits of study, or any real interest in

the more substantial parts of the subject taught, is an evil that besets primary teachers.

It is easy to interest children in wonders, but minds that are habitually aroused by novelty are almost sure to lapse into hopeless lethargy when the novelty has lost its charm. Many have experienced how hard it is to make anything of a class that has had the edge of its appetite for study blunted by feeding on scientific marvels for a few months. The curiosities of botany and zoölogy, the brilliant experiments of chemistry and physics, ought to be distributed along the whole course of study, and be utilized as a gentle and constant stimulus. It is as unwise to expect to develop a taste for scientific study by a course of highly seasoned, marvellous lectures, as to create a healthy desire for plain food by a preliminary diet of spice and confectionary.

Inverting the usual order, I give, as the close of this brief sermon, a pregnant text from the scripture of J. J. Rousseau, who says " Among the many admirable methods taken to abridge the study of the sciences, we are in great want of one to make us *learn them with effort.*"

13. HOW TO SAY IT.

The use of language is to set the mind free and send it forth that it may influence other minds. The mind in print flies around the globe. Words are deeds. He who speaks well, or writes well, does service as practical as the sowing of grain, the steering of a ship, or the curing of a wound.

Language is the most potent instrument that human power wields. The useful end of intellectual education is to learn to think, and the value of thought is measured by its adequate expression. Therefore teachers should not undervalue grammar and rhetoric. The art of saying, sums up and tests all mental acquisitions. " I know it but can't tell it " is the same as " I possess but cannot use." But the use of knowledge is *to use*.

Pupils must be trained to put their intelligence into the breath of life which awakens the vocal chords, and into the ink which talks from the written page. Young folks are apt to assume that they cannot make composition. It is easy to prove to the dullest child that he possesses power to speak and write. Take down in shorthand the answers he gives to your familiar questions, and you have a literary composition. Let the boys and girls translate tongue into pen ; let them put down from their fingers what just now fell from their lips. How teach a child to write sensibly and simply ? You had better study how to prevent him from losing the tact which comes to him naturally. Babies of five are often more expert at telling their meanings and feelings than are the students in the rhetoric class. Wonderfully fresh, idiomatic, and succinct is the oratory of the nursery. How beautiful, direct, and graphic the first letters written by boys and girls who have never been at school! Children love to communicate themselves. They are voluble and eloquent.

The class in composition should be the most interesting class in school, because it should bring into use all the pupils' knowledge, thought, feeling, and personality. But the fact is, the composition class, in the generality of schools, is abhorred by both teacher and pupils.

We begin wrong, and then go on from bad to worse until we have quite spoiled the natural faculty of language. We ought not to expect a pupil's school composition to be more correct or original than his average talk. When he can tell a story gracefully, then he may write it. Teach composition in every recitation. Awkward words and half-formed thoughts require correction in the geography class as much as in the grammar class. But criticism is not what is wanted so much as encouragement. Above all, do not expect learners to impart what they have not received. The substance of the composition is the main thing, the form is secondary. Perfection of form, elegant phraseology, bookish style, are never to be encouraged. The smooth, elegant, conventional essay, abounding in Latin derivatives, betokens feebleness and not power. Such finished productions are too often praised by teachers on Friday afternoon. No sham more pitiable than the ordinary school composition unless it be the ordinary graduating address, which is, indeed, the school composition gone to seed.

The written words of girls and boys should truly represent the habitual, intellectual, and moral status of the writer. First compositions should be like sketches from nature. They may *be* sketches from nature. Instead of requiring your pupils to write the description of a landscape, instruct them to go to a certain point and look out upon the scene, taking notes of what they see, to use in a genuine composition that shall actually portray a landscape.

Remember the blunt old maxim: "Have something to say, — then say it." And the way to say it will be found only by practice, practice, practice. Write, write, write. Art is long. One cannot learn to play the fiddle without years of practice, nor to play the harp of language.

Let us hang around the neck of this discourse a jewel from Macaulay. The jewel at least is worth your attention. Macaulay says, "The first rule of all writing — that rule to which every other is subordinate — is that the words used by the writer shall be such as most fully and precisely convey his meaning to the great body of his readers. All considerations about the purity and dignity of style ought to bend to this consideration."

IX

STUDIES IN THE HISTORY OF EDUCATION

I. CONFUCIUS

"Superior and alone, Confucius stood,
Who taught that useful science, to be good."

Pope's Temple of Fame.

EVERY process of teaching is suggested by some theory of human nature, consciously or unconsciously held by the teacher. Every system of education is an exponent of its author's philosophy. He who holds that the human faculties are essentially noble and capable of infinite improvement, will conceive profound and liberal schemes of culture; but he whose estimate of man's worth and destiny is mean will devise correspondingly mean plans of training, from which he will neither obtain nor expect great results.

There is no such thing as an uneducated people. The most primitive varieties of the human species have their notions of nature and existence, and make some effort to conform their lives to an ideal standard. The effort — even the desire — to become something that they think superior to what they are, is a step in education. Every influence exerted upon a person, from within or without, to cause him to act with the definite purpose of increasing his powers, is educational. The Indians have in mind a vivid picture of the true brave, and their young men are drilled to meet the severe exactions of the conception.

If we could range in a line of historic vision, running from the far past to the near present, the educational theories of representative men in various nations, many vain speculations would be abandoned and much wrong practice might be rectified. These theories, set forth in their relations to one another, would constitute the most valuable part of educational history, by showing what has been thought, and indicating what has been tried, and with what results, in the direction of culture and development. The views of the ancients on the educability of man are very instructive. What *was* helps to explain what *is*. The roots of the present lie buried deep in the past. No person is more likely to be " behind the times " than he who is ignorant of the great ideas and achievements of antiquity.

The industry of numerous investigators is gathering material upon which to base sound conclusions respecting the primitive condition of man and the beginnings of civilization. Bold hypotheses on the origin of species have pushed *that* question as far back as inquiry can go. How and when man originated science has not determined ; but there is a general agreement among learned men that the *place* of man's origin is Asia, as Moses declared it to be.

The Orient is the stage upon which the childhood of humanity exhibited its first demonstrations of power and purpose, — or shall we say, of weakness and wavering ?

We do not know in what precise locality human society first existed, or what was the first nation that played its part in the world's history. Hundreds and thousands of races and tribes may have made their entrance and exit prior to the time of those faintly revealed to us in the glimmering light of tradition. There is no doubt, however, as to which is the most ancient of *existing* nations. China is by far the oldest. Authentic records testify the existence of Chinese civilization nearly three thousand years ago. We have no reliable account of the beginnings of this nation. Far as her annals recede, —   .

"In the dark backward and abysm of time," —

China first comes into the range of study, a somewhat enlightened country. The condition in which we find her, when she first appears in history, justifies the presumption that she had been growing for centuries before. She possessed social and political institutions, science, art, .and literature, long ere Europe emerged from barbarism.

The word *isolating*, which philologists use to describe languages like the Chinese, may be aptly used also to describe the Chinese character. Until recently, it has been the policy of the Chinese to keep aloof from the rest of mankind. The great wall is typical of this isolating tendency, and of Chinese *stability*. The Chinese are the most industrious of people, and yet the nation has made but little progress for thousands of years. What Taine says of the scholars of the fourteenth century may be applied to the Chinese: " They seem to be marching, but are merely marking time." They do not get on, yet their energy is not lost. It is expended in turning the endless chain of a gigantic tread-mill. There are five hundred millions of them, and each keeps his place, and does his prescribed duty. Government, institutions, families, individuals, are fitted like watch-work into the respective places appropriated to them by inexorable law and usage. The myth that the world was cut and fashioned by Pwanka, the first man, with a chisel and mallet, symbolizes Chinese philosophy and enterprise.[1]

Five classes of duties are recognized by the Chinese as of universal obligation, — those between sovereign and minister, between father and son, between husband and wife, between elder brother and younger, and between one friend and another. There are, also, three virtues considered binding upon all : knowledge, magnanimity, and energy, or, "conscience, humanity, and moral courage, " as translated by Maurice from the French of M. Pauthier. To define and enforce these duties and virtues is the object of a great part of Chinese literature, especially of the so-called

[1] Confucius and the Chinese Classics, by Rev. A. W. Loomis, San Francisco, 1867, p. 17.

sacred Five Classics and Four Books. Chinese real life exhibits the approximate maintenance of these relations, as explained by the scholars and enforced by the emperor. The duties and virtues enjoined are acquired by imitation, and practised in a manner rather perfunctory than conscientious. As a necessary result of this system of external restraints and mechanical habits, the Chinese remain as they have been for ages. Tylor, in his " Primitive Culture," [1] asserts as a general fact that inferior grades of civilization are marked by strong conservatism He says, —

" The savage is firmly, obstinately conservative. No man appeals with more unhesitating confidence to the great precedent-makers of the past ; the wisdom of his ancestors can control against the most obvious evidence of his own opinions and actions. We listen with pity to the rude Indian as he maintains against civilized science and experience the authority of his rude forefathers. We smile at the Chinese appealing against modern innovation to the golden precepts of Confucius, who, in his time, looked back with the same prostrate reverence to sages still more ancient, counselling his disciples to follow the seasons of Hia, to ride in the carriage of Yin, to wear the ceremonial cap of Chow."

This quotation introduces the name, and indicates something of the character, of the best exponent of Chinese culture — Confucius. No countryman of his — Mencius possibly excepted — has ever grown to the intellectual and moral stature of this man. The world acknowledges him as undoubtedly great ; the Chinese regard him as greatest. Tsez Kung, one of his prominent followers, declares that the talents

1 Tylor, Primitive Culture, Am. Ed., vol. i, p. 156.

and virtues of other men are hillocks and mounds which may be stepped over, but that Confucius "is the sun or moon which it is impossible to step over." [1] The celebrated Mencius says, "What I wish to do is to learn to be like Confucius." And further, "Since there were living men, until now, there never was another Confucius." The very word Confucius, Latinized from the syllables Kung-fu-tze, signifies Kung the Master or Perfect Sage. This title is conferred by imperial authority.

Confucius was born in the year 551 B.C. The Grecian philosopher Pythagoras was then about thirty years old, and the Persian general, Cyrus the Great, had just begun his career of glory. The sage was descended from illustrious ancestors. His father died when Confucius was but three years old, leaving his son no patrimony except a precocious intellect and a studious disposition. A good mother conducted the child's education with care. At the early age of nineteen Confucius married. At twenty he was appointed "Keeper of the Stores of Grain," and at twenty-one, "Inspector of Pastures and Flocks," in his native place. At twenty-two he began to teach, receiving pupils at his own house. Shortly after this his mother died. He conducted her obsequies with great splendor, thus reviving an old custom, and, in further imitation of the ancients, he shut himself up and devoted three years to mourning and ethical

[1] This and other following quotations are taken from Dr. Legge's translation of the Chinese classics.

studies. Filial duty thus discharged, he resumed teaching; studied music under a renowned master; and began to travel about the empire, examining into the condition of the people, and visiting the courts of princes. He felt it to be his mission to instruct and elevate his generation. We are told that there were four things which the master taught — "letters, ethics, devotion of soul, and truthfulness." He poured out the cup of knowledge to all who were willing to receive, — kings or common subjects. The Master said, "From the man bringing his bundle of dried flesh for my teaching, upward, I have never refused instruction to any one." His fame and name spread. His disciples multiplied. Honor and office called him from his wanderings home to his native state, the kingdom of Loo. He was made successively magistrate, assistant superintendent of works, and minister of crime. He effected many reforms, and acquired vast influence. But the austerity of his principles proving too severe for the king, the Master finally lost power, and, at the age of fifty-six, sadly took his departure from a court at which he could be no longer useful. He resumed his journeyings, and continued for thirteen years the old work of preceptorial instruction. Poverty and neglect followed him. Once he narrowly escaped assassination. Often he suffered for want of food. At last, in his old age, he returned once more to Loo, and spent the few remaining years of his life quietly and happily, editing the sacred books. He died at the age of seventy-three.

In the Confucian Analects we find the following curious record of the moral progress of the sage:—

"The Master said, At fifteen, I had my mind bent on learning. At thirty, I stood firm. At forty, I had no doubts. At fifty, I knew the decrees of Heaven. At sixty, my ear was an obedient organ for the reception of truth. At seventy, I could follow what my heart desired without transgressing what was right."

With a Carlyle-inspired reverence for heroes, we approach this wise man of the East, to pay him such homage as his greatness can command. We survey him, and find him, indeed, colossal for his age and nation. He is extraordinary — but, after all, only an extraordinary Chinese. He did not grow freely to the form and dimensions of absolute human greatness. Like Pwanka's world, he bears marks of the mallet and chisel. He was born into an artificial world of inexorable requisitions and restraints. He was trained from infancy in accordance with traditional usage. The circumstance that his social rank was high subjected him the more entirely to the exactions of conventional life. His native capacity was remarkable, — he had cosmopolitan sympathies; he might have developed an original character even in spite of hereditary tendencies, but circumstances were always against it. He could only become a full-blown and superior specimen of what Chinese culture is able to produce from the most promising bud. He is the consummate flower of Chinese civilization.

Confucius accepted the theory of government and

society that he found riveted in the history and habit
of his nation. "There is government," he says,
"when the prince is prince, and the minister is
minister; when the father is father, and the son is
son." Believing that the relation of inferiors to
superiors should be that of the grass to the wind,
he submitted to the powers that be. Professing
himself only a lover of learning and a transmitter
of the wisdom of the ancients, he claimed no originality for himself. No one, he thought, could fall
into error who followed the example of the early
kings. As by the use of the compass perfect circles
may be made, so by the imitation of the ancient
sages may men be made perfect. "If some years
were added to my life," said the master, "I would
give fifty to the study of the Yih, and then I might
come to be without great faults." He endeavored
to walk in the path of the sage, which "embraces
the three hundred rules of ceremony and the three
thousand rules of demeanor." By these rules is to
be understood, not a mere code of etiquette, but an
elaborate system of conduct defining the highest
duties of life, civil, social, and moral. Etiquette
received an ample share of attention. Confucius
observed the directions of the manners-book with
scrupulous exactness. His behavior was exceedingly circumspect. He would not eat his mince-
meat unless it were properly cut, nor sit upon his
mat unless it were straight. He practised attitudes
and gestures suitable to each several occasion of life,

and required his nightgown to be half as long again
as his body.   A genius, naturally independent and
vigorous, thus tethered, reminds us of Gulliver
bound by the Lilliputians.

In the struggle to evolve, to rise to a better life,
Confucius broke many of his bonds.   The consciousness of his mission gave him strength.   His itinerant
life tended to disinthrall him.   With profound love
for humanity, he united a keen consciousness that
the world is not as good as it might be.   He acknowledges his own defects with humility, and laments the
degeneracy of others in language that recalls the
scriptural complaint, "There is none good, no, not
one." Yet, fully believing that good men have lived,
and that depraved human nature is capable of self-
rectification, he taught and admonished not without faith in the efficacy of his labor.   His system is
essentially moral.   ·

There are things in Confucius that make one think
of Plato, as, for instance, his devotion to hard study,
his eagerness to discover truth, his exaltation of
sincerity, his delight in music, and his scorn of
mercenary gain.   But he has none of Plato's poetic
faculty.   Like Socrates, he was a great talker, and
derived illustrations from the commonest objects.
His disappointment at not being able to bring men
to accept his doctrines reminds us of the despondent
moods of Socrates.   "What do you mean," asked
one of his favorite disciples, " by saying that no one
knows you?"   The Master replied, "I do not mur-

mur against Heaven. I do not grumble against men.
My studies lie low, and my penetration rises high.
But there is Heaven that knows me." Such is the
refuge of all great reformers, of whom men say they
were born before their time. Every earnest soul of
vast purpose sooner or later enters into the gloom
of its own peculiar Gethsemane.

While in some instances Confucius distinctly recognized a supreme power, it cannot be said that it
was his habit to appeal to Heaven, or that the notion
of a future life had any strong influence over his
actions. "To give one's self earnestly to the duties
due to men, and while respecting spiritual beings to
keep aloof from them, may be considered wisdom."
This is Confucian religion. It is eminently practical, if not very spiritual. It recognizes man as the
great object of man's love and service. All men are
accounted brethren, and owe one another the natural
debt of benevolence. The sage more than once
repeats the injunction, " Do not to others as you
would not wish done to yourself."

It is natural to suppose that Confucius, holding
such views as he did of human nature, should regard
education as an important means of bettering the
world. This he did. Following the ancients, he
taught that knowledge is conversion from evil to
good — that knowledge is the pathway to both wisdom and virtue. According to a vigorous modern
writer,[1] the religious idea is but one factor in the sal-

1 Dr. I. M. Wise: The Martyrdom of Jesus.

vation of the world, and science or culture is the
other. Many have relied wholly on the first, contemning the other; but Confucius may be said to
have regarded knowledge as man's chief concern,
even to the exclusion of a higher spiritual motive.
He would redeem mankind by instructing them in
secular knowledge. Education, in his creed, is a
means quite adequate to produce a perfect man.
"It is not easy," he says, "to find a man who has
learned for three years, without coming to be good."
Again, "The superior man, while there is anything
he has not studied, or while, in what he has studied,
there is anything he cannot understand, will not
intermit his labor." "Learn as if you could not
reach your object, and were always fearing, also, lest
you should lose it." "If a man keeps cherishing his
old knowledge, so as to be constantly acquiring new,
he may be a teacher of others." He puts more
stress on obtaining knowledge, on storing memory,
than on reflection. "I have been the whole day
without eating, and the whole night without sleeping; — occupied with thinking. It was of no use.
The better plan is to learn." Yet, in another place,
he says wisely, "Learning without thought is labor
lost; thought without learning is perilous."

Confucius would not confine the benefits of education to a favored few. The doctrine of universal
brotherhood implied the duty of universal instruction. We are told that, "when the master went to
Wei, Yen Yew acted as the driver of his carriage.

The Master observed, 'How numerous are the people!' Yew said, 'Since they are thus numerous, what more shall be done for them?'—'Enrich them,' was the reply. 'And when they have been enriched what more shall be done?' The master said, 'Teach them.'" He recognized in education an equalizing power. "There being instruction, there will be no distinction of classes." This proposition is to be taken with the mental reservation demanded in the modern use of its equivalent; for Confucius admitted a natural difference of capacity, and, indeed, classified mankind into higher and lower ranks, according to their quickness or slowness in learning. The lowest class, he says, are they who are dull and stupid and unwilling to learn.

It is a striking evidence of the sagacity of the sage, that he discerned the importance of mental prowess as a condition of military success. "To lead an uninstructed people to war," he declares, "is to throw them away;" but that if they be competently taught for *seven years*, they may be safely employed as soldiers.

We cannot resist the temptation to gather here a few more of the precepts of China's greatest philosopher. To us they seem suggestive, and of wide application; nor has modern culture grown entirely beyond the need of the truths they embody. The extracts are from the Analects : the headings are ours.

Learning like Building a Mound.

"The prosecution of learning may be compared to what may happen in raising a mound. If they want but one basket of earth to complete the work, and I stop, the stopping is my own work. It may be compared to throwing down the earth on the level ground. Though but one basketful is thrown at a time, the advancing with it is my own going forward."

What is Knowledge?

"Shall I teach you what knowledge is? When you know a thing to hold that you know it; and when you do not know a thing, to allow that you do not know it — this is knowledge."

False Pride.

"A scholar whose mind is set on truth, and who is ashamed of bad clothes and bad food, is not fit to be discoursed with."

Whom to teach.

"The Master said, 'I do not open up the truth to one who is not eager to get knowledge, nor help out any one who is not anxious to explain himself. When I have presented one corner of a subject to any one, and he cannot from it learn the other three, I do not repeat my lesson.'"

Teaching adapted to the Taught.

"The Master said, 'To those whose talents are above mediocrity, the highest subjects may be announced. To those whose talents are below mediocrity, the highest subjects may not be announced.'"

How Confucius taught.

"The Master, by orderly method, skilfully leads men on. He enlarged my mind with learning, and taught me the rudiments of propriety."

Experience confers Authority.

"Fan Ché requested to be taught husbandry. The Master said, 'I am not so good for that as an old husbandman.' He requested also to be taught gardening, and was answered, 'I am not so good for that as an old gardener.'"

Qualities of the Scholar.

"The scholar may not be without breadth of mind and vigorous endurance. His burden is heavy and his course is long."

Gravity and Instruction.

"If the scholar be not grave, he will not call forth any veneration, and his learning will not be solid."

Application.

"The Master said, 'Is it not pleasant to learn with a constant perseverance and application?'"

Duties of Youth.

" The Master said, ' A youth, when at home, should be filial, and abroad, respectful to his elders. He should be earnest and truthful. He should overflow in love to all, and cultivate the friendship of the good. When he has time and opportunity after the performance of these things, he should employ them in polite studies.' "

The Scholar's Rest.

" Let relaxation and enjoyment be found in the polite arts."

Blade, Flower, and Fruit.

" There are cases in which the blade springs, but the plant does not go on to the flower. There are cases where it flowers, but no fruit is subsequently produced."

Failure from Within.

" When the archer misses the centre of the target, he turns round and seeks for the cause of his failure in himself."

Virtue.

" If the will be set on virtue, there will be no practice of wickedness."

Law and Punishment.

1. " The Master said, ' If the people be led by laws, and uniformity be sought to be given them *by*

punishments, they will try to avoid the punishment, but have no sense of shame.

2. "'If they be led by virtue, and uniformity sought to be given them by the rules of propriety, they will have the sense of shame, and moreover will become good.'"

Higher Law.

"Without recognizing the ordinances of Heaven, it is impossible to be a superior man."

The Master did not suggest new methods of instruction, or lay down an original course of study. He only indorsed the scheme given in the Book of Rites, and other ancient classics, which it was the crowning work of his life to edit for the people's use. The technical branches taught were reading, writing, arithmetic, ceremonies, music, archery, and charioteering. At the age of seven, children learned to count and to distinguish the cardinal points ; at nine, to number the days of the month ; at ten, the *boys* were sent to live with teachers who instructed them for about ten years, first in numbers and writing, later in music and the odes, and lastly in archery and horsemanship. Lessons in filial duty and the rules of propriety were never intermitted.

Girls received little or no education of a literary kind, but plenty of advice on the duty of submission to the other sex. Mothers are honored in China as such ; but woman as woman is, and always has been, held in low esteem. Confucius hardly more than alludes to the female part of creation. He says somewhere, —

"Of all people, girls and servants are the most difficult to behave to. If you are familiar with them, they *lose their humility*. If you maintain a reserve towards them, they are discontented."

The system of lifelong studentship and competitive examinations, for which China is famous, though not instituted until many centuries after Confucius, naturally grew out of his doctrines, and has always been sustained by citing them. . . . The sage passed from earth nearly twenty-three centuries ago, but how vital his influence still is may be learned from the following passage taken from a biographical sketch by Dr. Legge : —

"At the present day education is widely diffused throughout China, and in all the schools it is Confucius who is taught. . . . The whole of the magistracy is thus versed in all that is recorded of the sage and in the ancient literature which he preserved. His thoughts are familiar to every man in authority, and his character is more or less reproduced in him.

"The official civilians of China, numerous as they are, are but a fraction of its students, and the students, or those who make literature a profession, are again but a fraction of those who attend school for a shorter or longer period. Yet so far as the studies have gone, they have been occupied with the Confucian writings. In many school-rooms there is a tablet or inscription on the wall, sacred to the sage, and every pupil is required, on coming to school on the morning of the first and fifteenth of every month, to bow before it the first thing as an act of worship. Thus all in China who receive the slightest tincture of learning do so at the fountain of Confucius. They learn of him and do homage to him at once. . . . During his lifetime he had three thousand disciples. Hundreds of millions are his disciples now."

2. EDUCATION IN ANCIENT GREECE.[1]

The fundamental conception that every child belongs to the state, and is destined to a prescribed public service, had great influence in suggesting laws and shaping institutions in early Greece. This is particularly true of Sparta, where the grasp of civic power was fastened upon the babe in the nursery, and was not withdrawn from the veteran of three-score years. Even in the Hellenic democracies personal independence was almost swallowed up in the duties of citizenship. The conception which the Greeks held of right life, the essence of their religion, . and the spirit of their education, tended to the suppression of individuality and the promotion of the state. The laws of Lycurgus assumed the power and glory of Sparta to be the objects for which the Laconian citizen existed. Military service was the Spartan's first and greatest duty. Hence military education was the chief concern of the state. Every male child born in Sparta was a potential soldier, or nothing. The children of the Spartans were subjected to an examination soon after birth ; the robust and promising were adopted by the family amid festive rejoicings, the feeble or deformed were exposed on bleak Taygetus. The barbarous custom of exposing infants was legally authorized in all Grecian states excepting Thebes. The laws and customs of Athens were

1 The principal authorities upon which this article is based are Curtius's " History of Greece," Becker's " Charicles," and Schmidt's " History of Pedagogics."

more liberal and humane than those of Sparta. The far-reaching mind of Solon recognized in the generous education of youth a guaranty of the growth and permanence of the Attic capital. His laws held fathers responsible for the education of their sons, and aimed to foster popular culture without subjecting it to stringent state control. The Athenian family was freer than the Spartan. Individual liberty and the prevalence of mental activity made Athens the centre of ancient culture. Athens stands for Greece; her life presents the best results of Hellenic civilization.

In the better class of Greek families the child, when formally accepted by the father, was intrusted to the care of a trained nurse, one from Lacedæmon being considered best. The nurse suckled her little charge, fed him honey, carried him much in the open air, dandled him in her arms, and sang him to sleep with lullabies. Great pains was taken to insure bodily health and symmetry in babyhood. The child's body and limbs were shaped with the hands. No haste was allowed in teaching children to walk. Nurture and growth were superintended with a wise moderation that aimed at the sure if slow development of a sound, strong body. The Greeks well knew that nature cannot be forced. They let the children have a long time and a good time in the nursery. Toys were provided in abundance, such as rattles, dolls, hoops, tops, and little wagons. Many juvenile games were in vogue, one of which was much like blindman's Luff. The misdemeanors of

the nursery were punished by the appropriate application of a slipper or sandal to the young Hellene's
person. Sometimes the offender was terrified into
submission by frightful stories corresponding to the
" Raw Head and Bloody Bones " of modern times.
On the other hand, obedience and docility were re-
warded by copious narratives, usually of a marvellous
sort, from the rich repertory of fable and myth. Skill
in story-telling was a chief accomplishment of the
nurse. At the age of about six, the boys were separated from the girls, put under the care of a pedagogue, and sent to school. The girls received little
or no education except from their mothers and
nurses.

The pedagogue was usually a slave of good character and education. "The democratic atmosphere
of Athens," says Dr. Curtius, "was in favor even of
the unfree class, and to the annoyance of the aristo-
crats encouraged the cultivation of humane and kindly
relations between the master and the slave." Polite-
ness and gracefulness of carriage were particularly
valued in the pedagogue, who was expected to serve
as a model of behavior to his charge. It was his
duty to accompany the boys to and from the school
and gymnasium, to carry their books and harp, and
to exercise a general superintendence over their conduct. He gave incidental instruction and advice,
but took no part in the regular work of the school.
This was intrusted exclusively to the preceptor. The
schools were all private. The state never entertained

the idea of building schoolhouses, or supporting teachers at the public cost. But education was demanded and encouraged by law, and recognized by the people as an element of power. Almost all the Athenian boys were sent to some sort of school for a longer or shorter time, according to the ability of their parents. The rich could command the best of teachers ; the poor were obliged to accept inferior ones. As a rule, the office of preceptor was not in high repute. It was regarded as menial, and often fell to persons who were thought unfit to make a living in any other vocation.

The elementary Hellenic education was simple in kind and method. The art of reading was taught, then the pupils were set to learn by heart passages from approved poets and moralists. The fables of Æsop and the poems of Theognis were among the text-books used. Homer, however, was the great fountain-head of instruction, the source alike of knowledge, patriotism, and religion. Next to Homer Hesiod furnished the Greek youth with material of education. This preliminary instruction was followed by a course including what were regarded as the two essential. parts of education — gymnastics and music. Gymnastics included wrestling, dancing, and many athletic. and graceful exercises ; also bathing, and whatever else conduces to perfect health, strength, agility, and physical self-control. Sceodamus says to Ulysses, in the eighth book of the Odyssey : —

"I think
Thou must be skilled in games, since there is not
A glory greater for a man while yet
He lives on earth than what he hath wrought out,
By strenuous effort, with his feet and hands."

Bryant's Od. vol. i., p. 187.

Music comprehended not only singing and practice upon the harp, but grammar, geography, and mathematics — in the language of Grote, "everything pertaining to the province of the nine Muses." Gymnastics and music, or physical and intellectual culture, were inseparably united. The body was considered as of equal importance with the soul. The sound body was thought essential to the sound mind. Curtius gives the following succinct characterization of the Athenian school culture:—

"Grammar, music, and gymnastics exhausted the circle of teaching, the first two of these departments being closely connected with one another. For, when the boy had learned to read and write, he read the poets; he learnt to declaim them, and with the words appropriated to himself the wealth of their subject-matter. Reason and feeling, taste and judgment, were developed by his habituating himself more and more to the ideas of poets of high and universal reputation. The declamation of poems led to the accompaniment on stringed instruments, and to the accurate acquaintance with the different rhythms. The power of the musical art proved its elevating and refining influence upon the minds of the young, without the intentional character of moral instruction disclosing itself to them."

3. PLATO AND EDUCATION.

All Greek culture points to Plato as the ripe result of its influence. He is the summing up and embodiment of the intelligence of his day. He knew all

that Athens could impart, all the science of the
Pythagoreans, and all the lore of the Egyptians. He
knew, and could use what he knew. Plato is the
greatest name in education, and his dialogues are the
true point of departure for whoever would trace
the winding road along which nations and individuals
have pursued human culture for the last twenty-
three hundred years. Pedagogy without Plato is like
a tree without a tap-root. Professor Jowett observes
that the Republic is the "first treatise on education
of which Milton and Locke, Rousseau, Jean Paul, and
Goethe are the legitimate descendants." It is a fact
curiously illustrative of the dearth of human inge-
nuity that twenty centuries have added almost nothing
to our knowledge of the mind and the right method
of its development.

According to the scanty record which history furnishes, Plato was born at Ægina, 429 B.C., the year
in which Pericles died. He lived through a period of
eighty-one years, and expired, it is said, in the act of
writing, or, according to another authority, with his
head pillowed upon some favorite books. He was of
doubly illustrious blood, his father being a descendant of Codrus, a Hellenic king, and his mother a
relative of Solon, the wise lawgiver. His book-edu-
cation was supplemented by extensive travel and
familiar intercourse with the most famous men of
his time, especially with Socrates, his great teacher.
How well was he fitted by nature, by study, and by
experience to comprehend the intellectual and moral

condition of the people of Athens, and to show them
the highway of reform! He was wise enough to be
moderate. He saw evil enough, but was no rash in-
novator. He could wait patiently for the leaven of
his transforming philosophy to work. It is working
to-day. Transmitted through centuries and nations,
it swells and flavors the educational loaf of Germany,
France, England, and America.

What we call our advance ideas in education were
anticipated by Plato. To the Greeks they seemed
Utopian dreams and poetic rhapsodies. All of
Plato's works abound in educational hints and suggestions; but the Republic and the Laws contain
direct discussions on teaching and training, and may
be considered, as a commentator declares, "theories
and plans of civic education rather than schemes of
legislation and details of laws." In his two great
works Plato develops a philosopher's conception of
a perfect human society—an ideal commonwealth.
His scheme of education reaches its grandest proportions in the Republic, though in the Laws, written
later, much of practical importance may be found,
and perhaps a nearer approach to the ordinary
modern conception of the aims and objects of
schooling. The materials upon which this article is
based are drawn mainly from the Republic.

It is not possible to separate in the Republic what
belongs purely to Plato from what belongs to the
prevailing system of education. In building his new
ship the philosopher would model it somewhat on the

old plan, and would use such of the old timbers as were sound and serviceable. The new ship was to meet all the useful ends of the old, and to be infinitely larger and grander.

As man, in Plato's view, was destined to live for the state, his training should fit him for civic duties, and it should be prescribed and enforced by the state. It was the state's duty to educate the citizen, as it was the citizen's duty to serve the state. Education should be compulsory. This was new doctrine. Teachers should be maintained at the public cost. This was new doctrine. The girls should be educated in the same way as the boys, for a woman is "but a lesser man." This was new doctrine. Plato urged women's rights and duties to an extent that would startle Mrs. Livermore. He would have women share in all the hardships of life, not excepting war.

His whole scheme of government and education is tinctured with a strong admiration of Spartan severity. In the Ideal Republic, the women and children were to be in common, and no parent was to know his own child. This is not the only Platonic notion repugnant to the modern mind. Like Wilhelm Meister, we are shocked and saddened at the discovery of a defect in a writer whom we honor. But a candid recognition of Plato's shortcomings, or of his *differences from us*, is necessary to a correct appreciation of his merits. He differs radically from enlightened moderns in regard to the relative rank and value of

men. He adopted the Oriental idea of caste. He
represented the different classes of men, under the
symbols, gold, silver, brass, and iron. The husbandman must remain a husbandman, the potter a potter.
He believed in the educability of men, not of man.
Brass and iron were born to menial stations, — born
to be governed and used. Gold and silver were by
nature susceptible of culture, were noble, were fit to
become guardians and rulers of the state. It is not
strange that with this aristocratic view of society,
Plato should associate contempt for common people
and manual labor ; or that he should see nothing
wrong in the fact that the proportion of slaves to free
burghers was as twenty to one in Attica.

Plato's primary conception of a state implies the
existence of a large number of ignorant, dependent,
but productive citizens, under the control and direction of a few select guardians and rulers of both
sexes. The guardians are to be soldiers as well as
civilians. The description of their nurture and
training constitutes Plato's scheme of education.
They are to be the offspring of the most perfect
parents. Their nurture even anticipates birth, and
prescribes that the conduct of a woman in pregnancy
should be moderate, gentle, and gracious ; and that
her physical habits should be such as to secure the
highest degree of health and vigor in her child.
The infant's first three years should be exempt from
fear and pain. Strong, prudent, and intelligent
nurses ought to be secured. The children require a

great deal of exercise and amusement ; and they
should be provided with toys and sports adapted to
their age.   Much stress is laid upon the importance
of *beginning* right.   Man is potentially a being beautiful, strong, and good.   If the body is healthy from
the start, if the mind is wisely directed in its first
motions, and if favorable influence continue, the
child will inevitably expand into the proportions of
a right man.   The primary education is to give the
body natural growth, to surround children with all
good and wholesome stimulations by which they may
develop into happy youth, as a rose blossoms.   Much
freedom is to be granted in childhood, but not license.
Respect for parents and elders must be maintained.
Punishments are sometimes requisite, but should
never be ignominious, or inflicted in anger.   As
children grow older, they are to be held with a
tighter rein.   "Of all animals, the boy is the most
unmanageable, inasmuch as he has the fountain
of reason in him not yet regulated.   He is the
most insidious, sharp-witted, and insubordinate of
animals."

At the age of six the sexes are to be separated,
and sent to school.   And, now, what shall the training be ?   Is there a better than the time-honored
curriculum, gymnastics for the body, and music or
literature for the soul ?

Literature is to be taught, not so much as a matter
of knowledge, as a means of forming correct moral
principles and mental habits.   Tales and poems are

to be committed to memory, but only such as convey a proper lesson. The young and tender mind must receive only right impressions. To this end mythology should be expurgated. Homer and the other poets are to be cleansed of all that encourages intemperance and lust, and all that tends to produce terror, such as horrible descriptions of Hades. The gods are to be represented, not as yielding to the passions and vices common to men, but as beings altogether pure and noble. Plato's education is based on a religious creed at once simple and sublime. God is good and unchangeable. All tales that teach the contrary are to be rejected, no matter how great their literary merit. True piety, sound morality, must be inculcated, whatever be left out. Do not Christian teachers stand rebuked by a solemn voice sounding across the lapse of twenty hundred years? With us intellect comes first, and morality is only incidental.

Music proper Plato would teach with reference to its effect on character, not as a mere polite accomplishment. The form and quality of music best adapted to educate are carefully considered. Words, melody, and rhythm are discussed. The only instruments thought desirable are "the lyre and the harp for the city, and a pipe for the country." The wonderful influence of music in regulating the human mind and heart is dwelt upon in eloquent strains.

" Is not this the reason why musical training is so powerful, because rhythm and harmony find their way into the secret places of the soul, on which they mightily fasten, bearing grace in their movements, and making the soul graceful of him who is rightly educated, or ungraceful if ill-educated; and also because he who has received this true education of the inner being will most shrewdly perceive omissions or faults in art and nature, and with a true taste, while he praises and rejoices over, and receives into his soul the good, and becomes noble and good, he will justly blame and hate the bad, now in the days of his youth, even before he is able to know the reason of the thing; and when reason comes he will recognize and salute her as a friend with whom his education has made him long familiar."

Under gymnastics Plato considers the general care of the body, recommending temperance and moderation in exercise and diet. Seasoning in food and all the "delicacies of Athenian confectionery" are to be avoided. Extreme simplicity in all things is enjoined. Simplicity in music "engenders temperance of soul;" in gymnastics, "bodily health." The rightly educated person should need neither magistrate nor physician. He should be a law to himself as to conduct and as to health. Soul-culture should keep him from violating the laws of the state; gymnastics should keep him physically well. Respecting the relative importance of literature and gymnastics, Plato departed from the established opinion of the ancients. He was the first to declare the absolute superiority of the soul to the body. "The good body," he says, "does not improve the soul, but the good soul improves the body. Then if we have educated the mind, the minuter care of the body may properly be committed to the mind."

Plato regards studies and exercises as a means and not an end. Every faculty exists in embryo in the child ; education calls it out. The fewer the methods of education, the better, provided they answer the purpose of giving body and mind the use of themselves. Quintilian likens the mind to a vessel to be filled ; Plato compares it to an eye turned toward objects, and thus made sensible of its power of seeing. Education is "not implanting eyes, for they exist already, but giving them a right direction, which they have not." How beautiful, how elevating this conception ! The soul is designed to compass the universe in its bright vision. Education is the adjustment of the soul to the eternal verities. Pursuing his own studies upon this lofty plane, even in the glimmering light of ancient science, Plato reached the grand generalization that all knowledge is one, — a proposition which we are in the habit of regarding as of purely modern development.

The preliminary education we have described is interrupted when the pupils arrive at the age of sixteen, and are subjected to a trial of practical life. When they reach the age of twenty, a selection of right natures is to be chosen, for a higher education. Sure, brave, fair, and noble persons, of keen and ready powers of acquisition and good memory, are

to be selected. These only can become good guardians. They must be " unwearied, solid men, lovers
of labor in any line." To these shall be imparted a
knowledge of arithmetic, geometry, and astronomy.
Plato attached great value to mathematics as developing the power of abstract thought. Dialectic was
next to be studied. This is " the coping-stone of the
sciences ; the nature of knowledge can go no further."
The dialectician is " one who has a conception of
the essence of each thing," an abstract true idea
of justice, truth, beauty, virtue, wisdom.

Again, education is to be interrupted, and its value
tested, by application to practical duties. The educated man is not to rest satisfied with the contemplation of his own attainments ; he must descend to the
aid of his fellows. He should be not only a right
thinker, but a perfect practical statesman. He must
not spend all his time in the " heaven of ideas ; " he
must serve the state in the " den of common life."

At the age of thirty, the best are once more to
be selected from the best, and put to school once
more. These choice natures finally become the
highest rulers, the kings of the state. Only ripe
philosophers can become kings. They are to devote .
themselves to study for five years. They are to
review, classify, and sum up all the knowledge here-
tofore acquired. They are then to devote fifteen
years to the highest concerns of the state, — to lead
armies, to govern cities.

" And when they have reached fifty years of age,

then let those who still survive and have distinguished themselves in every deed and in all knowledge come at last to their consummation. The time
has now arrived at which they must raise the eye of
the soul to the universal light which lightens all
things, and behold the absolute good ; for that is the
pattern according to which they are to order the
state and the lives of individuals, and the remainder
of their own lives also, making philosophy their chief
pursuit ; but when their turn comes, also toiling at
politics and ruling for the public good, not as if they
were doing some great thing, but of necessity ; and
when they have brought up others like them, and
left them to be governors of the state, then will they
depart to the Islands of the Blest, and dwell there;
and the city will give them public memorials and
sacrifices, and honor them, if the Pythian oracle consent, as demigods, and at any rate, as blessed and
divine."

Having led us to this mountain summit of human
possibility, Plato points, with encouraging cheerfulness, to ultra-mundane heights, and fresh fields of
endeavor beyond time. Not discouraged at the
meagre results which the culture of this life returns,
he makes the best of mortality happy to even begin
"something which avails against the day when we
live again and hold discourse in another existence."

Plato's scheme of education, as a system, is totally
inapplicable to our modern wants. Nevertheless,
separated from the state, or modified as to certain

impracticable features, and broadened at the base, so
as to embrace the many as well as the few, it might
serve us a very good purpose — at least as an ideal.
Modern educational theories are better than ancient,
chiefly because they are more humane and universal.
They assume that all men are educable, even crimi-
nals, mad men, and idiots. Modern society appre-
ciates brass and iron, and modern education is the
bold alchemy which transmutes base into noble, and
noble into nobler still.

Plato's educational value to us is discovered, not in
his system, but in particular discussions and suggestions. He is rich in maxims. He is the father
of object teaching and kindergartens. In the character of Socrates, he paints a model teacher. His
dialogues are acknowledged to be "the best examples
of the nature and method of dialectic." Joubert
says, " Plato found philosophy made of bricks, and
made it of gold." I know of no other work so profitable for the seeker of general culture to peruse as
Plato. Jowett's translation furnishes us with the
entire work in clear and beautiful English. So sensible, so invigorating, so amusing are these splendid
dialogues, that one involuntarily repeats Emerson's
question, "Why not educate our young men on this
book?"

4. ARISTOTLE AND EDUCATION.

Aristotle was born nearly four centuries before
Christ, at Stagira, a city on the coast of Thrace.

He came to Athens while yet in his teens, attracted by the genius of Plato. He became a disciple of the great philosopher, and soon distinguished himself for industry and ability. Plato called him the *mind* of the academy. With what a copious flow the stream of eloquent instruction must have run from such a master to such a pupil! The enthusiastic teacher will credit the tradition which affirms that when Aristotle happened to be absent from the lecture, Plato appeared spiritless, and complained that he spoke to deaf auditors.

Aristotle remained in Athens for about twenty years, devoting himself to study and philosophical pursuits. Shortly after Plato's death, which occurred in 338 B.C., he removed to the Mysian city of Atarneus, where he spent three years at the court of Hermias, his friend and fellow-student,—a philosopher king. Hermias, falling into the power of the King of Persia, was taken prisoner, sent to Asia, and hanged; and Aristotle fled for safety from Atarneus to the Isle of Lesbos. He was accompanied in his flight by Pythias, sister of Hermias, whom he had just married, and whom he is said to have loved with an extravagant passion. Pythias died within a year or two, and Aristotle soon afterward sailed to Macedonia, on the invitation of Philip, to undertake the education of the prince, afterward Alexander the Great. Philip and Aristotle were intimate in boyhood, and they continued lifelong friends. Upon the birth of Alexander, the king sent the philosopher this message : —

"Know that a son is born to us. We thank the gods for their gift, but especially for bestowing it when Aristotle lives; assuring ourselves, that, educated by you, he will be worthy of us, and worthy of inheriting our kingdom."

Alexander was fourteen years old, and Aristotle about forty, when they first came together in the relation of pupil and tutor. This relation continued for eight years, and we may conjecture that it was of no small benefit to Aristotle, as affording preparation for his future work. By imparting knowledge to others, we establish it in ourselves. What finer culture can be imagined than to be taught by Plato, and to teach Alexander!

Aristotle, ripened by years and a varied experience, returned to Athens and established his celebrated schools in the Lyceum. This Lyceum was a "gymnasium in the suburbs, well shaded with trees, near to which the soldiers used to exercise, and adorned by the Temple of Lycian Apollo, from whose peripaton, or walk, Aristotle and his followers were called Peripatetics." Aristotle, like other teachers of antiquity, had two forms of lecture, *acroatic* or *esoteric* and *encyclic* or *exoteric*. The acroatic lectures were set discourses addressed to his regular pupils, and were read in the morning at the Lyceum. The encyclic discourses were on the same or similar topics as the acroatic, but were popular in style, and adapted to the general learner. They were truly peripatetic lectures or talks, being given informally after supper, and while walking about for exercise of body and

relaxation of mind.   Only the acroatic treatises have
come down to us, and they in a mutilated condition.

For a period of thirteen years Aristotle continued
to instruct the young men of Athens in the science
and philosophy of his age.   His splendid career
then drew to a dreary close, as the sun sets in gathering clouds.   Like Socrates, he was accused before
the Areopagus of irreligion ; like Socrates, he was
misrepresented and persecuted, and recalling the
fate of Socrates, he went, self-banished, to Chalcis in
Eubœa, to prevent the Athenians, as he sadly said,
from committing a second sin against philosophy.
He died, in Eubœa, before the expiration of a year,
at the age of sixty-three.

It was inevitable that a man of Aristotle's associations and pursuits should consider deeply the
subject of education.   He did so, and some of his
conclusions on this subject may easily be gathered
from his preserved writings.   There is a severe unity
binding together his treatises on Ethics and Politics,
and by reading these works, we learn his conception
of man and the training that fits man for the highest
duties and truest happiness.

According to the ethics of Aristotle, the soul is
capable of two kinds of virtue, moral and intellectual.
Moral virtue rules that part of our nature which is
most closely connected with the body, —the instincts,
appetites, and passions.   It is not innate.   It is not
produced by nature, nor contrary to nature.   The
soul is passive to external influences.   Moral virtue

is simply habit. It is impressed by examples, by acts, by whatever may reach the mind through the senses ; and the impression is deepened by practice. If the tablet of the child's mind is not strongly inscribed with the characters of moral virtue, vice will write possession there. Hence the circumstances under which children are brought up are all-important, and parents, families, and states are responsible for their education until they reach the years of accountability. Children are incomplete, and their virtue is referable, not to themselves, but to their guardians. Adults are free agents, and their conduct should submit to the control of reason.

Intellectual virtue belongs to that part of our being which is farthest removed from the dominion of sense. It relates to the powers of thought and contemplation. The intellect is the noblest thing in man — it resembles the divine. Intellectual virtue is not a mere habit, like moral virtue, but it " has its origin and increase for the most part from *teaching*," and requires time and experience for its development. It is dependent upon the cultivation of the soul. Intellect grows thriftily only out of a moral soil. Goodness predisposes to right reasoning. The object of intellectual virtue is the discovery of truth, and Aristotle gives it as the distinguishing mark of a good or moral man, that "he can see the truth in every case, since he is, as it were, the rule and measure of it." This is a re-statement of one of Plato's ideas.

The exercise of the virtues, moral and intellectual, has for its end the supreme good of the individual by bringing him to a condition of almost perfect and constant happiness in the delightful contemplation of truth.   But the individual does not exist for himself alone, he exists for the state.   " To discover the good of an individual is satisfactory, but to discover that of a state is more noble and divine."   In Aristotle's system, as in Plato's, education is regarded as a public duty.   " No one ought to think that any citizen belongs to him in particular, but to the state, and it is the natural duty of each part to regard the good of the whole."   Aristotle's treatise on Politics applies to the state the same principles that his Ethics applies to men.   The good citizen is described as not essentially different from the virtuous man.   Politics, which is the greatest of sciences, should direct the citizen in all things that tend to a correct life according to a fixed ethical rule.   " It is evident that laws should be laid down for education, and that it should be public."   The laws must prescribe such regulations as will secure in the young those habits which confirm moral virtue, and predispose the mind to intellectual pursuits.   Further, they must dictate what individuals shall learn, and to what extent.

Aristotle, in Greek fashion, lays much stress upon the literal *breeding* of children, the advantages of good stock, fortunate birth, and careful nurture.   He specifies that infants ought to be fed with abundance of milk, without wine, allowed a free motion of the

limbs, and inured, very early, to the effects of cold.
Nothing should be taught the child, not even necessary labor, before he is five years old, lest it should
prevent his growth.   He must exercise freely, however, and his plays may be imitations of what he is
afterward to do as serious work.   The conflicts of
boys are not to be forbidden, since the "struggles of
the heart, and the compression of the spirits,"
which they produce, develop strength in a peculiar
manner.

The mental training of children requires the utmost watchfulness and circumspection on the part of
nurses, parents, and teachers.   Aristotle declares
that "it does not make a slight, but an important,
nay, rather, the whole difference," whether children
are brought up in right habits or not, from the beginning.   First influences are most important, because
"what we meet with first pleases best."   The fables
and tales told in the nursery should be of a proper
sort.   Children should be kept from the company of
slaves and all vulgar or vicious persons.   They must
hear no indecent language, see no obscene pictures
or statues, or be tempted, in any way, to violate good
morals or imitate bad manners.   They should be
guarded and tended within the pale of the family
until they arrive at the age of seven.   At that age
the first period of regular school education should
begin, to continue for seven years.   Another and
higher course of education, also of seven years' duration, should complement the training of boyhood,

and complete the citizen for the highest duties of life, both private and public.

The eighth book of Aristotle's Politics, evidently a fragment, treats of the studies suitable to the period of boyhood, and embraces many critical remarks on prevailing usage among the Greeks. Lacedæmon is especially recommended as being the only city in which education receives proper attention from the state.

Four branches are named, in the Politics, as comprising the matter which it was customary to teach children. These are reading, gymnastics, music, and painting. The utility of reading is taken for granted, not only for its own sake, but also as a means of acquiring other sorts of learning. The gymnastic exercises of boys, Aristotle thought, should be very gentle, as violent exercise is brutalizing, and, also, incompatible with study. "It is impossible," says our philosopher, "for the mind and body to labor at the same time, as each labor is productive of contrary evils : the labor of the body preventing the progress of the mind, and the mind of the body." Painting is recommended as of great and varied usefulness : for instance, to prevent mistakes in buying pictures or vases. It should be learned, moreover, not merely for its utility, but because it enables one to judge of the beauty of the human form. Some things are to be learned simply because they are noble and liberal ; for "to be always hunting after the profitable ill agrees with great and freeborn souls." The subject of music is discussed at considerable length, and the conclusion reached is, that children should be taught to sing and play music of a moral and elevating character, principally as a means of relaxation and amusement. This course of study seems meagre, and it is probable that Aristotle included much more under the term *reading* than we do.

After the youth shall have arrived at the age of fourteen, three years may be specially devoted to severe gymnastic exercises. This will leave four more years for the completion of education. Aristotle gives no outline of the course to be pursued during these four years, but it is safe to infer that he would have the young men instructed as he himself taught them at the Lyceum. Indeed, the school of Aristotle may be regarded as a sort of primitive university, conducted by a single professor. It was the Harvard of Athens, where the Stagirite read a continuous series of lectures to any and all who were seeking a higher education. These lectures were upon rhetoric, logic, metaphysics, ethics, politics, economics, mathematics, physics, and natural history.

Aristotle must have exercised a powerful influence upon his contemporaries, and especially his pupils. He was the first really scientific teacher of whom we have any account. His learning was vast. Quintilian refers to him as a prodigy of erudition. He gave form and method to studies before shapeless and confused. Centuries elapsed without adding

anything to the facts he left in natural history, and
Agassiz says that we must come down to Linnæus
before we find systematic zoölogy taken up where
Aristotle had left it. His system of logic, according
to Grote, "was not only of extraordinary value in
reference to the processes and controversies of his
time, but, also, having become insensibly worked
into the minds of instructed men, has contributed
much to form what is correct in the habits of modern
thinking." Burke declares, that of all Aristotle's
writings, only the treatise on natural philosophy is
unworthy of him, thus giving indirect testimony of
the sustained and varied power of the great philosopher. Another distinguished voucher for Aristotle's
worth, and that to the modern student, is the late
Dr. Arnold, who stated that he found the Politics
of great and direct use to him every day of his life,
and who further said that he would not consent to
send his son to a university where he would lose the
study of "dear old Tottle."

A just estimate of Aristotle's system of education
cannot be made unless we consider to what classes
the system is intended to apply. In the ideal state,
depicted in the Politics, the citizens are to be as
nearly equal as possible, and they are all to be educated. The citizens are to be served by slaves.
Slavery is recognized as the natural condition of a
portion of mankind. From the hour of their birth
some are marked out as slaves. This Aristotle em-
phasizes by frequent repetition. The slave is fated

to an abject life. His position is but a step above that of the lower animals. He knows that there is such a faculty as reason, but he is incapable of using it. He has no deliberative faculty. He has a natural need of a master, and his condition of servitude is right and just. The instruction which he is to receive is, of course, that of a menial, and is very limited.

And how about women? Are they to be educated? Aristotle's views are briefly these: The female of animals is, as a rule, inferior to the male. Woman is inferior to man, and in some respects opposite. She is weaker than man in body and in intellect. Man should exert a political government over his wife. His duties in the family are different from hers. It is his business to rule, hers to obey; his to acquire subsistence, hers to take care of it; his to deal with the outside world, hers to order the household within. As to children, it is no more the mothers' duty to rear them than the fathers' to educate them. That women should be educated, especially for the duties of the marriage relation, Aristotle distinctly affirms; but he nowhere describes the manner or place of their training. We may fairly conclude that he would confine their education to instruction in the domestic virtues, according to the dictation of the "man of the house."

5. QUINTILIAN.

Mommsen, the best authority on Roman education, draws a vivid contrast between the Grecian and the Roman character, showing the former eager to promote individual freedom, and the latter resolute to repress it. The historian says that the Roman judgment " deemed every one a bad citizen who wished to be different from his fellows." What culture was to Athens, law was to Rome. Hence the supremacy of civil power in Rome ; the subordination of people to potentate, and of family to father. The Roman husband was absolute monarch over wife and child, yet wife and child felt no degradation, since they regarded their subjection as inevitably fixed by the just ruling of the gods. How rigid the fabric of old Roman society ! It was as hard and inflexible as a suit of iron mail.

Rights, duties, obligations, being sharply defined, — the purpose of life being clearly recognized as service to the state directed by law, — education must force every child into the path prescribed for him. The training of Roman youth, in early times, was the shaping of Romans, not the developing of men. The Roman must fight — therefore his body was inured to hardship. His physical exercises were useful rather than graceful. The Roman must obey. The oldest Roman school-book was the " Twelve Tables," the code of laws. This was committed to memory by every boy. The Roman must speak in public.   Correct and forcible delivery was taught in every school.

There is no series of events in history more interesting or profitable to the student of educational philosophy than that embracing the intellectual relations of Rome with Greece.   Every youth in the high school knows that Greece conquered her conquerors by the might of culture.   Who can resist fate ?   The Romans at first feared and hated Grecian ideas.   They dreaded education, regarding it as a "disequalizer" of men.   They also feared, with good reason, the corrupting influence of luxurious Athenian life.   Cato, the censor, moved in the Roman Senate to dismiss certain Greek ambassadors, who, as Milton quaintly says, "tooke occasion to give the City a tast of their Philosophy."   Cato would none of that dangerous dynamite.   Yet he himself was induced to study Greek in his old age ; and his grandson spent his last hours reading the divine Plato.   The Roman conquerors were conquered indeed.   Their very slaves became their rulers, swaying the sceptre of intellectual power.   No force can be destroyed. The wave of Roman civilization combined with that of Grecian, and the cumulated billow rolled on.

Each nation has a predominant genius.   Each banks its capital, sooner or later, in the treasury of the world's progress.   The wealth of Rome was law and order.   The riches of Athens was culture. Modern nations draw interest on the two vast funds consolidated.

Athens elaborated noble systems of education. Socrates, Plato, Aristotle, created pedagogics for Europe. The Roman mind could not improve the theories which Grecian philosophy had devised. Hence there are no eminent Latin authorities on the principles of education.

Livius Andronicus translated the Odyssey into Latin 207 B.C., and this was used as a text-book. Greek schoolmasters flocked to Rome. Many were purchased as private tutors. A specially elegant article of Athenian pedagogue brought as high as two hundred thousand sesterces, or about ten thousand dollars. It became a custom for Roman youth to go to distant cities to pursue special studies, as modern American students go to London, Paris, or Berlin. Rhodes was famous for her schools of rhetoric; Athens, for philosophy; Alexandria, for science.

Pliny the Younger, in a somewhat celebrated letter to Cornelius Tacitus, writes: "Being lately at Comum, the place of my nativity, a young lad, son to one of my neighbors, made me a visit. I asked him whether he studied rhetoric, and where? He told me he did, and at Mediolanum. And why not here? 'Because,' said his father, who came with him, 'we have no professors.'" Pliny goes on to say how he argued with the boy's father and others to persuade them to establish a home college, offering to pay one-third of the cost himself. "Your sons," he says, "will by these means receive their education where they re-

ceived their birth, and be accustomed from their
infancy to inhabit and affect their native soil. You
may be able to procure professors of such distinguished, abilities that the neighboring towns shall be
glad to draw their learning from hence ; and as you
now send your children to foreigners for education,
may foreigners in their turn flock hither for their
instruction."[1]

The so-called " seven liberal arts " of antiquity were
grammar, rhetoric, philosophy, arithmetic, geometry,
astronomy, and music. These became the established
curriculum. They held their place as the essentials
of a finished training for hundreds of years, — in
fact, through the Middle Ages. They are still included as organic to every course of study.

I said there are no eminent Latin authorities on
the principles of education. Varro, the most learned
of the ancient Romans, a correspondent of Cicero
and a friend of Cæsar, wrote treatises on education,
but they are lost. ˙In his time the Greek system of
schooling prevailed in Italy. Cicero was deeply
interested in education, and wrote on the subject.
He honors the teacher's profession, and expressly
says, in his egotistic way, " As to whatever service I
have performed, if I have performed any to the state,
I came to it after being furnished and adorned with
knowledge by teachers and learning."

The man who embodied the principles of Roman-
ized Grecian education in language was not born

until more than eighty years after Cicero died.
Thoughts are lived before they are written. As
Plato came after Pericles, so Quintilian came after
Augustus. I do not mean to put Quintilian on a
par with Plato. Quintilian is the best exponent we
have of Roman education. He is not a great, original
philosopher, but an excellent summer-up of other
men's philosophy, — a shrewd, practical, common-
sense man of much learning and rare powers of
expression. He was a clever, communicative Roman
lawyer and teacher, with a "long" head, a good heart,
a sharp pen, a keen wit, and a commanding social
position.

Quintilian was born at Caluguras on the Ebro
River, about 40 A.D., some eight years before the
birth of Juvenal. He removed to Rome, where he
became a pleader, and afterwards a teacher of oratory.
He established a school in the eigth year of the reign
of Domitian, and received a salary of $4,000 out of
the public treasury. Moreover, his pupils, many of
whom were distinguished, must have paid him large
fees, for he amassed property. Juvenal, in one of
his satires, after speaking of the reluctance of fathers
to pay for their sons' education, and the miserable
condition of teachers in general, asks, "Where, then,
did Quintilian get money to pay for so many estates?
. . . It is good fortune! Yes! Quintilian was indeed lucky, but he is a greater rarity even than a
white crow." Quintilian spent about twenty years
in teaching, and his famous work on the "Instruction

of an Orator" shows on every page evidence of the author's experience. The treatise is not a fine-spun theory, but a well-woven record of actual school-mastering. The book is saturated with the life of its writer, and this personal element makes it entertaining to this day. I find its charm to hold after a second and a third perusal, and I venture to transcribe a few of the passages that seem worthy of study as literature and as pedagogical science.

While engaged in the composition of his "Institutes,"-Quintilian was intrusted with the education of two of Domitian's grand-nephews. In the introduction to the sixth book he laments the death of his wife and children. He says, "My youngest son dying when he had just passed his fifth year, took from me, as it were, the sight of my eyes. . . . Such a child, even if he had been the son of a stranger, would have won my love. It was the will, too, of insidious Fortune, with a view to torture me the more severely, that he should show more affection for me than for any one else ; that he should prefer me to his nurses, to his grandfather who educated him, and to all such as gain the love of children at that age. . . . I then rested for my only hope and pleasure on my younger son, my little Quintilian, and he might have sufficed to console me, for he did not put forth merely flowers, like the other, but, having entered his tenth year, certain well-formed fruits. I swear by my own sufferings, by the sorrowful testimony of my own feelings, by his own shade, the deity that my grief worships, that I discerned in him such excellences of mind that the dread of such a thunder-stroke might have been felt even from that cause, as it has been generally observed that precocious maturity is most liable to early death. He had, also, every adventitious advantage, agreeableness and clearness of voice, sweetness of tone, and a peculiar facility of sounding every letter in either language, as if he had been born to speak that only. But these were still only promising appearances ; he had greater qualities, — fortitude, resolution, and strength, — to resist pain and fear; for, with what courage, with what admiration on the part of his physicians, did he endure an illness of eight months ! How he did console me at the last ! How, when he was losing his senses, and unable to recognize me, did he fix his thoughts in delirium only on learning." [1]

The reader, if he be a man of feeling, will not get over this touching passage without emotion ; to me the last sentence seems pathetic, in a way of which the writer, perhaps, was unconscious, for it suggests the probability that the gentle " little Quintilian " may have been educated into eternity. The hardest thing for an ambitious father, or an enthusiastic preceptor, is to forbear urging a precocious child.

Quintilian indorsed Plato in the belief that youth is the time for toil. He says it is not to be apprehended that boys will suffer from overwork, bodily

[1] This and the extracts which follow are taken from Watson's literal translation of Quintilian's Institutes.

or mental. "The temper of boys is better able to bear labor than that of men." "Yet some relaxation is to be allowed to all : not only because there is nothing that can bear perpetual labor, but because application to learning depends on the will, which cannot be forced. Boys, accordingly, when reinvigorated and refreshed, bring more sprightliness to their learning, and a more determined spirit, which for the most part spurns compulsion. Nor will play in boys displease me ; it is also a sign of vivacity ; and I cannot expect that he who is dull and spiritless will be of an eager disposition in his studies, when he is indifferent even to that excitement which is natural to his age." While Quintilian advocates a stalwart training, and scorns "that delicacy of education which we call fondness, which weakens all the powers of the body and mind," he strongly objects to corporal punishment. "That boys should suffer corporal punishment," he says, "though it be a received custom, I by no means approve ; first, because it is a disgrace and a punishment for slaves, and in reality an affront ; secondly, because, if a boy's disposition be so abject as not to be mended by reproof, he will be hardened even to stripes ; and, lastly, because if one who regularly exacts his tasks be with him, there will not be the least need of any such chastisement."

Our Roman schoolmaster thinks that "no part of a child's life should be exempt from tuition." "Let us not lose even the earliest period of life, and so much the less, as the elements of learning depend

on the memory alone." "The chief symptom of
ability in children is memory; the next is imitation."

Quintilian takes a very encouraging view of the
educability of the average boy. He says : " Let the
father, as soon as his son is born, conceive, first of
all, the best possible hopes of him, for he will thus
grow the more solicitous about his improvement
from the very beginning ; since it is a complaint
without foundation, that 'to very few people is
granted the faculty of comprehending what is imparted to them, and that most, through dulness of
understanding, lose their labor and their time.' For,
on the contrary, you will find the greater number of
men both ready in conceiving and quick in learning,
since such quickness is natural to man ; and as birds
are born to fly, horses to run, and wild beasts to
show fierceness, so to us peculiarly belong activity
and sagacity of understanding, whence the origin of
the mind is thought to be from Heaven. But dull
and unteachable persons are no more produced in
the course of nature than are persons marked by
monstrosity and deformity ; such are certainly but
few. It will be a proof of this assertion, that, among
boys, good promise is shown in the far greater number ; and, if it passes off in the progress of time, it
is manifest that it was not natural ability, but care,
that was wanting. But one surpasses another, you
will say, in ability. I grant that this is true ; but
only so far as to accomplish more or less, whereas

there is no one who has not gained something by study." •

Discussing the relation of natural ability and culture, our author says : " If you suppose either to be independent of the other, nature will be able to do much without learning ; but learning will be of no avail without the assistance of nature. But if they be united in equal parts, I shall be inclined to think that, when both are but moderate, the influence of nature is nevertheless greater ; but finished orators, I consider, owe more to learning than to nature. Thus the best husbandman cannot improve soil of no fertility, while from fertile ground something good will be produced even without the aid of the husbandman ; yet, if the husbandman bestows his labor on rich land, he will produce more effect than the goodness of the soil itself. Had Praxiteles attempted to hew a statue out of a mill-stone, I should have preferred it to an unhewn block of Parian marble ; but if that statuary had fashioned the marble, more value would have accrued to it from his own workmanship than was in the marble itself. In a word, nature is the material for learning, — the one forms, the other is formed. Art can do nothing without material ; material has its own nature even independent of art ; but perfection of art is of more consequence than perfection of material."

Quintilian treats the important subject of diversity of natural gifts with wonderful discrimination and clearness. "Two things," he remarks, "are especially to be avoided, — one to attempt what cannot be accomplished, and the other to divert a pupil from what he does well to something else for which he is less qualified." Yet he believes in harmonious development, and does not think "that any good quality, which is innate, should be detracted, but that whatever is inactive or deficient should be invigorated or supplied."

Some pungent observations are made on precocity. "That precocious sort of talent scarcely ever comes to good fruit. Such are those who do little things easily, and, impelled by impudence, show at once all they can accomplish in such matters. But they succeed only in what is ready to their hand; they string words together, uttering them with an intrepid countenance, not in the least discouraged by bashfulness, and do little, but do it readily. There is no real power behind, or any that rests on deeply fixed roots; but they are like seeds which have been scattered on the surface of the ground and shoot up prematurely, and like grass that resembles corn, and grows yellow, with empty ears, before the time of harvest. Their efforts give pleasure, as compared with their years; but their progress comes to a stand, and our wonder diminishes."

Quintilian's model pupil is described in these words: "Let the boy be given to me whom praise stimulates, whom honor delights, who weeps when he is unsuccessful. His powers must be cultivated under the influence of ambition; reproach will sting him to the quick; honor will invite him, and in such a boy I shall never be apprehensive of indifference."

The "Institutes" does not stop with the portraiture of different types of pupils; the teacher is also painted in lively colors. Here are some passages of keen truth; "The ablest teacher can teach little things if he will; first, because it is likely that he who excels others has gained the most accurate knowledge of the means by which men attain excellence; secondly, because method [ratio], which with the best qualified teachers, is always plainest, is of great efficacy in teaching; and, lastly, because no man rises to such a height in greater things that lesser fade entirely from his view. . . . It generally happens that instructions given by the most learned are far more easy to be understood and more perspicuous than those of others. . . . The less able a teacher is, the more obscure will he be. For none are more pernicious than those who, having gone some little beyond the first elements, clothe themselves in a mistaken persuasion of their own knowledge, since they disdain to yield to those who are skilled in teaching."

"Above all, and especially for boys, a dry master is to be avoided not less than a dry soil for plants that are still tender. Under the influence of such a tutor they at once become dwarfish, — looking, as it were, toward the ground, and daring to aspire to nothing above every-day talk. To them leanness is in the place of health, and weakness instead of judgment ; and while they think it sufficient to be free from fault, they fall into the fault of being free from merit. Let not even maturity itself, therefore, come too fast ; let not the malt while yet in the vat become mellow, — for so it will bear years, and improve by age."

Here is Quintilian's outline of the ideal teacher : " Let him adopt, above all things, the feelings of a parent toward his pupils, and consider that he succeeds to the place of those by whom they were intrusted to him. Let him neither have vices in himself, nor tolerate them in others. Let his austerity be not too stern, nor his affability too easy; let dislike arise from the one, or contempt from the other. Let him discourse freely on what is honorable and good, for the oftener he admonishes the more seldom will he have to chastise. Let him not be of an angry temper, and yet not a conniver at what ought to be corrected. Let him be plain in his mode of teaching and patient of labor, but rather diligent in exacting tasks than fond of giving them of excessive length. Let him reply readily to those who put questions to him, and question of his own accord those who do not. In commending the exercises of his pupils, let him be neither niggardly nor lavish ; for the one quality begets dislike of labor, and the other self-complacency. In amending what requires correction let him not be harsh, and least of all not reproachful ; for that very circumstance, that some teacher's blame as if they hated, deters many young men from their proposed course of study. Let him every day say something, and even much, which, when the pupils hear, they may carry away with them,—for though he may point out to them, in their course of reading, plenty of examples for their imitation, yet the *living voice*, as it is called, feeds the mind more nutriment, and especially the voice of the teacher, whom his pupils, if they are but rightly instructed, both love and reverence. How much more readily we imitate those whom we like, can scarcely be expressed."

Quintilian's directions for instructing children are full and minute. As memory and imitation are the faculties first developed, the talk of the boy's nurses must be on proper subjects, and correct in grammar. The next things to be learned after the nursery stories are the fables of Æsop. Verses from the poets should be committed to memory. As soon as a boy has learned to read and write he should be instructed by the grammarians, — that is, Greek and Latin, — Greek first. This instruction includes the art of speaking. The directions for teaching elementary grammar, and what we call rhetoric and composition, are practical, suggestive, and luminous. I know of nothing better of their kind in any modern book. The suggestions on reading are most excellent, and as applicable now as in ancient times. " For my part," says our author, " I would have the best authors commenced at once, and read always; but I would choose the clearest style and most in-

telligible." "It has been an excellent custom that
reading should begin with Homer and Virgil, al-
though, to understand their merits, there is needed
much of mature judgment ; but for the acquisition of
judgment there is abundance of time, for they will
not be read but once." "Those writings should be
the subjects of lectures for boys, which may best
nourish the mind and enlarge the thinking powers ;
for reading other books, which relate merely to education, advanced life will afford sufficient time."
"The love of letters and the benefit of reading are
bounded, not by the time spent at school, but by the
extent of life."

Teachers of composition may find a useful hint in
the following : "Let that age [youth] be daring,
invent much, and delight in what it invents, though
it be often not sufficiently severe and correct. The
remedy for exuberance is easy ; barrenness is incur-
able by any labor. That temper in boys will afford
me little hope in which mental effort is prematurely
restrained by judgment. I like what is produced to
be extremely copious, profuse even beyond the limits
of propriety. Years will greatly reduce superfluity ;
judgment will smooth away much of it ; something
will be worn off, as it were, if there be but metal
from which something may be hewn and polished
off ; and such metal there will be, if we do not make
the plates too thin at first, so that deep cutting may
break it." In another place we find this very true
maxim : "By writing quickly we are not brought to

write well, but by writing well we are brought to write quickly."

After the foundations are well laid in reading, writing, and grammar, the education is built up on the old Greek plan. The superstructure consists of music, geometry, astronomy, philosophy, eloquence. Quintilian had in view the training of a perfect orator, as Plato had that of a perfect philosopher. Both conceived an ideal, completely accomplished man. Plato's mind, however, was altogether poetical, while Quintilian's was altogether practical. Quintilian's finished man is the successful man of the world, but Plato's man is winged for other worlds.

The "Institutes" is one of the very best books on pedagogy that was ever written, and I do not see how it can ever be altogether superseded. It seizes upon the vital and the permanent. It is crammed full of sound sense. It broaches almost every important question in education. I could excuse the average lecturer on "Theory and Practice" for stealing Quintilian to substitute for his own advanced views. Where will we find better methods of instruction than those given in the old treatise? Where finer bits of criticism? Quintilian actually teaches the art of literary criticism. His comments on the principal writers of antiquity have been the delight of generations of scholars.

It would be a service to the teachers' profession, and to the reading public, if some competent hand would compile a little volume of Quintiliana.

6. GOETHE AS AN EDUCATIONAL LIGHT.

Goethe was only twenty-eight years of age, when Jefferson brought to Carpenter's Hall that social and political document which announced to the world the independence of America and the inalienable rights of individual men. We may say that the powerful influence of Goethe began its active operation in Germany about the time that democracy became an actual shaping energy in the New World. Both forces worked together for freedom, humanity, and culture. Goethe's influence was scarcely felt in England or America until after 1824, the year in which deep-discerning Carlyle translated "Wilhelm Meister" into English. During the last half century the luminous message of Germany's profound thinker has been conveyed throughout all civilized lands ; and in this country it has become, if not popular, at least known and appreciated by the reading and thinking class. Probably such books as "Wilhelm Meister's Apprenticeship and Travels" will never attract the multitude ; neither will Plato, Dante, nor Milton. Nevertheless, from such supreme sources of knowledge, thought, and taste, come the ideas, theoretic and practical, which fill secondary books and finally permeate the common mind, as from mountain lakes issue vital springs and sparkling streams that flow downward to irrigate and fertilize forest and field.

Goethe has been called the Apostle of Self-culture.

Though his name is not often mentioned among those of renowned educational reformers, he may be ranked high in the first class of teachers of mankind; rather a former than a reformer, he deals with fundamentals, — grasps the great first principles of life and culture, and indicates the wisest modes of activity for men collectively and man the unit. The lesson of his life is most stimulating; contact with his vigorous mind, even through the medium of his books, leads to hopeful effort. How cheering, how exhilarating, how strength-giving, must his presence and intimate conversation have been to his associates. His personality surcharged the air. One imagines that from him to his capable disciple, a liberal education might flow by spiritual induction. He was intensely alive physically and mentally to every external impression, and, to his apprehension, everything around, above, and below was also throbbing with life. "His education," says one biographer, "was irregular; he went to no school, and his father rather stimulated than instructed him." Yet his surroundings were favorable. His receptive nature took in knowledge from all sides. He began consciously to *live* as soon as he began to grow. Teachers in schools and colleges propose to fit boys and girls for living. His strong, spontaneous, and happy being did not separate the fitting from the living, but lived the fitting and fitted the living from the start to the close of his career. The motto on which he constantly dwells in his great work is this,

" *Think on living.*"   The burden of his song is in
the words : —

> " Life's no resting, but a moving ;
> Let thy life be deed on deed ! "

Sincerely desiring to know and understand nature
and mankind in all their aspects, he sought and
studied languages, literatures, science, art, and institutions.   Minerals he examined in mountain and
mine, plants wherever they grew ; libraries were his
workshops, books his tools.   Goethe's museum con-
tained all the Muses.   The encyclopædia of human
nature he mastered by reading its speaking volumes,
— men, women, and children.   The human heart was
to him Bible and hymn-book.   The world was his
orange, and he richly enjoyed the nourishing juice of
it.   So great a brain as his, so richly endowed by
nature, and so amply furnished with the accumulated
knowledge of the past, corrected by present observation, could not fail to give out value to other
brains.   There is hardly a topic within the wide
range of pedagogical science, or within the still
wider field of human culture, that Goethe has not
touched somewhere in his writings.   And whenever
he touches a theme of this character, light appears,
as when a conducting medium approaches an electri-
fied body.   Light and heat appear, and the warm,
luminous shock makes an impression and is remembered.   Commonplace writers say many true things
and many important things, but say things in an
ordinary and unsurprising way ; but men of origi-

nality and special force utter themselves home to the
heart and memory. Goethe does this. His conceptions are striking, his images novel, his expression is
large and suggestive. Whatever a really great man
says on any subject is precious; what Goethe said
and thought about education deserves our reverent
attention. We need not worship him, nor adhere to
his errors ; but his serious opinions demand respect,
because he was a lover of his race, because he strove
to discover and announce the truth, and because he
had the rare gift to express his thought in artistic
and therefore admirable form.

"Wilhelm Meister's Apprenticeship and Travels,"
while it purports to be merely a novel, is a somewhat
fantastic treatise in poetic prose on life and culture
in general; it abounds in philosophical speculations,
criticisms on literature and art, and subtle disquisi-
tions concerning the innermost meanings of things
human and divine. Like the enchanted cask in the
drama of Faust, which yielded all varieties of wine
according to the drinker's taste, and even spurted
fire into daring cups, this miraculous vintage of
thought and imagination furnishes a flagon to suit
every palate. Here is geology for the scientific, art
for the artistic, literature for the literary ; here are
real life and ideal dreaming ; here are men and
women of common and uncommon types ; and here,
also, are allegorical creations of merely symbolic
character.

The entire work may be regarded as an attempt

to portray the processes of human development, and
to indicate the duty of the individual to himself, and
his relation to his fellow-man, and to the divine
power. Meister's apprenticeship is the apprenticeship or preparation for a no less serious trade than
the art of living. The conception is the grandest
with which human thought can concern itself. Is not
education the supreme science of life, and conduct
its application? The second volume of the book
deals directly with the motives and processes of instruction and training as applied to youth, which we
recognize as education or schooling. The author
gives a picture or model of what he conceives to be
the best general mode of education. In a prolonged
episode detailing the nurture, instruction, and discipline of little Felix, Wilhelm Meister's son, we are
introduced to an imaginary province of vast extent
and great beauty, which Goethe says he might justly
call a Pedagogic Utopia. The description of this
region, its institutions, officers, and appliances for
the development of boys into the full possession of
their powers, occupies many chapters of the book,
and constitutes a most admirable discourse on the
principles and practice of education. Nothing more
charming in the whole range of pedagogical literature than these vivid chapters, unless we except
the somewhat similar and equally lofty discussion of
the same subject by John Milton in his celebrated
" Tractate," depicting an ideal academy, or in the
immortal " Republic " of Plato. It may be remarked

that both Goethe and Milton adopt many of Plato's
views; or shall we rather conclude that sublime
minds naturally see and think alike, as eagles soar in
planes of nearly the same altitude.   Goethe attaches
to music an educational importance as high as that
which the great Greek philosopher conceded to it.
He says, " Song is the first step in education ; all the
rest are connected with it and attained by means of
it."   In the exact practice of musical technic, he discovers not only a general harmonizing of the faculties, but a preparation for the precise understanding
and use of arithmetic and other mathematical studies.

In Goethe's scheme, no exercise, bodily or mental,
is divorced from practical ends, no energy is to be
wasted in abortive pursuits ; all learning is for the
sake of doing; all theory should be practicable.
The poet was himself a man of affairs, honored as
well for executive skill in business as for literary
genius.   The power which created Faust could also
manage a theatre or transact a diplomatic commission. He somewhere says, " Practical activity and
expertness are far more compatible with sufficient
intellectual culture than is generally supposed."

A leisurely excursion through the Pedagogical
Province would certainly prove profitable, but to enjoy such journey completely, each excursionist will
be his own best guide, travelling with book in hand.
With Carlyle's translation as staff, I have wandered many times through Goethe's wonderful educational Utopia, and each tour has revealed new

objects of interest, and also, it must be confessed, new mysteries. Few books are more intricate and puzzling, and at the same time more fascinating. That must be an exceptional mind which is not lured by one thing or another in this book ; the man who understands it all is wiser than the author claimed to be.

Without attempting a full or systematic survey of the Pedagogical Province, I shall give a few of its leading features, or, rather, some of the general ideas which governed its imaginary denizens. In the first place, Goethe believes in the educability of human nature. Culture, though it cannot create capacity, can develop the human powers to an unlimited degree. The main business of life is an active training of whatever faculties in the individual respond to an external or an internal call. The universe is the soul's necessity. When the child is born, he is in school, and his training is begun by every object and influence that surround him. The best that his parents can do, is to provide the most wholesome and happy circumstances among which the infant may grow and enjoy. Freedom and opportunity are the necessary conditions of fortunate development ; vitality and activity are what the developing body and soul of the child must bring to his own aid. It is a thought of the French writer Joubert, that " Man might be so educated that all his prepossessions would be truths, and all his feelings virtues." Goethe maintains the like faith. He says, " Well-formed, healthy children bring much into the world with them. Nature has given to each whatever he requires for time and duration ; to unfold this is our duty ; often it unfolds itself better of its own accord." And again, " Let no one think that he can conquer the first impressions of youth. If he has grown up in enviable freedom, surrounded with beautiful and noble objects, in constant intercourse with worthy men ; if his masters have taught him what he needed first to know, for comprehending more easily what followed ; if he has never learned anything which he requires to unlearn ; if his first operations have been so guided that without altering any of his habits he can more easily produce what is excellent in future ; then such a one will lead a purer, more perfect and happier life, than another man who has wasted the force of his youth in opposition and error. A great deal is said and written about education ; yet I meet with very few who can comprehend and transfer to practice this simple yet vast idea, which includes within itself all others connected with the subject."

The passage just quoted sounds the keynote to Goethe's symphony of education. Freedom, — freedom, — freedom ! action, — action, — action ! these are the master-words of his discourse and exhortation. Give the individual elbow-room and breathing space. Let him seek and find the learning and the vocation which God designed him to use. First of all, discover if possible what is in the child, what nature suggests concerning his proper destiny, what he can probably do, what are his potential adaptations to life. He cannot be everything ; he must be one thing, or some few things at most. Though he must develop to the utmost all that lies germinal within him, and become a symmetrical and perfect man, he is but *one man*, a small part of the many that make up society and produce civilization. In Goethe's language, " It is all men that make up mankind ; all powers taken together that make up the world. These are frequently at variance ; and, as they endeavor to destroy each other, nature holds them together, and again produces them. From the first animal tendency to handicraft attempts, up to the highest practising of intellectual art ; from the inarticulate crowings of the happy infant, up to the polished utterance. of the orator and singer ; from the first bickerings of boys, up to the vast equipments by which countries are conquered and retained ; from the slightest kindliness and the most transitory love, to the fiercest passion and the most earnest covenant ; from the merest perception of sensible presence, up to the faintest presentiments and hopes of the remote spiritual future ; all this, and much more, also, lies in man, and must be cultivated : yet not in one, but in many. Every gift is valuable, and ought to be unfolded. When one encourages the beautiful alone, and another encourages the useful alone, it takes them both to form a man. One power rules another: none can cultivate another : in each endowment, and not elsewhere, lies the force that must complete it :

this many people do not understand, who yet attempt
to teach and influence. Let us merely keep a clear
and steady eye on what is in ourselves; on what en-
dowments of our own we mean to cultivate: let us
be just to others; for we ourselves are only to be
valued in so far as we can value."

Keeping in mind the clearly distinguished relations of man, first to mankind in general and then
to himself, we can understand why it is that Goethe
places so much stress upon the importance of dis-
covering innate capacity. His philosophy would not
attempt to make silk purses of sows' ears, or sows'
ears of silk purses; would not expect to grow thistles
on fig-trees, or figs on thistle-bushes; would not
promise to fit every man for all positions; or, in a
word, labor to frustrate the designs of nature, or
substitute the schoolmaster's will for the command
of Almighty God, written in the book of the child's
manifest idiosyncrasy. The teacher should endeavor
not to make his pupil over according to a preconceived model, but to discover what pattern the divine
Creator has outlined for the guidance of human
instruction. "For to uniform we are altogether
disinclined," says the overseer of the pedagogical
province; "uniform conceals the character, and, more
than any other species of distortion, withdraws the
peculiarities of children from the eye of their superiors." This was said in reference to dress, but the
spirit of it applies to any external that may tend to
obliterate individuality. Goethe looks with horror

upon the fatal mistake of disregarding the natural differences in men. He would have all teachers dread the ever-present possibility that their pupils may waste effort by attempting what they can never hope to accomplish. "In all men," he declares, "there is a certain vague desire to imitate whatever is presented to them ; and such desires do not prove at all that we possess the force within us necessary for succeeding in these enterprises. Happy they who soon detect the chasm that lies between their wishes and their powers."

Once more he asks, "What mortal in the world, if without inward calling he take up a trade, an art, or any mode of life, will not feel his situation miserable? But he who is born with capacities for any undertaking, finds in executing this the fairest portion of his being." And again, "Is there not good hope of a youth who, on commencing some unsuitable affair, soon discovers its unsuitableness, and discontinues his exertions, not choosing to spend toil and time on what never can be of any value?" Further still I quote on this important point, "We should guard against a talent which we cannot hope to practise in perfection. Improve it as we may, we shall always, in the end, when the merit of the master has become apparent to us, painfully lament the loss of time and strength devoted to such botching." Does not the truth of this come home with sad emphasis to many a disappointed person who has squandered time, money, health, and enthusiasm in the forlorn attempt to cultivate a power the seeds of which nature never planted deeply in his being?

Now, since children know not their own powers, since everything seems easy to them, since they readily imitate whatever they behold, since they are liable continually to mistake wishes for capacities, is it not the first duty of the teacher to discover their true dispositions and tendencies, to set them right when they chance to go wrong, and to keep their activity exercised in lines that lead to the best results? The parent must at first think and judge for his child; the teacher, in place of the parent, must assume the same delicate and difficult responsibility. To blunder at the beginning of the journey is to wreck the possibilities of a life; therefore the science of sciences, and the art of arts, so far as education is concerned, is the science and art of approximating to the correct discovery of the promising capacities of pupils. The teacher needs to differentiate his boys and girls. They may all be taught from the same books, but not with the expectation that all will make the same use of the same learning, or attain the same ends in life. Not uniformity but diversity will result from an education which recognizes unlikeness in the very nature of minds. The pupil who is so fortunate as to find for himself, or to have discovered for him, his true bent, and who sets about doing that which there is good hope he can do, will not be long in coming to a full consciousness that he is on the right track. Every instinct, every hunger and thirst of his being, will find daily gratification, and will grow by what it feeds on. The student who is making progress towards the vocation he was born to follow, will delight even in the drudgery of his necessary task. His life's work will be a vocation indeed, — a calling, — a joyous career of activity to which the inner voice invites him. All this is enforced, over and over again, by the author of " Meister." He iterates and reiterates, "Every capability, however slight, is born with us; there is no vague, general capability in men. It is our ambiguous, dissipating education that makes men uncertain. It awakens wishes when it should be animating tendencies ; instead of forwarding our real capacities, it turns our efforts towards objects which are frequently discordant with the mind that aims at them. I augur better of a child, a youth, who is wandering astray on a path of his own, than of many who are walking aright on paths which are not theirs. If the former, either by himself or by the guidance of others, ever finds the right path, that is to say the path that suits his nature, he will never leave it ; while the latter are in danger every moment of shaking off a foreign yoke, and abandoning themselves to unrestricted license."

Goethe admits that it is extremely difficult to determine the child's natural bent, and therefore difficult to select the course of culture best suited for each one's development. He seems to recommend that some special art or occupation should precede that general culture which belongs to the completed man.   In the imaginary Province of the novel, when Meister presents his little son Felix to the directors, he asks advice thus, "'If I thought of sending Felix for a while into one of these circles, which would'st thou recommend to me?'—'It is all one,' replied Jarno; 'you cannot readily tell which way a child's capacity particularly points. . . . In all things to serve from the lowest station up is necessary.   To restrict yourself to a trade is best; for the narrow mind, whatever he attempts is still a trade; for the higher, an art; and the highest, in doing one thing, does all; or, to speak less paradoxically, in the one thing which he does rightly, he sees the likeness of all that is done rightly.   Take thy Felix through the Province: let the directors see him; they will soon judge him, and dispose of him to the best advantage.'"   In another place we find this more general statement: "In order to accomplish any-thing by education, we must first become acquainted with the pupil's tendencies and wishes; that these once ascertained, he ought to be transported to a situation where he may, as speedily as possible, con-tent the former and attain the latter; and so if he have been mistaken he may still in time perceive his error; and at last, having found what suits him, may hold the faster by it, may the more diligently fash-ion himself according to it."

The reader cannot fail to observe that Goethe, though he places upon the teacher much responsi-

bility in aiding the child to discover its true field
of activity, does not conceive it possible that the
teacher should think and act for the learner in the
vital processes of education. Human culture is necessarily self-culture. The teacher may point out what
to do, and even explain how to do it, but the learner
must do his own thinking and feeling. One can no
more understand or enjoy for another, than he can
digest or sleep for him. " Each man has his own
fortune in his hands ; as the artist has a piece of
rude matter which he is to fashion to a certain shape.
But the art of living rightly is like all arts ; the capacity alone is born with us ; it must be learned and
practised with incessant care." These are Goethe's
words. He warns all earnest souls that eternal activity is the price of culture. "Nothing upon earth
without its difficulties !" he exclaims. The best culture is attained by the hardest work and at the expense of much time. " Steep regions cannot be sur-
mounted," says the poet, "save by winding paths ;
on the plain, straight roads conduct from place to
place."

We must not hastily conclude that because a youth
is slow in manifesting talent or genius, he is destitute of natural ability. " He in whom there is much
to be developed will be later in acquiring true per-
ceptions of himself and of the world. There are
few who at once have *thought* and the capacity of
action. Thought expands, but lames : action ani-
mates, but narrows."

The several passages quoted will serve to bring out in sufficiently strong relief two or three of the leading principles of Goethe's educational doctrine. These principles are exceedingly suggestive and fruitful; and while we may not all agree with all the deductions derivable from them, they undoubtedly contain much of the essence of eternal truth. He who agrees with them in theory, will not go far wrong in practice, and he who raises objections to them will at least get the benefit which comes from high thinking; for these supreme questions cannot be intelligently and candidly discussed without advantage to both sides.

Passages from Wilhelm Meister.

The Superficial Teacher.

" Wilhelm signified his wish that Montan would impart to him so much as was required for the primary instruction of the boy. 'Give that up,' replied Montan. 'There is nothing more frightful than a teacher who knows only what his scholars are intended to know. He who means to teach others, may indeed often suppress the best of what he knows; but he must not be half-instructed.'"

Where to find Perfect Teachers.

"'Where then are perfect teachers to be found?' one says. 'Where the thing thou art wishing to learn is in practice.'"

Good Work takes Time.

"'Was the world not made at once, then?' said Felix. 'Hardly,' answered Jarno; 'good bread needs baking.'"

First Steps in Teaching.

" To fix a child's attention on what is present; to give him a description, a name, is the best thing we can do for him. He will soon enough begin to inquire after causes."

Head Versus Hands.

"Drawing was not hard for me : I should have made greater progress, had my teacher possessed head and science ; he had only hands and practice."

Conversation.

"What you do not speak of, you will seldom accurately think of."

Surmounting Difficulties.

"We look upon our scholars as so many swimmers who, in the element which threatened to swallow them, feel with astonishment that they are lighter, that it bears and carries them forward; and so it is with everything that man undertakes."

Æsthetic Culture.

"Men are so inclined to content themselves with what is commonest; the spirit and the senses so easily grow dead to the impressions of the beautiful and perfect, that every one should study by all methods to nourish in his mind the faculty of feeling these things. For no man can bear to be entirely deprived of such enjoyments : it is only because they are not used to taste of what is excellent, that the generality of people take delight in silly and insipid things, provided they be new. For this reason, one ought, every day at least, to hear a little song, read a good poem, or see a fine picture."

Men's Teachers.

"What in us the women leave uncultivated, children cultivate when we retain them near us."

Reverence.

"One thing there is which no child brings into the world with him ; and yet it is on this one thing that all depends for making man, in every point, a man. Reverence ! Reverence for that which is above us, for that which is below us, and for that which is around us."

How to regard Others.

"When we take people merely as they are, we make them worse; when we treat them as if they were what they should be, we improve hem as far as they can be improved."

The Best.

" Words are good, but they are not the best. The best is not to be explained by words. The spirit in which we act is the highest matter."

Religion.

"I look upon religion as a kind of diet, which can only be so when I make a constant practice of it, when, throughout the whole twelve months, I never lose it out of sight."

X

THE UTILITY OF THE IDEAL[1]

THE subject of my address is The Utility of the Ideal. I employ the word Utility to signify something more than mere material usefulness. Manures upon land are of utility ; so also are evanescent tints upon dissolving clouds. The economic maxims of Poor Richard are of utility ; so also are the dreams and reveries of Ik Marvel. Comprehensively speaking, we say that whatever can better the character or condition of man is of utility. Whatever can elevate thought, purify taste, awaken aspiration, or wean the faculties from low and unworthy tendencies, is of incalculable utility.

" And yet," exclaims Ruskin, " people speak, in this working age, when they speak from their hearts, as if houses and lands, and food and raiment, were alone useful, and as if sight, thought, and admiration were all profitless ; so that men insolently call themselves utilitarians who would turn, if they had their way, themselves and their race into vegetables ; men who think, so far as such men can be said to think,

[1] Annual Address before the Ohio Teachers' Association at Columbus, O., Wednesday, July 6, 1870.

that the meat is more than the life, and the raiment more than the body; who look to the earth as to a stable, and to its fruit as to fodder; vine-dressers and husbandmen who love the corn they grind, and the grapes they crush, better than the gardens of the angels upon the slopes of Eden; hewers of wood and drawers of water who think that the wood they hew, and the water they draw, are better than the pine forests that cover the mountains like the shadow of God, and than the great rivers that move like his eternity."

To such persons, the title of this discourse, The Utility of the Ideal, is an absurd collocation of words. To such the word Utility has but a meagre meaning, and the term Ideal is but empty breath, or, at most, but a convenient negative, signifying the utter absence of the actual. Such do not recognize the Idealist as a rational being. They deny the existence of the vast invisible world of which he speaks and sings. Their experience acquaints them only with things tangible, visible, sapid, odorous. They are cognizant only of forces obvious to animal perception. They believe, as Emerson humorously states it, "that mustard bites the tongue, that pepper is hot, friction matches incendiary, revolvers to be avoided, and suspenders hold up pantaloons." With Plato's "earth-sprung" Athenians, they contend "that whatever cannot be squeezed together in the hands is wholly nothing." They indorse the opinion of Dupaty, of the French Association, who declared to the astronomer La Place, that the discovery of a new pudding is of much more importance than the discovery of a new comet. In gross and sensuous scepticism, they hardly stop short of the Bosjesmen of South Africa, who, when told that there is a God, incredulously exclaim, " Show him to me!"

Common to the matter-of-fact class is a disposition to divest even the external world of whatever contributes to sentiment or taste. Not satisfied with contemning the adornments of art, they even seem to regard nature's exuberant loveliness as useless superfluity. Instead of rejoicing in the all-pervading beauty of the earth, they frown upon it as though it were a chief manifestation of God's curse upon a disobedient race. They would make anchorites of the sons and daughters of men. In the name of all the virtues, they would clip off the golden edges of the summer clouds, change the many hues of vegetation to a uniform blue-gray or butternut, veto the melodious carols of the birds, plough up your flower-bed and sow it with turnip-seed, batter the ornamental cornice from your house, pull down the pictures from your wall, cast your fashion magazine into the fire, and coin your jewels into Federal money.

It is foolish to underrate the value of material good. Property is power. Houses and lands, food and raiment, machinery and money, are excellent so far as they go, and they go far. But these things take care of themselves. No man needs arguments to convince him of the utility of eligible town-lots,

paying mines, and bank-stock producing big divi-
dends. All admit that man is a fine *animal*, the finest,
—and that he is worthy to live in material splendor,
ease, and luxury. He must lie soft, feed rich, dress
royally. But is not man something more and better
than a superb animal ? more and better than vitalized
earth ? Nay, he is also vitalized Heaven. He has
a soul in his body. He has spiritual faculties as well
as senses. All his powers and susceptibilities should
be recognized and nurtured. Who shall presume to
set aside any element of his nature as useless, evil,
or unworthy of care ? Dare one assert that any
ingredient that God has put into the human constitution is misplaced ? Nay, every faculty of body and
soul contributes to the perfection of our nature, and
demands a legitimate sphere of action. It is true
that faculties may be abused or perverted, but that is
no reason why they should be suppressed, or why
their normal function should be denied.

Ideality, as Tuckerman truly observes, is as much
a heaven-implanted faculty as conscientiousness.
They mistake who suppose that it is a noxious weed,
springing up in the mind to the injury of practical
sense, morality, or religion. Divine Wisdom drops
the tender seed of imagination into the unconscious
soul of the infant. The morning of life quickens the
seed, and it becomes an early flower, indigenous to
childhood, the very spring-beauty of that auspicious
season. Children imagine as naturally as they laugh
and cry. To them a few sticks laid around the stump

of a tree become lofty walls, enclosing noble apart-
ments; in shapeless blocks and broken stones they
possess elegant furniture ; in bits of shattered crock-
ery and refuse fragments from the tin-shop they
behold costly sets of china and magnificent silver
service. One little girl prattling in a playhouse by
herself, is multiplied by the swift arithmetic of her
busy fancy into a parlorful of ladies and gentlemen,
voluble in polite conversation, and mindful of every
courtesy of society. Isn't a broomstick a veritable
horse to little Tommy? and isn't Tommy a locomotive when he noisily pulls three cigar-boxes tied together in a row along the gravel walk, puffing as
he runs? Does not Annie's doll understand as well
as anybody? Is there not a crock of gold at the
end of the rainbow, and a Santa Claus at the end of
the year? Do not the birds talk and the winds whisper a language intelligible to the children? In the
clouds they see cities, and armies flying, and marvellous mountains; and when it thunders, the mountains
change to stormy battlements, and the armies bom-
bard the cities, and set them afire with torches of
lightning. To them in other mood, the awful thunder may seem the voice of omnipotent God uttering
unto the ends of the earth, *I AM, I AM.* Oh, credulous, creative childhood! who would rob it of its
irradiant atmosphere of imagination? Who would
dispel the golden and roseate clouds that flush and
float along its marvellous horizon? Ideality is to the
child the very perianth of his young existence, as

necessary to his healthy development as are floral appendages to the rudimentary fruit which they surround. In due time the petals of youthful fancy are scattered by the wind of experience, and a new mode of growth begins. But, alas for the fruit, if the flower be prematurely removed! alas, if it be repressed!

> " There was a time when meadow, grove, and stream,
>   The earth, and every common sight,
>   To me did seem
>   Apparelled in celestial light,
>   The glory and the freshness of a dream."

Soon enough come the years that compel the sad continuation of the verse : —

> " It is not now as it hath been of yore;
>   Turn wheresoe'er I may,
>   By night or day,
>   The things which I have seen, I now can see no more."

It is the spontaneous act of the child's mind to transmute the real into the ideal. The radiance of unobscured faith changes common earth into fairyland for the young and innocent. The magical world of ideality moves along with the child as a halo moves along with the moon. It guards the new existence from worldly harm while it is yet too weak to guard itself. It even alleviates pain and steals away the monotony of irksome duty. Did you never when a child, engaged in some disagreeable task, banish the thought of present weariness by calling the wizard Fancy to your aid? Did you never, while drudging over some repulsive work, fly away in glad revery to wander amidst the delights of Aladdin's palace? What sensitive child has not, when sick or lonely, or grieved or afraid, found comfort and peace by summoning a host of imaginary attend-. ants to sympathize with him, and perhaps gently lead him out of himself into the healing paradise of dreams? There was a lad to whom the anguish of a great bereavement would have proven insupportable, had it not been for a comforting belief, dependent upon an excited fancy, — the belief that a beloved sister, though gone from earth, sometimes played for him her angel harp, so that he could hear it faintly sounding — oh, how faintly! — in far-off mansions of the Blest.

Charles Dickens has written more frequently and pathetically than any other author in behalf of children, and their divine right to exercise their faculties in a natural and happy way. He has also given us many graphic pictures of the stern materialist and the unpoetic worldling. Perhaps he has drawn no character of this kind more truly representative than that of Thomas Gradgrind, "the man of facts and calculations," whose favorite words are, " Now, what I want, is facts. Teach these boys and girls nothing but facts. Facts alone are needed in life. Plant nothing else; root out everything else. You can only form the minds of reasoning animals upon facts; nothing else will be of any service to them. This is

the principle upon which I bring up my own children, and it is the principle upon which I bring
up *these* children. Stick to facts, sir!" You who
have read the story recollect how Thomas Gradgrind's model son and daughter lived in Stone
Lodge, and had a little conchological cabinet, and a
little metallurgical cabinet, and a little mineralogical
cabinet, with the specimens all labelled and arranged ;
and how, almost as soon as they *could* run, they had
been made to run to the lecture room ; how they had
never seen a face in the moon, nor said, —

> " Twinkle, twinkle, little star,
> How I wonder what you are ; "

for they were never permitted to wonder anything.
You remember how the children's instinct struggled
against a training at once rigorous, austere, and repulsive ; how too much restraint turned their better feelings inward, to work slow destruction upon
the character ; how their repressed fancy became a
maimed and distorted faculty ; how Louisa, step by
step, became morbid and sullen, then desperate and
reckless ; how Tom, the father's idol, naturally of
noble tendency, grew, by degrees, selfish and exacting, then hypocritical and dishonest, then mean and
whelpish, and how he at last died a wretched vaga-
bond.

Is not the story logical and wise ? Does it not
afford a warning that many a mother and father,
public teacher, and gospel minister should heed?

Nay, Thomas Gradgrind, not facts alone should oc-
cupy the growing mind, but fancies also, as nature
imperatively demands. Not realities alone, as you
define realities, but ideals too, as the well-being of
the soul requires. Man is not a calculating machine,
not a patent memorizer of dead facts, not a passion-
less, reasoning animal; not a creature of few and
simple capacities easily estimated and readily supplied.
His spiritual dimensions cannot be taken ; his powers
and needs cannot be summed up. Above the plane
of ordinary sensations and conceptions lie the vast
plateaus of thought and affection, the towering summits of imagination, the fiery craters of passion, the
snow-white peaks of heavenward aspiration. Man is
the centre of a boundless sphere of which but a little
inner circle is to him actually and scientifically known.
Infinity encompasses him round about. He is conscious
of a mysterious relationship which his own nature
bears to a whole universe of material and non-material
things. His faculties strive uneasily towards attract-
ing forces created for them. By and by they grow
stronger, and reach toward the object of their desire
with assured confidence. The senses are not happy
until they know how to observe, and are furnished
with proper objects. The memory demands material
to memorize. The reason craves subjects upon which
to exercise its peculiar function. Love is feeble
without a beloved. Taste remains latent without
the beautiful to call it forth. The All-provident has
created in the vast storehouses of human resource

abundant supplies to answer every possible demand
of our nature. Perfect human culture would result
from the adjustment of all the faculties to the functions which they are designed to perform. In other
words, right education finds out for man conditions
in which he can obtain suitable exercise for every
power — suitable supply for every innate want. If
these conditions are already favorable, man will not
need the offices of the educator. Only close the cir-
cuit of right influences around him, and, like the
electro-magnet, he becomes strong by a species of
induction that no man can explain.

While we condemn the philosophy of Gradgrind,
it does not follow that we adopt its extreme opposite.
The child's imagination, though it should be recognized and cherished, needs but little artificial stimulation. Unless impaired by hereditary neglect, or
paralyzed by false training, or enfeebled by baleful
surroundings, it will spring into activity, provided it
is only set free, and allowed a field of reasonable
extent in which to range.

There is in our day no good excuse for permitting
children to read books of indifferent quality. Many
most excellent juveniles have been written within
the decade. The highest genius in the world has
exercised itself in behalf of the children. But it is
with books as with money, — the less valuable circulate
to the exclusion of the intrinsic best.

Among the commendable things undertaken in
busy Boston, is the establishment of a commission

of cultivated women to sit in judgment upon the
merits of Sunday-school and other juvenile books.
Every volume submitted to the commission for examination is read and recommended by at least five
critics, before it is approved and entered upon the
catalogue of unexceptionable publications.   It is to be
hoped that this commission and others like it, if they
should be formed, will make a thorough winnowing
of the chaff from the wheat in children's story-books.
We must not inconsiderately reject all fictitious juvenile literature because much of it is worthless, or
even worse.   I would not deprive children of fairy
or dwarf, hunchback or magician, Jack the Giant-
killer, or Cinderella.   Mother Goose, unexpurgated,
is good reading, and furnishes an excellent foundation for primary education.   The history of the
Babes in the Woods, as related in the quaint old
ballad, should be treasured in every nursery.   How
many tears have moistened the page which records
the last sleep of the lonely children in each other's
arms, and the mournful rite of the sympathetic robins!
Such tears are spring rains that quicken plants of
affection to bloom and bear fruit in the summer of maturer years.   One great function of the story-books is
to touch the feelings and evoke the moral sentiments ;
to convey ideas of justice and injustice, reward and
retribution, sacrifice and sufferance of wrong.   The
sympathies and antipathies are aroused ; the young
reader measures himself by an ideal standard ; good
motives prevail, and character grows.   The crying

part in many of the old nursery ballads is the valuable part. This fact the publishers do not seem to appreciate; hence we have so many mutilated editions of standard story-books. The prevailing custom is to leave out, or at least greatly to soften down, the tragical portion of the stories, in the mistaken belief that nothing painful should be presented to the mind of the little reader. There is a version of the pathetic ballad just alluded to which, instead of terminating with the death of the wandering babes, represents them as only sleeping one night in the forest, to be discovered next day and carried in triumph to the palace of their inheritance. There is a rehash of the romance of Red Riding Hood, according to which the little maid did not go down the wolf's throat at all, after the last fearful exclamation, " O grandmother, what great teeth you have ! " Instead of eating Red Riding Hood, the wolf is killed by a valiant wood-cutter, and the child is rescued without a scratch. This is as bad as bringing Romeo and Juliet to life after the scene in the Capulets' tomb, or restoring the king to reason and Cordelia to life in the tragedy of Lear.

We can ill spare from the armory of educational instruments such compositions, fictitious or true, as serve to fire young people with noble enthusiasm and heroic ambition ; or which cultivate in them a delicate sense of poetic justice. The romantic ballad, the trenchant fable, the florid allegory, the thrilling narrative of imaginary brave adventure, are all serviceable allies of the prudent parent or instructor.

When we emerge from the enchanted wonderland
of youth into the more sober region of adult years,
the imagination changes somewhat in character, and
we naturally seek a different method of gratifying it.
Reason and experience, passion and sentiment, mod-
ify our ideal conceptions. Fancy is restrained. We
begin to judge fiction and poetry by a standard of
taste and propriety. In short, the lordly faculty,
imagination, which before was our ruler and master,
is now itself subject to cultivation, and made subser-
vient to the will. Still it continues, as it was, a pur-
veyor of profit and pleasure to the soul, and a magic
shield between its possessor and much that is offen-
sive in life. At maturity we minister to the ideal
faculty in many ways, but chiefly by means of fiction,
poetry, and the other æsthetic arts, appealing to the
imagination.

The time is not yet passed in which the novel is
occasionally arraigned before the tribunals more or
less representative of popular opinion, to answer for
its moral character and its influence upon the mind.
Many witnesses have from time to time given testimony
concerning it. Rousseau said that romances induced
in him fantastic and false notions of life, whereof he
was never entirely cured by experience and reflection. Samuel Johnson minutely depicts the pernicious effects of indulgence in revery, and shows how
" by degrees the reign of fancy is confirmed; how
she first grows imperious, and in time despotic.
Then fictions begin to operate as realities, false opin-

ions fasten upon the mind, and life passes in dreams of rapture or anguish." Multitudes of writers of less note than Johnson have asserted that the habit of reading fiction unfits the mind for severe application, and destroys a healthy interest in the practical affairs of life. The novel has not unfrequently been denounced from the pulpit as an unmitigated evil, inflaming the passions and tending to confound all moral distinctions. On the other hand, there are not wanting weighty authorities in favor of fiction. Hazlitt declares that "there are few books to which he is oftener tempted to turn for profit and delight than the standard novels. We find in them," he says, "a close imitation of men and manners; we see the very web and texture of society as it really exists, and as we meet it as we come into this world. We are brought acquainted with the motives and characters of mankind, imbibe our notions of virtue and vice from practical examples, and are taught a knowledge of the world through the airy medium of romance."

The novelist has not only to study the manners of men, and the construction and visible operations of society, but also to discern the laws of mind, and to describe the sources and consequences of human actions. He illustrates the possibilities of life by supposing persons of various character influenced by various situations and conditions. He depicts the power and operation of the passions. He exhibits in striking contrast the different states of humanity.

He portrays the struggles of pride and duty, the triumph of virtue and heroism, the deformity of crime, the omnipotence of love. To create such a work as " Don Quixote," " Tom Jones," "Ivanhoe," "David Copperfield," or " The Newcombs," is no easy or frivolous task. On the contrary, it is a labor which calls for an intimate knowledge of human nature, clear judgment, and continued application, to say nothing of the wonderful inventive faculty upon which, more than upon all the rest, it depends. The plot of a good novel must accord with the possibilities of things. Like a perfect landscape painting, the novel must truly represent reality, though no part of it need be directly copied from nature.

There are many very excellent people who cannot get rid of conscientious scruples against reading a novel, so long as there is a history or a biography to be had, not conceiving that a true record of thought and sentiment may be as valuable as a record of word and deed. They do not see, for example, how Charlotte Brontë's " Jane Eyre " can be a better book and a truer biography than Mrs. Gaskell's " Life of Charlotte Brontë," as it certainly is.

Fielding wittily said, in a satirical comparison of his novels with the works of professed historians, that, in their productions, nothing was true but names and dates, while in his everything was true except the names and dates.

Charles Reade boldly claims that fiction, " whatever you may have heard to the contrary, is the highest, widest, noblest, and greatest of all the arts;" that it "studies, penetrates, digests, the hard facts of chronicles and blue books, and makes their dry bones live."

By their fruits shall ye know men and books. That is the truest and most valuable book which most benefits the character and enlarges the mind of the reader. Precious is that reading which opens the heart to humane influences, which widens our sympathies for our fellow-creatures, which, by presenting lovable ideals, increases our reverence for human nature and our belief in its perfectibility. Precious also is that reading which contributes to innocent amusement; for cheerfulness disposes to goodness, and a hearty laugh is the best gymnastics for both body and soul. Let us be grateful for the profit, the pleasure, the inspiration, which we derive from the works of great novelists. Among the literary benefactors of mankind, while we number famous philosophers and historians and essayists and bards, may we not forget to include the celebrated authors of fiction, — Cervantes and Richardson and Fielding and Scott and Thackeray, and above all — the greatest novelist that ever lived and died, whose name is in your warm hearts before my lips pronounce it — Charles Dickens.

The objection to the novel on moral grounds is seldom urged in the present day, since clergymen and other public teachers, avowedly the champions of virtue and religion, have taken to the invention of stories as a direct means of Christian instruction, and the religious novel finds a place on the centre-table of the strictest deacon.

The conveyance of moral precepts or of practical information is not a necessary object of fiction. The so-called " novel with a purpose " is generally a failure. The *novel proper* is not a didactic treatise under an assumed name, nor a sermon travelling incognito, nor a new philosophy sugar-coated. The novel is a work of art, as a poem or a statue is. It is enough if it be true to itself. Its unity explains its purpose ; its consistency vindicates its character.

The literary creator hears the question, " What do you mean ? " with a feeling of humiliation. If he has succeeded in producing what he aimed at, a work of art, that work is self-explanatory to all who can appreciate it ; to those who cannot, no amount of explanation will prove satisfactory. What does any work of fine art mean ? It means simply approach toward the realization of an ideal. Is there not satisfaction in the mere contemplation of a harmonious, consistent plan ? — skilful development of supposed events ? — lively and accurate representation of character and manners ? — felicity of expression ? " Eat thou honey because it is good," is the counsel of Solomon. There is an æsthetic taste ! Its honey is the artistic, the well-related, the beautiful, the ideally true. If Lord Brougham makes the pleasure of the mind a sufficient motive for the study of philosophy, if Sir John Herschel is indignant when asked " whither his researches tend," and feels that there is a lofty and disinterested pleasure in his speculations that ought to exempt him from such questionings, how shall the literary artist humiliate himself to explain the value of his productions? The true work of art has its practical uses. It signifies many things to many minds. Each reader may interpret Faust and Hamlet as he can, but Goethe and Shakespeare only create.

> " Say to what uses shall we put
>   The wildwood flower that merely blows,
> Or is there any moral shut
>   Within the bosom of the rose ?
> But any man that walks the mead,
>   In bud, or blade, or bloom, may find,
> According as his humors lead,
>   A *meaning suited* to his mind ;
> And liberal applications lie
>   In art, like nature, dearest friend ;
> So 'twere to cramp its use, if I
>   Should hook it to some useful end."

Leaving the realm of prose fiction, we find the next manifestation of ideality in the field of poetry. Here imagination takes her noblest flights, and fancy roams at will. The grossest air of poesy is ether ; her eye is microscopic, and her ear catches the sound of flowers blossoming. She breathes the odors wafted from Paradise, and feeds on dews impalpable, shed from unseen skies, spanning the mystic land of dreams ! Vex not the bard with questions of time and sense. He dwells in spirit and in eternity. Commiserate him not, though he seem poor and lowly. The poet is forever blest. He loves all things. His is the joy and peace of infinite hope and faith. Surround him with poverty and squalor and sin and woe, he will discover in the vilest face some angelic lineament, and in the saddest spot some ray of consoling beauty. Put him in dungeon depths, yet will his starry thoughts light up the gloom, transforming it to glory. *Poeta*, maker — he is like a god. Out of the void he creates immortal forms.

> " The poet's eye in a fine frenzy rolling,
> Doth glance from heaven to earth, from earth to heaven;
> And as imagination bodies forth
> The forms of things unknown, the poet's pen
> Turns them to shapes, and gives to airy nothing
> A local habitation and a name."

The Utility of the Ideal! How the glowing theme expands as we strive to compass it! In every high department of human cultivation it is apparent. Proud, calm science, poised in an atmosphere of actual phenomena, is often borne to loftier heights than reason kens, on the daring wings of imagination, as the discoveries of Kepler prove. Max Müller declares that " the torch of imagination is as · necessary to him who looks for truth, as the lamp of study ; " and Sir David Brewster admits " that, as an instrument of research, the influence of imagination has been much overlooked by those who have ventured to give laws to philosophy." And a great exponent of modern science says that " Bounded and

conditioned by co-operant reason, imagination becomes the mightiest instrument of the physical dis-
coverer. Newton's passage from a falling apple to
a falling moon was a leap of the imagination. When
Sir William Thomson tries to place the ultimate
particles of matter between his compass points, and
to apply them to a scale of millimetres, it is an exercise of the imagination. And in much that has recently been said about protoplasm and life, we have
the outgoings of the imagination guided and controlled by the known analogies of science."

Ideality is necessarily developed in the pursuit
of the æsthetic arts. Music, that divinest human
possession, is it not language without words? one
degree nearer to the absolute expression of our pas-
sionate longing for unutterable sweetness and harmony? Painting and sculpture, are they not attempts to set forth conceptions more perfect and
lovely than any that are derived from natural objects? Are not all great works of art, as Edgar Poe
has exquisitely expressed it, efforts "to apprehend
the supernal loveliness? to grasp, now wholly here
on earth, those divine and rapturous joys of which
we obtain but brief and indeterminate glimpses"?
Is not the infinite desire with which we seek to realize the ideal, a species of worship?

The favorite subjects of high art have ever been
sacred. From the time of Solomon's Temple to this
day, the resources of architecture have been lavished
upon cathedrals dedicated to serving the Lord.

Rubens's masterpiece was the Descent from the
Cross. Michael Angelo's last work represented the
same beautiful and touching subject. The designs
of Raphael are chiefly drawn from Scripture history.
The last touches of his hand rested upon the head
of Christ in the picture of the Transfiguration. " It
was," says Vasari, " the greatest effort of an art
which could go no farther; and this last term of
the painting marked also the term of the life of the
painter. He never touched pencil more."

The sublimest musical composition of Haydn is the
oratorio " Creation ; " Beethoven's Symphonies are
the rapture of devotion ; the spirit of Mozart breathed
itself to Paradise in a prophetic requiem.

Tasso is immortal in " Jerusalem Delivered."
Dante in the " Divina Commedia ; " Milton's genius
culminated in the production of " Paradise Lost ; "
and the sacred Book concludes with the magnificent
imagery of the Apocalypse.

Thus does the ideal evermore ascend. Thus does
it struggle up through earth's restraints and pains,
aspiring to immortal estates. The holiest efforts of
our lives are strivings towards the ideal good which
we vaguely comprehend. That which we call the
ideal is the only eternal actual. Is not the body the
simulacrum, and the invisible soul the real existence ?
Are not the essential truth, beauty, good, love, of
this Universe abstract, indefinite, pure ideal ? The
fairest visions that float above the low confines of
earth, are they not hints and suggestions of heaven ?

Mysterious heaven! eye hath not seen, nor ear heard, neither have entered into the heart of man the things which God hath prepared; yet when with pure desires we climb the dazzling stair of Ideality, up by the golden steps of spiritual culture, we feel the airs of the city of rapture blowing in our souls, and almost see, with spirit vision, the glory-tinted pinnacles of the temple of perfection gleaming afar!

Mount higher yet, O soul, on trembling wings of faith and adoration! pierce further yet, O anxious eyes, into the uncreated light! The music of the spheres rings in celestial harmony around. The infinite and eternal Paradise is entered, but the Ideal is not attained. It evermore recedes, ascends. It is inaccessible. From everlasting to everlasting we shall pursue it, and the pursuit shall be one of endless happiness. For the ideal of those who have put on immortality, is not other than God, the sum and essence of all perfections.

XI

SYLVAN MYTHOLOGY, POETRY, AND SENTIMENT [1]

JACOB GRIMM, in his "Teutonic Mythology," proves that the Aryan word for *temple* means also *grove*.

"The groves were God's first temples."

Our ancestors held the woodland sacred, and worshipped individual trees. A grand conception of Norse mythology is that of the tree Igdrasil. The intense prose-poet of Craigenputtoch puts the gigantic idea in scenic words. "I like, too," he says, "that representation they have of the tree Igdrasil. All life is figured by them as a tree. Igdrasil, the Ash-tree of Existence, has its roots deep down in the kingdoms of Hela, or Death ; its trunk reaches up heaven-high, spreads its boughs over the whole universe ; it is the Tree of Existence. At the foot of it, in the Death Kingdom, sit three Nornas, Fates,— the Past, Present, and Future,— watering its roots from the Sacred Well. Its boughs, with their buddings and disleafings, — events, things done, catastrophes, — stretch through all lands and times. Is

[1] An Arbor Day Essay — Read before the Ohio State Forestry Association.

not every leaf of it a biography, every fibre there an
act or word? Its boughs are histories of nations.
The rustle of it is the voice of human existence,
onward from of old. It grows there, the breath of
human passion rustling through it; or storm-tossed,
the storm wind howling through it like the voice of
all the gods. It is Igdrasil, the Tree of Existence."

The primitive people of Northern Europe consecrated groves. They felt the solemn influence of
imperial trees, and deemed that the gods throned
themselves among the sky-reaching branches. The
instinct is natural. Architects conjecture that the
gothic arch was suggested by the majestic aisles of
the cathedral-forest. The camp-meeting of recent
days depends for much of its picturesque and inspiring power upon the essential dignity and sublimity
of the forest. The local worship of trees as symbols
of some mysterious power, survived in Germany
long after the introduction of Christianity. The
holy oak of Geismar, in Hesse, was cut down by
certain missionaries in about 725 A.D., and the timbers hewn from it were built into a church edifice
dedicated to Saint Peter. As King Olaf

" Preached the gospel with his sword,"

so the militant priests preached with the axe. Many
a crusade was ordered against particular sacred
groves. The pagans held tenaciously to their sylvan superstition. Grimm states, that " in the Prin-
cipality of Minden, on Easter Sunday, the young

people of both sexes used, with loud cries of joy, to dance a rigan or rig around an old oak." Again, he says, "In a thicket near the village of Wormeln, Panderborn, stands a holy oak, to which the inhabitants of Wormeln and Calenburg still make a solemn procession every year." This recalls to mind our English May-pole and its religio-social character. And how inevitable the transition of thought to the American liberty-pole, and the partisan pole-raisings, in which hickory and ash represent, if not religion, at least politics and patriotism! Surely the tree yet maintains a wonderful hold on imagination as a much-suggesting emblem.

We call the oak King, but our forefathers named it Divinity. Possibly the young oaks that Baron von Steuben sent from Saxony to Eden Park, Cincinnati, may be the progeny of some tough old Northern god. Or may not the acorns that produced them have been shaken down by some weird wood-wife, clad in white garments, sitting in the tree-tops? Such wonderful maidens, old legends say, dwelt in the woods, — sometimes were seen of men at an uncertain hour, — either amid the thick foliage or half-hidden in a hollow tree. The Christian priests of the Middle Ages caused images of the Madonna to be fixed on trees, that pagan adoration might be drawn from the old religion to the new — from Odin to Christ.

The Druids of Britain figured existence by a tree — not the ash, but the oak. The very word Druid is said to be derived from the Greek, meaning *an oak*. The Druids worshipped one god, Hesus; his emblem on earth was the oak-tree. The parasite mistletoe, growing on the tree, is man, the helpless creature, dependent on the bountiful Source.

The Hindoos held the banyan in veneration. They called it the sacred tree, the "Bohdi tree"— we may say the Igdrasil of the Brahmans. When Gautama, the founder of Buddhism, underwent the blessed transformation by which he attained a perfect virtue — became divine — he sat under a banyan-tree. The miraculous event is described in the magnificent sixth book of Arnold's "Light of Asia."

In the Persian Bible, "Zend Avesta," are many invocátions to Ameretat, god of trees, one of the six leading divinities, "Praise to Thee — Tree, good, pure, created by Mazda."

Ruskin in his greatest book, "Modern Painters," thus glorifies the pine-tree : "The tremendous unity of the pine absorbs and moulds the life of a race. The pine shadows rest upon a nation. The northern peoples, century after century, lived under one or other of the two great powers of the pine and the sea, both infinite. They dwelt amidst the forest as they wandered on the waves, and saw no end nor any other horizon. Still the dark, green trees, or the dark, green waters jagged the dawn with their fringe or their foam. And whatever elements of imagination, or of warrior strength, or of domestic justice were brought down by the Norwegian or the

Goth against the dissoluteness or degradation of the
South of Europe, were taught them under the green
roofs and wild penetralia of the pine."

And Emerson treats the same idea poetically in
these lines from his " Wood Notes :" —

> "Old as Jove,
> Old as Love,
> Who of me
> Tells the pedigree ?
> Only the mountains old,
> Only the waters cold,
> Only moon and star,
> My coevals are.
> Ere the first fowl sung,
> My relenting boughs among,
> Ere Adam wived,
> Ere Adam lived,
> Ere the duck dived,
> Ere the bees hived,
> Ere the lion roared,
> Ere the eagle soared,
> Light and heat, land and sea,
> Spake unto the oldest tree."

The holy books of all nations symbolize much by
the tree. The first book of the Hebrew Scripture,
and the last book of the Christian, employ the tree
metaphor most impressively.   In Genesis we read of
the "tree of Knowledge" with its fatal fruit, and
Revelation supplies a contrast, "The tree of Life,
which bore twelve manner of fruits, and yielded her
fruit every month ; and the leaves of the trees were
for the healing of the nations."

The mythology of Greece and Rome affords a

beautiful and most fanciful system of mild belief in sylvan divinities. The wood-wives of the German forest are kin to the Hamadryads of Southern Europe. The Grecian wood-nymphs dwelt in trunks of trees, from which they sometimes escaped, as a ghost from a body entranced; but the destruction of the tree marked the term of the Dryad's life. The crackle and groan of a falling tree is the death-struggle of the imprisoned nymph.

Mythology, ancient and modern, abounds with stories of the metamorphose of animate creatures, divine, human, and brute, into plants. Virgil relates in the "Æneid" that when the pious Trojan began to pluck up a wild myrtle in Thrace, the voice of his old friend Polydore cried out from the torn stock, to the amazement and grief of Æneas.

Dante consigned the souls of suicides to eternal bondage in gnarly, infernal trees, on the sentient boughs of which the harpies perch. In the thirteenth canto of "Inferno," the poet describes his doleful personal experience in one of these terrible man-tree forests: —

> "Then stretched I forth my hand a little forward,
> And plucked a branchlet off from a great thorn;
> And the trunk cried, ' Why dost thou mangle me?'
> After it had become embrowned with blood,
> It recommenced its cry, ' Why dost thou rend me?
> Hast thou no spirit of pity whatsoever?
> Men once we were, and now we are changed to trees:
> Indeed thy hand should be more pitiful,
> Even if the souls of serpents we had been.'

As out of a green branch that is on fire,
At one of the ends, and from the other drips
And hisses with the wind that is escaping,
So from the splinter issue forth together
Both words and blood."

Tasso, in "Jerusalem Delivered," narrating the adventures of Tancred in the enchanted wood, describes a sorrowful murmuring in the leaves of the cypress; the sound of a half-articulate, lamenting voice that filled Tancred

"With pity, sadness, grief, compassion, fear."

Overwrought with awe and indefinite apprehension, the hero drew his sword and cut a deep gash in the tender rind of the cypress. Drops of blood trickled from the wound, a groan escaped, and a voice complained in accents of tender reproach :—

"Tancred, thou hast me hurt."

It was the voice of Clorinda, the lost, loved mistress of the unhappy knight.

Ariosto, in that astounding string of cantos, called "Orlando Furioso," also leads a hero, Rogero, into enchanted realms of "false Alcina's Empery," where the man of arms ties his courser to a myrtle-tree. The stud made the myrtle shake, and brought down a shower of leaves about his feet. Drops of sweat appeared on the bark of the tree. At length the myrtle spoke and told a long story, in which it, or he, for this tree was of the ruder sex, claimed to be heir to the crown of England, debarred his rights by the

unfriendly power of magic. This gallant myrtle had
no mean opinion of his own personal attractions, for
he said,

> "More dames than one my beauty served to warm."

All readers are familiar with Shakespeare's Ariel,
whom the witch Sycorax imprisoned in a "cloven
pine," from which he was rescued by Prospero, who
afterwards threatened : —

> "If thou more murmurest, I will rend an oak,
> And peg thee in his knotty entrails till
> Thou hast howled away twelve winters."

The belief that plants may possess a life, spirit, or
soul similar to that of man has almost faded out of
the world. Yet poetry still retains the mythical
conception in a refined form. Bryant sings : —

> "Nay, doubt we not that under the rough rind,
> In the green veins of those fair growths of earth,
> There dwells a nature that receives delight
> From all the gentle processes of life,
> And shrinks from loss of being. Dim and faint
> May be the sense of pleasure or of pain,
> As in our dreams; but, haply, real still."

Wordsworth, in delicate sympathy with nature,
trod the woodland with deep reverence, and admonished thus : —

> "Move along these shades
> In gentleness of heart, with gentle hand
> Touch — for there is a spirit in the woods."

Tylor, in his "Primitive Culture," says, "The
notion of a vegetable soul, common to plants and to

the higher organisms possessing an animal soul in addition, was familiar to mediæval philosophy, and is not yet forgotten by naturalists." May it not be added that the facts and speculations of biology and evolution not only revive the ancient theory, but attempt to extend it?

The new philosophy may prove that man is organically akin, not only to baboon and bird, but also to pine-tree and palm. Protoplasm is marvellously democratic. There is no doubt that all matter is alike. Resolving nature puts all her kingdoms on familiar and equal terms.

> " Imperial Cæsar, dead, and turned to clay,·
> May stop a rent to keep the wind away."

Some years ago I visited in Providence the spot where Roger Williams is buried. I was told that an attempt had been made to exhume his body. A small tree was the monument that marked the grave. The sexton's spade discovered neither coffin nor bones, but instead was found a plexus of roots, so massed and shaped as to bear the form of a human body. Ten thousand rootlets, with their spongioles, had eaten up the dust of Roger Williams, and arranged themselves so as to preserve the exact outline of his frame. Here was a direct transformation of human flesh into wood, bark, and leaves ; maybe, into flowers and fruit.

Considered merely as material changes, the metamorphoses of Ovid are not wonderful ; they are but chemical experiments. One might actually taste the blood of Thisbe in a ripe mulberry, or see the pale cheek of Narcissus in the flower into which that melancholy youth was transubstantiated.

When we consider how nearly allied in substance are nerve and wood fibre, and how interwoven with the religion, philosophy, history, and poetry of the race the forest is, we may begin to understand why trees and their associations so deeply interest a thoughtful, and especially an imaginative or sentimental man. We can understand why the poets, great and small, delight in celebrating woodland scenery, and in idealizing individual trees. From the simple lyric, "Woodman, spare that tree," to the transcendental "Wood Notes" of Emerson, the wide range of sylvan sentiment runs up and down the whole gamut of poesy. Volumes could be compiled of excellent poetry relating to the woods. Literature fosters love for trees, and is, therefore, a most practical ally of forestry as a science. The idea of associating the memory of authors with the preservation and admiration of trees is really an inspired thought. Nothing more appropriate can be conceived.

I do not forget that there must be saw-logs as well as sentiment, planks as well as poetry. Forestry is a useful art, and common-sense cultivates trees for timber. While we honor the spade, we must not withhold the praises of the axe. Yet now it is well that the axe should rest with the rifle which slew the wild beasts and wild men that threatened the pioneer.

Hitherto, the very huzza of patriotism and progress has been raised for that same sharp axe. " Be Yankee doodle doo and the felling of Western forest remembered," wrote Carlyle to Emerson.

It now becomes startlingly apparent that the chopper's strokes have resounded too long in the primeval glooms ; that the war on the woods is likely to prove a war of extermination. No more is it so great a virtue to chop. " A man was famous according as he had lifted up axes upon the thick trees." Luckily the patient earth will restore the majestic armies slain ; recruit troops of trees on hill and plain. To this end, we must cultivate a sentiment for planting, as our fathers stimulated a passion for clearing.

XII

WILLIAM DOWNS HENKLE—MEMORIAL ADDRESS[1]

PORTIA. Is it your friend. . .?
BASSANIO. The dearest friend to me. . .
Merchant of Venice.

A FASCINATING interest attaches to inquiries concerning the origin of the human species; still more intense is the interest when applied to the origin of the individual. By what process of evolution, through what series of natural selections and conflicts for survival, did this or that particular man come to being? What were his hereditary aids or hindrances? Who and whence his ancestors?

We are our forefathers. The prophecy of intellectual power is in the fortunately organized brain. Good organization is bettered by culture. The perfect work of education can be accomplished only in the person well born of a stock rightly educated.

We are astonished at the rapid growth of a mind apparently neglected. A country lad, without schools or school-masters, suddenly absorbs the knowledge and culture of the age, and gains recognition as the flower of the college faculty.

[1] Read at the thirty-third annual meeting of the Ohio Teachers' Association, at Niagara Falls, N.Y., July 7, 1882.

The tree accounts for the branch. In the root and the soil which nourishes it, seek for an explanation of the flower and the fruit.

William Downs Henkle was fortunate in his ancestry. Many streams of good blood found confluence in him. We shall understand him the better by studying his progenitors.

Tracing his paternal lineage back six generations, we reach Rev. Gerhard Henkle, a German theologian of Frankfort, chaplain to a grand-duke. Gerhard Henkle espoused Lutheran doctrines, lost credit at court, gave up his chaplaincy, and between the years 1720 and 1730 emigrated to America, for conscience' sake and freedom's. He settled first at Germantown, Pennsylvania, but later, removed to the county of Lancaster, where he became pastor of a Lutheran Church. He is said to have founded St. Michael's Church in Philadelphia.[1]

Gerhard Henkle's great-grandson, Moses Henkle, born in Virginia, and educated in the College of William and Mary, beçame a Methodist, and preached Methodism in a day when the sect was not popu· lar. He married Margaret Montgomery, a descendant of a distinguished family, and near of kin to the poet. Moses and Margaret Henkle had five sons, all of whom, following their father's example, became preachers of the gospel. One of these five sons,

---

[1] Rev. Socrates Henkle, D.D., of New Market, Va., possesses a silver spoon three hundred years old, that belonged to Gerhard Henkle. It bears the Henkle coat-of-arms.

Rev. Lemuel Green Henkle, was the father of the late Hon. William Downs Henkle.

The name Downs comes from the maternal line of Henkle's ancestry. Mary Downs was the maiden name of his mother. She was of Quaker parentage. Her mother, Elizabeth Morse, was a direct descendant of Mary Wright, of whom we have this quaint account in authentic Quaker records: "In the year 1660, Mary Wright, a young maiden of Oyster Bay, Long Island, travelled several hundred miles and preached openly to John Endicott and his Council, in Boston, against the bloody work of executing several of our ministers for no other crime than preaching the gospel of Jesus Christ; for which she was imprisoned near a year, and then, with twenty-seven other Quakers, released from jail and driven into the wilderness."

Henkle, Montgomery, Downs, Morse, Wright — good sources are these from which to derive a man and compose a character. These names represent simplicity of conduct, progressive ideas, sensitive conscience, and tenacious adherence to principles. The religious element dominates.

William D. Henkle was born Oct. 8, 1828, at Pleasant Hill, six miles from Springfield, Clarke County, O. His father's possessions were but small; he owned a humble cottage, besides which his horse, saddle- and bridle, comprised about all his worldly wealth, for he was an itinerant preacher. Obeying a call to Louisville, Ky., Rev. Lemuel Henkle removed to that city with his family, and was there stationed pastor of the Methodist Protestant Church. There he died, of confluent small-pox, in the year 1835. William was at the time a lad of seven. He had three sisters, one nine, one five, and one three years old.

After her husband's decease, Mary Downs Henkle returned to her father's home at Urbana, O., where she resided for two years, and then she removed to her own cottage in Springfield. While living at his grandfather's, in Urbana, William, or "little Bill Downs," as he was familiarly styled, manifested that disposition to inquiry which distinguished him in manhood. His father had taught him to read, and he conceived a love of books. The first school he attended was at the old Urbana Academy, in which he afterwards tried his "prentice hand" as a teacher.

William's aptitude for numbers, and his persevering habit, were shown while he was a very small boy. Failing one evening to get the right answer to a question in arithmetic, he went to bed dissatisfied. In the night he was heard, calling out to his sister, "I have the answer! I worked it out in my sleep!" His memory was excellent, and often when at the old Downs homestead, the family assembled in the large, cheerful room, made bright by the roaring fire in the wide fireplace, he entertained the company by reciting "On Linden when the sun was low." It is no surprise to learn that the future editor of *Notes and Queries* was fond of working out puzzles. He was very quickminded, and made ready application of what he

learned. His sister relates that "nothing delighted
him so much 'as getting a company of children together and making a speech to them, generally on
temperance." From this we learn that the institute
lecturer began practice very early, and on a very important subject, to a very impressible audience.
When the widow and her son and daughters began
their independent struggle for subsistence, in Springfield, it was well for them that they were bound together closely in the bands of family love. Toil was
their portion. They were acquainted with privation.
The mother's needle helped to earn the children's
bread. Adjoining their place there was a brick-yard,
and some of the hands who worked at the kilns were
boarded at the widow's house. The owner of the
brick-yard hired William to drive a cart, paying him
a trifle for his service. To what use do you think the
black-haired, rosy boy put the first wages he received?
He bought a bonnet for his mother.

His mother! The gentle Quakeress who had
given her hand to the earnest Methodist preacher,
— the mild, thoughtful, intrepid descendant of Mary
Wright! From her William inherited his sweet-
est and his strongest qualities. From her he derived his quiet way and his even temper. Her brain
transmitted to his the mathematical aptitude. Mary
Downs was potentially the author of the Algebra
which her son actually produced. "She could do
head-work more accurately than any other woman
I ever saw," writes one who knew her. Her daugh-

ter, Mrs. Spain, says, "Mother, when she was left a young widow with four children, resolved to devote her life to educating them ; she managed, by untiring industry, to eke out the slender means left her in such a way that we were kept constantly together. . . . Losing our father as we did, we gave a double share of love to our mother ; and having only one brother, he was the idol of the family. I am sure no happier family ever lived. Mother was always the centre, ready to take an interest in all our lessons or games ; but Will was the life of the circle, ever willing to amuse and to instruct." The tribute which Mrs. Spain pays to her brother has deep significance, for relations peculiarly touching existed between her and him. They were playmates from infancy, and were tenderly attached to each other always. When Ella was a child of four she one day fell into a mill-race, and was rescued from drowning by Will, who plunged into the water and saved her. He was her only teacher. When he expired, this devoted sister was at his side, and, with his wife and daughter, caught the last whispered "farewell" from his dying lips.

Mr. J. M. Milhollin, a second cousin of Mr. Henkle, gives interesting recollections of his kinsman's boyhood and youth. He says, "When we used to gather about the streets of Springfield, Will was never a ringleader. His favorite attitude was to stand, leaning against a wall or other object, with his hands behind him. He generally inclined his head a little, and always smiled when addressed, or when he himself spoke. His own share of the talk was small, and was composed of questions, answers, and *very* short sentences. Often he saw a point where others did not. Then he would be very apt to mention something about it to the boy next to him, but not to the whole crowd."

To those who have watched the growth of Mr. Henkle's library, and who know how his very heartstrings were twined round his precious books, the story of his first collection is very affecting. The slender boy that drove a cart, hauling clay in the brickyard, spent part of his scanty purse in buying books. His bookcase was a candle-box with a sliding lid. Happy boy! symbolic box! the candles have shed their glimmering light and are gone out; but the books, — inextinguishable torches, — shall shine on, to illuminate heart and mind.

Young Henkle went to school in Springfield, first to Mrs. Bassett, then to a teacher named Adams, and for a short time to his uncle, Alfred Reed. The effect of the school routine upon him was not stimulating. He appears to have conceived a disgust, not for learning, but for the teaching he received. Possibly he felt a dim consciousness that school was retarding his progress rather than promoting it. Such feelings do possess the unquiet mind of youth at the period when conscious acquisition begins. There comes a time when the pupil gets outside of himself, looks at himself, and sees the necessity of conducting his own education, using books and teachers as essential means, but not as wholly responsible for his education, or as substitutes for his own industry and will. We are told that the docile, ingenuous boy passed into a state of obstinacy. He is dissatisfied with the aridity and the narrowness of the school. Surely there are better modes than this, he grumbles. Better nothing than this dull round.

He roves the streets, and rambles away to the hills and woods of the wide country. But it is not listless wandering. It is not indolent dreaming. The boy is in quest of the living fountains. He longs to know; to seize fast hold of realities. His restlessness is owing to that pang which Plato describes as the constrained effort of the soul's wings striving to expand and bear the man up and away.

Now the book-store, like a strong magnet, draws him to its loaded shelves. The candle-box is no longer large enough to hold the volumes that come to Widow Henkle's cottage, and Will has a black walnut box made and placed on the top of the bureau, for books. As one awakened to a conviction of sin feels that all his past virtues count for nothing, so the boy, aroused to a sense of ignorance, begins humbly to study and learn. His quick ear has caught scraps of conversation between thoughtful men, and he finds out who are the intellectual lights of the town. He hears of this doctor, and that lawyer, and yonder professor, who possess treasures of special knowledge. The strong desire to become a scholar warms his being. He is ready now for teachers and schools. Do we not know that the work is all but done? Henkle is born into the kingdom of the intellectually saved!

When we are ready for them, our teachers come. How, like a good genius in a fairy tale, came the young high school student, T. D. Crow, to William Henkle. "I noticed the lad," says Mr. Crow, "sitting in his mother's kitchen, intently poring over such old books or newspapers as he could lay his hands upon, and, indeed, seeming to care for naught else. So I said to him one day, 'William, if you will come to my room once each day, I will hear you recite in anything you want to study.' . . . Next evening he entered my room with three books under his arm, viz., Smith's English Grammar, Talbot's Arithmetic, and Comstock's Natural Philosophy." This fairy tale had its just, poetic sequel when, after long years, Mr. Henkle made Mr. Crow acting commissioner of common schools, at the State capital.

Grammar, arithmetic, philosophy, — these only provoked the desire for other branches. The passion for learning increased by what it fed on. Young Henkle sought the acquaintance of Mr. White, a scholarly gentleman then teaching in Springfield, who afterwards became a supreme judge. Mr. White led his eager student into the mysteries of algebra and the charms of Latin grammar. Ambition now pointed to the Springfield High School as the next goal. Chandler Robbins, afterwards professor of languages in Augusta College, Kentucky, was principal of the high school when Henkle attended it. The continuity of Henkle's high school course was interrupted by his teaching his first school in the winter of 1845–46. He was about sixteen years old. He boarded with his mother, ate breakfast early, walked four miles to school, came home to supper, and then went one mile to a night school to recite German and French, — ten miles' walking a day, besides the labor of teaching a country school and learning lessons in two foreign languages !

His teaching term ended, Henkle returned to the high school, from which he was graduated August 7, 1846. At graduation the rising scholar delivered a Latin salutatory. A proud occasion was that for the Henkle family. Mother and sisters attended the exercises, which were given in the Methodist Church. "How happy we all were !" reports Mrs. Spain. "I knew Will's salutatory as well as he did himself, and could have prompted him had there been need of it."

From the high school Will went to Wittenberg College, but he did not finish the college course. In the catalogue for 1847 his name stands highest among the classical students. He always cherished grateful recollections of Wittenberg and of his instructors there. "But what, in faith, make you from Wittenberg?" an intimate friend used to ask him playfully, quoting Hamlet ; to which he would quickly reply, "A truant disposition, good my lord."

Late in 1847 he taught a private school at Urbana, and not long afterwards he was chosen principal of the academy. His mother sold her house in Springfield and followed him to Urbana.

One obtains a curious impression from reading formal recommendations given to eminent men before they became eminent. Mr. Henkle's old teacher, Chandler Robbins, in a document dated September, 1847, "takes pleasure in stating that Mr. William Henkle was formerly a pupil of his," and "believes him to be well qualified to teach youth in literature and science as far as to prepare them to enter the freshman class in college," and, finally, "cordially recommends him to the community as a young man every way worthy of confidence."

While at Urbana, Henkle one day came into Doctor Howell's office and discovered the doctor's brother with a large work on anatomy in his hands. "I am trying to learn the names of five hundred muscles and two hundred and fifty bones." — "Give me a dozen of them," said Henkle; "I'll remember them for you." His avidity for all knowledges led him to undertake the study of medicine, in which he made considerable progress. Dr. Howell was astonished at the extent of the young schoolmaster's information, and said with emphasis, "*He is thorough.*"

The Henkle family connections in Clarke County were numerous ; and it was a custom for all the kith and kin to assemble at stated times, and to hold what

Will called a "Henkle Jubilee." A memorable gathering of this kind took place while William was teaching in Urbana. He hired a substitute on the day of jubilee, for on no account could the family festival go on without him. He was the inspiration and joy of the company. It was long remembered by those present that Will made a wonderful, comic speech, from a swinging perch in the branches of a big white-oak tree that had just been cut down. Certain teasing girl cousins made fun of the orator's newly sprouted whiskers, and he retorted by smoothing a large imaginary beard, and exclaiming, "My whiskers! oh, my whiskers!" The day was drowned in laughter.

One day an excursion was made, up the midde branch of Buck Creek, by a dozen young people, in a two-horse farm-wagon. Will Henkle was the soul of the party. "What we lacked of having sport that day it would be hard to supply," reports the cousin who drove the horses. A shower came up. William borrowed of a farmer an enormous overcoat, nut-brown, old-fashioned, short in the waist and long in the skirts, with tail split almost up to the shoulder-blades. In this coat did the future doctor of philosophy masquerade, to the infinite amusement of the others. He started a spelling-school in the wagon, and gave out such words as *shoo*, the exclamation used to drive away chickens. Arriving at his uncle's house he played beggar, imploring his aunt to

"Pity the sorrows of a poor old man."

Then there was strolling over the hills, and singing "Uncle Ned" and "Old Virginny," and recitations, the whole concluding with a pathetic selection
by Will about an Alpine vulture carrying away a
child, ending with the lines, —

> "The scarlet cap it wore that morn
> Was still upon its head."

Such were the cheerful, innocent, social recreations of William D. Henkle at the age of twenty.

He now puts on the toga of manhood, and with
true Roman valor begins the campaign of mature
life. In 1848 he made his first appearance as institute instructor, giving a series of lectures on English
grammar. When the union system went into effect
he was employed as principal of the Urbana High
School.

In 1850 he went to Greenfield, O., and for one
term taught in the seminary there. From Greenfield he went to Mechanicsburg, whither his mother's
family also removed. He taught in a seminary, in
which he was associated with a superior scholar,
Mr. Robert Wilson, a graduate of Queen's College,
Belfast, Ireland. Prof. T. C. Mendenhall tells us
that "it is highly probable that Mr. Henkle there
learned, for the first time, through his association
with Mr. Wilson, the great value of accurate, thorough, and exhaustive scholarship, a lesson which he
himself, in after-life, unconsciously taught all who
were so fortunate as to sustain intimate relations

with him." While at Mechanicsburg, Henkle gave
much of his mental energy to mathematical work. In
a letter to one of his mathematical correspondents,
Miss Fitch, now Mrs. A. F. Rabb, dated March 12,
1852, he says, "We have here a glorious mathematical trio, composed of Mr. Stribbling, an engineer;
my partner, Mr. Wilson; and your friend, W. D.
Henkle. Our attention is devoted almost entirely
to geometry. Neither of them is an amateur in
algebra. Geometry is their forte. Hence, whenever
I receive an algebraic problem for solution, I don't
hand it over to them, but keep it all to myself. . . .
We go in for mathematics here among the ladies. I
took a class of girls through the Calculus."

His devotion to mathematics did not prevent
him from investigating other special subjects. In
December, 1853, he attended the second annual
meeting of the Ohio Phonetic Association at Columbus, and read an able report on Phonetic Teaching.
At the third annual meeting of the same body, held
in Cincinnati, in 1854, he also took a leading part,
presenting a curious and elaborate paper on The
Bearings of Phonetics on Etymology. The paper was
published with the proceedings of the Association.

While living at Mechanicsburg, Mr. Henkle was
married to Miss Kate A. Estabrook of Dayton, O.,
Oct. 13, 1851.

In the summer of 1854 Mr. Henkle and family
removed from Mechanicsburg to Green Mount, near
Richmond, Ind., where a college had been organ-

ized, in which he occupied the chair of ancient languages.

One of Mr. Henkle's pupils at Green Mount was Wm. Henry Smith, afterwards secretary of state in Ohio, and now manager of the Associate Press. Mr. Smith prepared a sketch of Mr. Henkle's life for the *Type of the Times.*

In a letter to his correspondent, Miss Fitch, dated Oct. 15, 1854, Mr. Henkle speaks of visiting Cleveland to attend the Ohio State Association, and of going to Urbana, Mechanicsburg, Dayton, Oxford, and Eaton. "I taught algebra at the Eaton Normal School about two weeks, after which I conducted a Teachers' Institute at Richmond. Professor Stoddard and Dr. Cutter were with us the first week. It was the best institute I ever attended. Our school began on the 3d of September, since which time I have read about seven works, delivered three scientific lectures, attended to school duties, and written quite a number of pages of algebra, in series and indeterminate analysis. I suppose you know that Stoddard and myself intend to publish a University Algebra. . . . Perhaps you would like to know what works I have been reading. I will tell you. Trench, Tuckerman, 'Characteristics of Literature,' two vols., 'Plurality of Worlds,' 'More Worlds than One,' and Chapin's Grammar."

The institute at Richmond alluded to in this letter was really the first session of the Wayne County Teachers' Association. Mr. Hiram Hadley says, "The

Wayne County Association, through the impetus which Henkle more than all others imparted to it, held its meetings uninterruptedly for more than ten years, and set in motion educational forces that have contributed largely, not only to the enviable rank which Wayne County holds, but to the educational progress of the whole State."

Mr. Henkle aided in the organization and maintenance of the Indiana State Teachers' Association, of which he was a charter member. He was called from Green Mount to Richmond, in which city he organized the Union schools and became their superintendent. The Supreme Court of Indiana, through its representative, Judge Perkins, crippled or killed the public schools by the decision, that local taxes levied for school purposes are unconstitutional. His schools broken up at Richmond, Mr. Henkle went to Indianapolis, and started a private academy.

In 1856 the first number of the Indiana *School Journal* was issued, with Geo. B. Stone as editor-in-chief, and W. D. Henkle one of the associates. Stone left the State in 1858, and Mr. Henkle became the editor. But the educational field in Indiana was blighted by the Perkins decision. Mr. Henkle said, with dry wit, "I examined the Constitution of Indiana with extra care, to see if I could not find some way of getting rid of Judge Perkins's decision. I could not, until I found that emigration from the State should not be prohibited. I got rid of the decision by coming to Ohio."

The autumn of 1859 found Mr. Henkle teaching mathematics in the South-Western Normal School, at Lebanon, O. The "University Algebra" had just been issued. It was the privilege of his classes to use that exacting text-book, and the author was the teacher. The class assembled in the basement room of the old academy building, and with enthusiasm teacher and learners went through the book, though not many of the learners could have made much headway without the guidance of the master. Guidance it was, and that merely, for Henkle did not carry his pupils. He marched ahead, showing the way, blazing now and then a tree in the wilderness of difficulty, but never removing the knotty logs or the thorny underbrush. If at times the students lost sight of the path, they felt no misgivings in regard to their leader's knowledge ; there was no losing him, however labyrinthian the way.

Mr. Henkle was perhaps at his best in Lebanon. He was past thirty years of age, and in full physical vigor. He surprised the students on the play-ground, by his gymnastic skill, especially by his jumping and quoit-pitching.

To the pupil who wished to learn he opened the full storehouse of his mind ; but he was not distinguished for inspiring the sluggish, or sharpening the dull. While patient and impartial in his class work, he held the esoteric opinion that not all who had the calling of students were elected to scholarship. And, like Confucius, he thought it waste of time to " carve rotten wood."

His chosen disciples worshipped him. A true philomath, he stimulated investigation and promoted acquisition. Not only the professors and pupils in the Normal School recognized him as an authority; he was sought by the best intelligence of Lebanon and of Warren County. He revived the Mechanics' Institute, an organization that had been famous in the days of Thomas Corwin's boyhood. He influenced the press, the bar, the pulpit of Lebanon. Not the less he reached the very rabble of the street ; for, like a new Socrates, he went about in such a simple, honest, candid way, that he won the confidence and esteem of all.

In the Normal School the "Test Speller" was evolved. The curious lists that are printed in that odd book were pronounced to the students of the Normal School long before Mr. Henkle had an idea of publishing them for general use.

W. D. Henkle was a great reader. Not content with grasping the general scope and significance of a volume, his penetration extended to the subtlest thought of the author, while he took note also of every verbal peculiarity, and of such mechanical items as most concern the accurate proof-reader. The pages of his books are marked with many symbols, significant to him. On his back would this omnivorous reader lie, stretched out upon a lounge, with his book held above his face, with a pencil by his side, and a paper-knife in his hand, and there would he read, and read, and read. He luxuriated in the *Quarterly Reviews*, all of which he took. Any book or magazine was delightful to him. The idea of dry or tedious literature he could not conceive. He bought the eighth edition of the Encyclopædia Britannica, and this vast work he actually read, in regular course, omitting only the minor articles.

Dr. Mendenhall, as he has told us gracefully, was attracted to Lebanon by the fascinations of Henkle's tough algebra, and the fame of its modest author. E. O. Vaile, nephew to Mr. Henkle, and now editor of *Intelligence*, was for a time a member of the household at Lebanon.

In 1862 the Republicans nominated Mr. Henkle for State commissioner of schools, but at the election he was defeated with the whole State ticket. After the campaign he became superintendent of the public schools at Lebanon.

In 1864 he received and accepted an invitation to go to Salem, Columbiana County, as superintendent of schools there. He held this position until 1869, when, on the resignation of John A. Norris as State commissioner of schools, Gov. R. B. Hayes appointed Mr. Henkle to fill the vacancy for the remainder of the term. From Columbus he returned to Salem, resuming the duties of superintendent of schools. About this time he began the publication of the serial *Notes and Queries*. In 1875 (September), when Dr. E. E. White disposed of the Ohio *Educational Monthly* in order to accept the presidency of Purdue University, Mr. Henkle purchased the periodical, and from that time until his death he was its editor.

In 1868 Mr. Henkle was president of the Ohio State Teachers' Association. He was a prominent member of the National Educational Association, of which he was the secretary for six years. In June, 1876, the degree of Doctor of Philosophy was conferred on him by Wooster University.

Full of honors, but not of years, he died, aged only fifty-three, at his home in Salem, Nov. 22, 1881.

At the beginning of his last illness, his wife discovered him lying upon the lounge in the library, and on the floor lay a book which he had just been reading, and which had fallen from his tired hand.

The telegraph's tongue of fire told the sudden news : " Henkle is dead !" Ohio's teachers bowed and wept. We had not thought of him as mortal.

> " Oh, what hadst thou to do with cruel Death,
> Who wast so full of life, or Death with thee,
> That thou shouldst die before thou hadst grown old ? "

Few had thought to praise him in his lifetime, so unobtrusive was his serene wisdom, so unassuming his philosophic repose. As soon would one think of praising the wholesome air or the starry sky ! But, gone, he was missed. " There is but one Henkle."

Not only from his personal friends and fellow-workers in Ohio came the echo of sorrow and the tribute of admiration. Wm. T. Harris sent his lament from Concord, Mass., saying, " I am one of a very, very large brotherhood of educators, living all over this nation, that are unspeakably shocked and pained to hear of Dr. Henkle's illness and death. He was universally beloved and respected." From Worcester the veteran A. P. Marble wrote, "Every word of eulogy meets a response in my heart; but they all fail to do justice to the noble man that he was." Mr. Bicknell, from his desk in Boston, said, "We shall long remember his noble life and valuable services for education, and his place none can fill with equal ability and fidelity." And from Pennsylvania, Mr. Wickersham sadly voiced a general thought, "The National Association will miss him greatly — no other member would have been missed so much."

William Downs Henkle, not seeking, won his high rank by doing a true man's honest work. In a world where sham often seems to be preferred to reality, it is comforting to note a marked instance in which merits such as his are recognized and honored. Not for his education, or for his ability, or for his public services, was he loved chiefly, but for his humanity.

The range of Mr. Henkle's studies was wide, and in nothing was he superficial. As a mathematician, he was regarded by mathematicians as first-rate. As a linguist he was proficient, being able to speak in five languages and to read in nine. So extensive were his researches in philology and lexicography, that in these and kindred studies he was regarded as an authority, even among specialists. He gleaned from his reading many words not found in the great American dictionaries until he added them. He established the pronunciation of many words, especially proper names. Professor Marsh of Lafayette College wrote to him, "I do not believe that I have expressed to you my pleasure at the introduction of so much good spelling, and so good rules for it, into the last volume of the American Educational Association. We are much indebted to you for that, as for so many other things."

The minute investigation he made in several departments of study, particularly in grammar, enlarged the boundaries of exact knowledge, and gave impulse to right methods of research among teachers. He did not concede that there is any such thing as useless knowledge. In his "Educational Notes and Queries" he did what perhaps no other man in the United States was capable of doing. His insatiate desire to ferret out final facts made the man *sui generis*. At one time he became interested in ascertaining the exact pronunciation of the names of fixed stars. Exhausting his own sources of knowledge, he wrote to William S. Wheeler, the editor of Webster's Dictionary, but Wheeler's vast resources could not supply the desired information. Henkle wrote next to W. D. Whitney, who replied that the subject "floats in an insoluble uncertainty." That was the very reason why Henkle desired to clear the matter up. His mind could not rest until he could put the proper diacritical mark upon the name of every star.

His curious interest in facts remotely connected with common activity did not prevent him from attending to affairs familiar and practical. While he sought the names of the stars in boundless space, he also knew how butter is made, and what variety of potatoes is best.

While living in Salem he put his astronomical knowledge to practical account. He announced in the town newspaper, "I have established a true meridian on Lundy Street, by observation on the north star, making a correction for azimuth." The school clock at Salem kept true time, and it was suggested that the mayor order the town bell to be rung on true time. Thus would Henkle adjust himself and the community to that order which is the first law of the material heaven. Let us be *right* by the north star.

Scrupulous accuracy attended him in his travel, his business affairs, and in all his habits. His wife says, "Whenever he left home he always told me on what train he would be at home. Even if he were gone for a week or ten days at a time, he would tell. He knew the railroad lines and connections so well, that when he went to Atlanta last summer he told me when he would be at home, and he came as he told me." He was extremely punctual and exact in all money matters. He kept himself and wife supplied with clean, new fractional currency, to discharge every score to the cent, and on the second. The north star of undeviating honesty controlled his transactions.

His painstaking precision was visible in all his private affairs. Mrs. Henkle says, speaking of the condition in which he left his papers, etc., "If he had arranged his business with a view of leaving it, he could not have done it better."

As an educator Mr. Henkle was practical as to what he advocated and what he did. While State commissioner he said in a speech, "Not much legislation is needed. If we were granted three things, we would not ask for anything more for fifty years. First, county supervision. Second, abolition of the sub-districts. Third, a State normal school."

In an address at Sandusky he advised the teachers never to abandon any feature of instruction simply because it was old. They must remember that it is always new to pupils. Determine what is proper to infuse in your schools and then keep it. In the same address he said, "No teacher should be employed on account of sympathy." Mrs. Henkle gives the incident which perhaps fixed this principle in his mind. She says, "I remember at one time when he was county examiner in Warren County, a young lady was trying to pass the examination. He was doing all he could to give her time, etc., and she, of course, was in tears. I ventured some remark in her behalf. I shall never forget his reply, nor the manner in which it was given. I do not think that I ever knew him to speak with so much force or feeling. "Don't say a word ; I see the little children all over the land holding up their hands to me and saying, 'Don't send us such teachers.'"

In his inaugural address, before the State Association at Dayton, in 1868, Mr. Henkle expressed tersely what may be regarded as the fundamental philosophy of his educational belief. "I confess," he says, "I have no great admiration for the word *discipline* when its primitive meaning is banished to give place to another. Discipline and disciple both have their root in the Latin *discere*, to learn, and hence, primitively, discipline is learning. I firmly believe that if the ordinary idea of discipline were traced critically to its source, it would be found to be knowledge — a knowledge of methods, modes of thought, etc., as contra-distinguished from the simple knowledge of facts without their relations. My opinion as to what we should learn, to be thoroughly and liberally educated, may be stated as follows: As discipline is a knowledge of methods, our studies should be sufficiently extended to embrace all species of discipline. This is the ideal towards which we should approximate."

There was a flavor of rather sweet irony in Mr. Henkle, and a rich vein of humor. He was the laughing philosopher, never the cynic. He distinguished a "joke with a point" from a "joke with a sting," and never enjoyed the latter. His sense of the ludicrous found frequent gratification in real life and through books. He relished reading "Tristram Shandy" and "Humphrey Clinker." Sometimes he amused his friends by giving a burlesque lecture on Spencerian Penmanship, illustrating on the blackboard with hypercritical discriminations the vital importance of slope, shade, and terminal *curlycue*. Sometimes he would ridicule the extravagances of elocution by declaiming in the prevailing style, but with many absurd exaggerations as to intonation, facial expression, and gesture.

Without a touch of affectation, he yet had personal eccentricities that often turned the laugh upon himself. Interested in conversation, he forgot to serve his guests at his own table. He ate mechanically, and, after dinner, sometimes asked his wife whether he had eaten or not. One morning he came to school with two shirt-collars on, one buttoned outside the other.

In morals, Mr. Henkle was rigorous with himself and exacting of others. It angered him to see men debase themselves. He indulged no vice, large or small. Temperate, chaste, pure in speech, he resembled the Zarathustra of the Persian Bible.

In politics and religion he was conservative. His habit of uttering paradoxes, of setting half-forgotten truths in a strong light ; his love of the curious ; the wide range of his information, which took in all ages, nations, and creeds ; his critical faculty, which deemed nothing too high for its exercise, led many to set him down as much more radical than he really was. Conservative himself, and holding convictions firmly settled, he yet encouraged controversy on all subjects. Nothing of the bigot, nothing of the dogmatist in him ; he was open to conviction at all times.

He had special pleasure in discussion, not debate, with clergymen of different denominations. He was a member of the Methodist Protestant Church. Well acquainted with the arguments of materialism, he did not consider them conclusive. Believing in evolution, he did not reject the First Cause. He revered the holy Bible, and had faith in the efficacy of prayer. All his religious views and observances partook of the informal simplicity of his mother's Quaker creed.

Socially, Mr. Henkle was delightful. Wherever he went there was good society. Never to be forgotten are certain golden days and ambrosial nights spent at the hospitable home of Hon. J. P. Siddall of Richmond, Ind., when Henkle, Dr. John Hancock, good old Dr. Hoshour, A. P. Russell, the genial author of "Library Notes," and other gentlemen, with a bevy of bright women, made life seem not only worth the living, but made an hour seem worth a lifetime. And without Henkle these rare symposia could not have been. In Lebanon and Salem it was the same. This self-made scholar, this serene gentleman, wherever he went created friends and made them happy. His was a home-staying heart. His sojourn at Columbus, away from his family, was a cross to him. Kate and Clara, his wife and daughter, were his angels, — home his earthly paradise. He writes to Clara from the office of state commissioner, Columbus, Nov. 30, 1869, at four minutes after five, Tuesday : —

DEAR DAUGHTER CLARA, — When I began to write to mamma, I had just come from a large children's meeting. It rained when I went, and was raining when I came back. There were present a great many children, come through the storm. Mr. Chidlaw, of Cincinnati, talked first, and then Mr. Moody, of Chicago, the latter a great man for holding children's meeting. Mamma will tell you what the latter means. The children voted to have another meeting to-morrow or next day. I have not seen Cousin Ed yet. He was at the lecture last night, but I did not see him. Mr. Mendenhall and Brown were here and went with me to the children's meeting.

Last Sunday I saw a little girl on the street dressed in a scarlet plaid like yours, with high blue shoes, and a blue hat with a white feather. A man was with her. Do you think that man was her papa? I do. I hope you are getting to be a better and better girl every day. I will see how far you have read when I get home. Remember, you were to be where it says, " I saw a house and a mill," or something like that. I must close. It is half-past five and I must soon go to supper. From your papa.

Good evening.

Alas ! good evening, thou kindest of men !

His humanity extended to dumb animals. The family horse always showed a preference for him, and the household cat had her favorite resort near his chair in the library. After his death the cat continued for a week to visit his room and to lie in her customary place, but, finding at last that her master did not return, she came no more to the empty chair.

My task is nearly accomplished. Once more association draws us to the library. The library! In it he lived ; from it his dead body was carried to the grave. His life was consecrated to books. Let us name him Henkle, the Reader. Would you see the sacred room ? the place of study ? the penetralia of his intellectual life? You are his friends, and it will surely not profane my trust if I read to you his wife's touching words : —

"I am sitting just where he used to sit, in his library, at his table. Every available space in this large room is filled to the ceiling with cases full of books. Just as soon as Mr. Henkle was dressed he was right here at work. Never idle one moment. His last entry in his written catalogue of books is, Peck's Ganot's Natural Phil. Revised, Num. 4426. His books, as you know, were accumulated one at a time. Sometimes he would see advertised a book that he wanted, and would order it, and after long waiting it came. It was always the contents he wanted ; he cared nothing for the binding. . . . I wish I knew just what to tell you. I wish I could tell you what a pleasant home he made. He was always pleasant. Every day it seemed to me he grew dearer and dearer, — we lived so *together* — worked together. I cared so little for anything so he was at home with me. . . . Always the same busy, quiet man, but so bright and happy ; often has he spoken to me in these months of how his love for me grew as the years went by. I think you will not think me foolish in telling you these things. . .. . Yes, it is hard to think of him cold in death, that active, cheerful, happy, big-souled man."

So speaks his wife, out of the fulness of memory and love and devotion and bereavement. Her words are the appropriate conclusion to this memorial.

www.ingramcontent.com/pod-product-compliance
Lightning Source LLC
Chambersburg PA
CBHW021046030726
47496CB00006B/1706